# DARKWATER LIES

Center Point
Large Print

Also by Robin Caroll and available from Center Point Large Print:

*Torrents of Destruction*
*Darkwater Secrets*
*Strategem*

# DARKWATER LIES

DARKWATER INN • BOOK 2

## Robin Caroll

CENTER POINT LARGE PRINT
THORNDIKE, MAINE

This Center Point Large Print edition
is published in the year 2019 by arrangement with
RC Productions, Inc.

The text of this Large Print edition is unabridged.
In other aspects, this book may vary
from the original edition.
Printed in the United States of America
on permanent paper.
Set in 16-point Times New Roman type.

ISBN: 978-1-64358-360-0

The Library of Congress has cataloged this record
under Library of Congress Control Number: 2019944733

*For Pam . . .*
*my partner in crime in my*
*research trip for this series*
*my brainstorming buddy*
*my sanity during conference season*
*. . . my friend.*

# 1

## ADELAIDE

"We've been hacked!"

Adelaide Fountaine looked up from her notes and tightened her grip on the phone. "I'll have to call you back, Daddy." She hung up the phone without waiting for her father's response and stared at Lissette Bastien. "We've been what?"

"Hacked! Our computer system." Lissette's eyes were wider than usual, her smooth mocha skin flushed.

Taking a deep breath, Adelaide refused to stand or give in to the alarm threatening to rise. "Explain, please."

Lissette had been learning the hospitality business to take over as managing owner of the hotel for less than a year, not enough time to accurately gauge panic-worthy events. Not like Adelaide, who had nearly six years under her belt at the Darkwater Inn and had weathered the most serious—and almost career-ending—events.

"We thought it was just a glitch when the room-service orders all came in, but it's so much more than that."

Adelaide held up a hand. "Wait a minute. Slow down and back up. What room-service orders?"

7

The younger woman sucked in air, then let it out in a rush. "That's what started everything. Dimitri got one hundred and six room-service orders all at once in the system."

One hundred and six? "That's improbable." The hotel hosted two hundred and seven rooms, including the suites, and as of this morning, with it being Mardi Gras season, they were at ninety-eight percent occupancy. So it was *possible* to have that many orders, but the likelihood was very slim. It was carnival season and after 6:00 p.m., so a large majority of the hotel guests were out celebrating in the city.

Lissette nodded. "Right. Dimitri figured it was a glitch in the system, so he called over to tech support. They ran some tests remotely and told him the system was operating properly, but he knew that had to be wrong, so he called me. We rebooted the system and followed all the advice tech support gave, but the orders were still there. Dimitri rang four random rooms that had orders on the system and asked if they'd placed a room service order. None of them had."

Of course not. Adelaide nodded.

"Together we called the software support team. They walked us through everything to try. Rebooting. Resetting. Even starting in safe mode. Nothing worked."

Adelaide let out a pent-up breath. "It sounds like perhaps we need a representative from the software company to come check the program, but it doesn't sound like we've been hacked." Thank goodness, because she certainly didn't need anything like that. Nothing that would give Claude Pampalon a reason to, once again, doubt her capability to run the hotel as general manager. He'd been gracious enough to grant her request to take a six-month sabbatical to train at a five-star hotel in Europe as long as she returned for the busy Mardi Gras season, but she'd been back a month now. It wouldn't bode well for her if anything went majorly wrong at the Darkwater Inn that she couldn't handle after having been gone.

Lissette shook her head. "That's just what Dimitri thought, too, until he ran over to security to see if Hixson would look and see if he could figure it out."

Smart move on Dimitri's part. Hixson, the barely legal young man in the Darkwater's security department, had been taking online classes in computer coding. Finally, Dimitri seemed to be doing what Adelaide had been harping on him to do for a couple of years—learning the staff. Maybe her time away had helped Dimitri as well.

Lissette continued. "Hixson was able to get into the system and figured out there were corrupt lines of code, and he's pretty sure they were put in there deliberately to mess with the system."

That was a game changer. Adelaide pushed to her feet, snatching her cell phone from her desk. "How long ago did the room service orders show up in the system?" She jerked open her office door and headed down the hallway.

Lissette fell into step beside her, staring at her watch. "I think they all appeared about five or so."

Adelaide glanced at the time on her phone: 6:13 p.m. They'd been down over an hour, and she was just now hearing about it? Unacceptable. She quickened her already fast pace toward the security office.

"Ms. Fountaine!" Barb, the night-desk manager, came from behind the counter and rushed to her. "We've had several guests complain that their room keys aren't working."

Adelaide paused to look the woman in the eye. "I need to see to a pressing situation at the moment. For the time being, just get new cards and reprogram as needed, Barb. I'll check back with you as soon as I can."

Barb nodded and went back to the front desk while Adelaide returned to her fast pace toward the security office. She glanced at Lissette. "You said the orders showed up around five? Over an hour ago?"

"But we only figured out it was a hack in the last thirty minutes or so." Lissette's steps faltered.

Pausing with her hand on the security office

door handle, Adelaide glanced over her shoulder. "At which time you should have alerted me. We've lost thirty more minutes now, putting the hotel and all of our guests at risk."

Lissette's eyes narrowed, and the muscles in her jaw flexed. Adelaide didn't have time to address the chip that had been on Lissette's shoulder ever since Adelaide had returned from Europe.

Not now. Not when they'd already lost so much time. She jerked open the door and stepped inside. The first thing she saw was acting chief of security Sully Clements typing frantically on dual keyboards and murmuring to himself. Or to Hixson, who sat at a computer as well, fingers flying over his own keyboards.

A hack could compromise all the sensitive data on hotel guests, staff . . . the hotel itself. Mr. Pampalon would have a fit. This could be just what he needed to prove Dimitri wrong and deny Lissette control over the hotel. He'd probably fire Adelaide for good measure since it had happened on her watch.

Adelaide moved to stand at Sully's right arm. "I've just been made aware of the situation. Any progress?" She didn't want to get in the way, but her heart caught in the back of her throat. She needed results.

"Ms. Fountaine, I've run every debugging program we have, performed every virus scan, and called everybody that I can, but no one knows exactly what happened. Somehow, someone got into our system remotely and locked it up. I can't figure out what all is included."

Adelaide chewed her bottom lip. If only Geoff weren't in jail, if only this had waited five months to happen until he was out . . . No, she was the general manager of the Darkwater, and she would figure out a way to handle the situation.

"We've rebooted the system three times, even bringing it back up in safe mode." Hixson shook his head. "It loads, but then messes up. It either freezes everything or just locks up random actions. I've never seen anything like it, and I've studied hack prevention."

She looked at her watch again. The system had been compromised for over an hour and a half. Protocol dictated that she notify the police cyber-crimes unit, especially with the particular guests she had in house at the moment. Still, she hesitated.

It'd been barely a year ago that she'd confronted the biggest problem she could ever have imagined she'd have to face. Her four years of hotel management education at Northwestern State University hadn't prepared her to handle a murdered body found in one of the rooms. Many changes had followed at the hotel, including one that left them without their chief of security and made Adelaide leery to call in the police too soon. But she had to protect the hotel, first and foremost. "What all is affected?" she asked both men . . . neither . . . anyone.

Hixson leaned back in the chair and looked up at her. "The way the Darkwater's set up is that everything is running on two systems. One system runs the room reservations, the accounting systems, outlets, and stuff like that. Those programs on that server don't seem to be affected by whatever is knocking out the other one, so all those things are up and running without a problem. The one that's messed up maintains the programs for customer satisfaction like housekeeping, requests, and room service. This server also runs all the security programs— monitors, electronic locks, mass notification system, and the room-key program."

Oh, lovely. Now Barb's front desk problems made sense. "So no guest room keys are going to work?" She pinched the bridge of her nose. "Everyone is going to be locked out of their rooms?" This was like her worst nightmare come to life.

"I'm sorry, Ms. Fountaine." Sully nodded. "The keys can be reprogrammed, and I think they'll work, but I'm not positive. It looks that way now, but . . ."

No time to be sorry, actions produced results. She turned to Lissette. "Call the police cyber-crimes unit and report the problem." She looked at Hixson. "Keep trying to get the system working." She turned to Sully. "Who is at the vault?"

"Leon."

"Has he reported anything unusual?" Adelaide could hear Lissette on the phone giving the basic information to the police amid the backdrop of Hixson's tapping on the computers.

"I haven't talked to him since Dimitri spoke with us." The tips of Sully's ears reddened. "I'm really sorry, Ms. Fountaine."

Adelaide ground her teeth silently. Geoff would've checked with the vault immediately, according to procedure. But she wouldn't panic yet because surely if there'd been any disturbance, Leon would've called. "Will you please check in with him?" At least she could mark that off the protocol checklist.

"They're sending someone right over." Lissette clutched her cell in front of her as if it were a life preserver and she was in deep waters. "The dispatcher said detectives would be here within fifteen minutes."

Fifteen minutes they really didn't have. Not if everything had been hacked remotely.

"I can't get Leon to answer the radio or his cell phone." Sully pushed to his feet. "That's unlike him, ma'am. Maybe the hacker took out our radio and blocked the call somehow. I'll go check."

Adelaide's heart pounded against her ribcage. "I'll go with you." She tried not to glare at

Lissette as she spoke. "Hixson, please continue to work on the system. Lissette, call Dimitri and have him meet us at the vault."

She followed Sully out of the security room, matching his long stride as they crossed the lobby. The hustle and bustle of people outside the hotel's open front doors, enjoying carnival season in the French Quarter, was deafening. Or maybe it was just Adelaide's pulse pounding in her head that filled her ears.

She and Sully passed the front desk and headed toward the back of the building and the area restricted to only a few hotel employees and a very select few guests. It was in this dark back area that the vault sat, secure and guarded. Even more than usual at the moment, considering one special guest in particular had brought their own guard as well.

Adelaide followed Sully so closely that when he stopped suddenly, she ran into his back. With no explanation and in one fluid movement, Sully pushed her against the hallway wall, drew his gun, and spun toward the door to the vault. He took a step over the threshold into the vault room.

What the— Adelaide pushed off the wall and eased behind Sully. She immediately saw two bodies on the floor. She sucked in air as her steps faltered. The door to the vault stood open before her like a gaping, dark void.

They'd been robbed!

Sully, gun still drawn, squatted beside Leon on the ground and pressed two fingers against the downed guard's throat. His shoulders sagged a little as he glanced back at Adelaide and shook his head before checking the second figure.

Her eyes burned. Not again. "Hey."

She spun around, every muscle in her body taut.

"Whoa." Dimitri smiled as he closed the distance between them. "Sorry, didn't mean to startle you. Lissette said you were heading here. What's going on?" He joined her, looked over her shoulder into the room. "Oh, no." He pushed around her and dropped to his knees beside Leon.

"They're both dead. Lots of blood loss." Sully holstered his gun. "There's nobody else in here. I'll call it in." He pulled his cell and dialed 911.

Unable to hold back any longer, Adelaide rushed into the room. Leon . . . And Princess Katerina von Pavlovna's private guard dead too . . . What had been taken?

Dimitri was on his feet in a flash, his arms around her. "You can't help them. They're gone. We need to wait in the hall."

"But Leon—"

Dimitri steered her back out of the vault room. "It's a crime scene now."

This couldn't be happening. Not again.

Sully joined them in the hall. "The police are sending over detectives right now. Their cyber-

16

crimes team had already been dispatched, so this is a priority since the two incidents are probably related."

Adelaide's stomach twisted. Bile burned the back of her throat. This was worse than last year's dead body in a hotel room. This was two bodies, a hacked security system, and a probable robbery, and she'd been back on the job for barely a month. Claude Pampalon, owner of the Darkwater Inn and Dimitri's father, was sure to fire her now. Not that that was more important than the two dead men—of course not—but . . .

As if reading her mind, Dimitri pulled her into his arms, providing her warmth and comfort. She let herself draw from his strength as she closed her eyes and breathed in, relaxing in the familiar scent that was all Dimitri. Just for a moment she needed this. Needed him. Just for this minute she needed not to have the weight of responsibility bearing down on her. Just for a second . . . two . . . three.

Adelaide exhaled slowly and eased out of his embrace. She was the general manager of the Darkwater Inn, at least for now, and she had a job to do. She squared her shoulders. "I need to see what's been taken from the vault. I'm not going to touch anything." She hesitated. The fewer who entered a crime scene, the less chance the police would have an issue. Three of them had already been inside the room.

She slipped off her heels. "Come on, Sully. We'll just do a walk-in to get an initial idea of how much has been taken. Dimitri, would you please head to the lobby to meet the police?"

Dimitri raised a single brow, but nodded and left.

Great. She hadn't really thought about that aspect. Homicide at the Darkwater Inn—that was sure to bring Detective Beau Savoie to the scene. About this time last year, Beau and Dimitri had both shown a romantic interest in her, but she'd told them both that she'd needed time to focus on herself. After a few months of trying to continue with the status quo, however, she'd found the situation too difficult and awkward, realizing she was keeping them hanging. It was then that she'd found the opportunity to train at the hotel in Europe, which Claude had thankfully allowed. She'd returned home about a month ago, having had some space both physically and mentally, and known she had cleared a lot of the emotional baggage that had kept her from taking the next step with either relationship.

"Ms. Fountaine, are you sure you don't want to wait for the police?" Sully pulled her from her musings.

She shook her head. "If what I suspect has been taken, we'll need to call more than just the New Orleans police department."

The inside of the vault was dimmer, the lighting

more muted than the harshness of the hallway. The right and left walls housed floor-to-ceiling shelves where items were stored for safekeeping. The back left corner held the five-and-a-half-feet-tall safe. The door stood open, and Adelaide's heart pitched to her toes.

She wasn't quite sure how she was going to handle what was about to become an international incident, but Adelaide was certain of one thing: she was about to find out.

# 2

## BEAU

Detective Beauregard Savoie stepped from the cruiser onto the parking lot of the Darkwater Inn at exactly 7:19 p.m. The early evening February moon split through the clouds that had covered the Louisiana sky for most of the day. He sighed into the gentle breeze as he took in the hotel. Addy's hotel. A strong sense of déjà vu made him shudder as he strode toward the glass lobby doors.

His partner, Detective Marcel Taton, fell into synced steps alongside him. "Crime scene unit is on its way, along with the coroner."

"Who from CSU?" Beau didn't slow as he flashed his shield at the uniformed doorman and strode into the lobby. While all the technicians in the crime scene unit were good, Beau had his favorite team and preferred working with them. Especially on a double homicide.

Marcel chuckled. "Nolan, Robert, and Erik."

"Good." Beau drew to a sudden stop as his eyes met those of Dimitri Pampalon, who stood in the lobby with Lissette Bastien, his half sister.

Dimitri's father owned the Darkwater Inn, so he and Lissette were technically owners as well, which made them Addy's bosses. But that didn't bother Beau. What did bother him was Dimitri's obvious interest in Addy and his close proximity to her every day. While it hadn't been so bad while she was in Europe the last several months, she was back now, and Beau couldn't stop the feelings of jealousy that threatened to strangle him. He'd been in love with Addy since they were kids. He'd finally broken his silence about his sentiments last year, but Addy hadn't made any determination between him and Dimitri. She'd explained she needed space, and they'd both respected her wishes. And then she'd been gone for half a year training at that hotel.

But she was back now.

And there were two dead bodies reported at the Darkwater Inn.

"Adelaide sent me to meet you." Dimitri's voice didn't waver, yet it held the inflection that he had better access to the woman they both were attracted to.

Beau chose to ignore that for the time being. He was here to do a job at the moment. "If you'll take me to the crime scene, we can start. Our unit will be here shortly."

"I'm assuming the crime scene unit will be in their van?"

"Of course," Marcel replied.

Dimitri turned to his sister. "Why don't you go out front and direct them to park in the alley near the back entrance? It'll be much closer for them to access the vault. And the coroner as well."

Parking the CSU and coroner's vans in the alley would also help keep the homicides and robbery out of the public eye. Better for the hotel. Better for business.

"This way." Dimitri didn't wait for Beau or Marcel to answer as he led them down the hallway behind the front desk. Beau couldn't stop his detective's mind from sizing up the man, even though he knew him.

Dimitri Pampalon, thirty-three years old, only son to hotel mogul Claude Pampalon. Bred and groomed to take over the family fortune but thwarted daddy's retirement plans when he opted to play Chef Boyardee and bring in his long-lost but newly found half sister to take his place. Daddy Pampalon hadn't been happy then, and Beau doubted much had changed.

Dimitri turned into the maze of hallways hidden from customer view behind the front-desk counters. "Your cyber-crimes team arrived a few minutes ago and is in our security area going over the computer system that was tampered with."

"I know." Beau had spoken with Zach, the lead investigator on the team, on the drive over, and they would coordinate their teams, with Beau taking the lead since he'd been promoted not too long ago to lead detective.

As was his habit, Beau didn't want to be told

details, preferring to make his own observations and notes. Some might think his method old school, even if he was only thirty-four years old and on the job for a decade, but the process worked for him. He had one of the highest percentages of cases solved in the precinct, so he had to be doing something right. He pulled out his notebook and pen, still refusing to use a pencil regardless of what anybody else did, and gave a curt nod to his partner.

Marcel, who had almost total recall so never had to write anything down—an ability Beau wished he had—acknowledged the nod by quickening to step beside Dimitri. "I know you've reported all the times and pertinent information regarding the hack to our team, but can you give me a basic rundown?"

Dimitri's pace slowed a little. "We had over a hundred room service orders hit our system simultaneously. Guests' room cards stopped working. We thought at first there was a glitch, but our team soon realized that the system had been hacked. Adelaide requested security contact the man at the vault. When there was no response, our acting chief of security, Sully, and Adelaide came to investigate. They found our security guard and the private security guard of one of the hotel's guests both lying dead in the vault. That's pretty much where we're at now." He turned the corner and stopped.

Addy and the tall bulk of a man stood outside the vault door. She looked at Beau as he approached. Fear and horror glistened in her eyes. Beau pulled gloves and shoe covers from his pocket and busied himself putting them on, stopping himself from any unprofessional actions toward her despite everything in him tensing to pull her to him.

Marcel paused beside Beau. "Who all has been inside since this happened?"

"Me," the large black man said.

"This is Sully Clements, our acting chief of security," Addy volunteered. "Sully checked to see if the men were alive, as well as to see if there was anyone else inside."

"There wasn't." Sully nodded.

"You're the only one who's been inside?" Marcel asked.

Addy shook her head. "Dimitri stepped inside to check on Leon, our security officer there, and I went into the vault to check the safe."

Beau tightened his jaw. She knew better. "Why?"

Her gaze flashed against his face. "Because it's my job to know what's missing, especially items that belong to guests." She wavered. "I took my shoes off before I went in, though, so I wouldn't mess up any evidence."

Beau's lips tingled toward a smile. Typical Addy to try her best to do what she thought

24

was right, even when it really didn't make a difference. Instead, he turned to a fresh page in his notebook. "So, Sully, you, and Dimitri all have entered the crime scene?"

Addy lifted her chin and stared at him. "Yes." He made a note.

"Mr. Pampalon, if you would come down the hall a little with me, I can get your statement." Marcel gently turned Dimitri away from the vault room. Most people were more thorough with their statements when they retold them without someone else present to muddy the memory. Beau and Marcel usually worked to separate witnesses if at all possible.

Beau pulled out another pair of the foot coverings from his pocket and passed them to Addy. "You can walk me through it." He turned to Sully Clements. "Please stay here. Detective Taton will take your statement as soon as he finishes with Mr. Pampalon."

As he stepped into the vault alongside Addy, he took a moment to allow himself one personal question. "Are you okay?"

She nodded. "I'll be okay. Unlike Leon." She ran a hand over her hair. "I need to call his family. I don't want them to hear about this on the news."

"We'll take care of that."

"I appreciate that, but they're part of the Darkwater family."

"You can call after we make the official notification. We'll also need to speak to everyone who had access to this room, as well as to the security system."

She nodded but kept her gaze averted from the two dead men on the floor.

It probably seemed very odd to her for them to work around the bodies, but Beau had a job to do, and the quicker he did it, the quicker there would be justice for her employee. He moved into his detective mindset. The coroner and CSU would be here soon to collect every bit of evidence. Right now, he needed an idea of what he was dealing with.

"So, what was kept here in the vault?" He tapped his pen against the notebook and faced Addy, effectively blocking her view of the dead men on the floor.

She nodded toward the shelves on the right side of the room filled with large cardboard boxes. "Those are basically old records for the hotel. Things Mr. Pampalon wanted to keep. Old things belonging to the hotel that we bring out on special occasions." She nodded to the bank of shelves lining the left side of the room. "Those wooden crates store pieces of art and paintings that we rotate through certain areas of the hotel. Some of them are quite valuable."

Yet they didn't look disturbed at all. They were,

by all initial observations, untouched. "Nothing belonging to guests kept in here?"

She shook her head. "Since we installed safes in each room, we don't store much in the vault for guests anymore. Only on rare occasions and special events like an art showing or something." She nodded toward the open safe in the back corner. "If it's something extremely valuable, we store the items in there."

The black metal safe was about five or so feet tall, three and a half feet wide, and a couple of feet deep. The door stood ajar, revealing two shelves and a drawer, which was also open. Beau, careful to not touch the door, studied it. "I'm assuming there were items in here?"

Addy nodded. "A personal item belonging to Mr. Pampalon, about fifty thousand cash, and as of two nights ago, the crown tiara of Princess Katerina von Pavlovna of Liechtenstein."

What? "Wait a minute. Let me get this straight. First off, you keep fifty grand in cash?" Who did that?

"Most hotels do keep a bit of cash on hand. Twenty-five to fifty thousand is the usual for most hotels our size. We just don't advertise that, for obvious reasons."

"That's a lot of money to sit around in a safe, Addy."

"It's customary. Has been that way since the day I started working here."

That seemed like a large amount of cash. He couldn't help but wonder who all knew that kind of money was kept in the safe.

Still careful not to touch the actual safe itself, Beau moved closer and inspected it. No scratches on the outside of the door. None on the drawer pulled out. Both the door and the drawer had an electronic lock. Either someone knew the codes to open it or knew how to gain access.

Like a hacker.

Beau turned back to Addy. "The tiara?"

Her face paled against her long, dark hair as she nodded. "Princess Katerina von Pavlovna is here from Liechtenstein as a special guest of Mr. Pampalon. She is scheduled to ride on his krewe's float this weekend. Her crown was stored in the drawer until the parade on Saturday at noon."

"Hello, Detective Savoic."

Beau turned to greet Nolan, head of the CSU team dispatched. "Glad to see your team here."

"Erik's taking pictures of the outside of the vault door first so Robert can dust it for prints." Nolan was all business, one of the reasons Beau liked his particular team so much. They were fast, thorough, and good. Very good.

Beau took note that Nolan was already in his full evidence-collecting gear. "I'm guessing Walt should be here soon."

Nolan nodded. "We passed his van on our way

in." He pulled out evidence bags from his kit. "Why don't I start here at the safe?"

"Thanks, Nolan." Beau turned back to Addy, taking her arm and leading her back into the hall, passing Erik as his camera flashed almost continuously on his way inside. Robert already had his little brush out, dusting over the vault's handle.

"So the crown was in the drawer of the safe?"

Addy nodded. "Right. We put it in there two nights ago. When they arrived on Monday evening."

"They?"

"Princess Katerina von Pavlovna and her fiancé, Edmond Jansen."

"Claude Pampalon brought in a real princess for his Mardi Gras krewe?" Beau knew the older Pampalon had an ego as big as the Big Easy—had made that fact clear five or so years ago when he started his own krewe that had to have the longest parade on Saturday afternoon, the biggest floats, and the most outlandish party. Even so, a real princess? How did one even go about *hiring* a real princess?

Addy smiled, her eyes connecting to his in the familiar way of two people very comfortable with one another. They should be, since he and Addy had been friends since they were children. Their pasts were as interwoven as any could be. "One of Mr. Pampalon's business associates is Edward Jansen, Edmond's father. Apparently the princess has been wanting to come to the States to visit. Mr. Pampalon made it happen for her."

"Which also benefitted his own standing with his business associate?" Because Beau couldn't imagine that man doing anything for anyone that didn't directly benefit himself.

"Of course." Addy's smile reached her eyes for a fraction of a second . . . until the coroner and two of his assistants wearing jackets with the coroner's office logo emblazoned on the back walked down the hall.

"Hey, Beau."

Beau turned. "Hey, there, Walt. How's it going?"

The old coroner, whose brows formed a bushy fringe over his eyes, shook his head. "I'm not retired and living at an old fishing cabin, so that tells you something."

Beau chuckled at their familiar back-and-forth dialogue. "Same here, my friend. Same here."

"Two bodies, I hear?"

Beau nodded.

"Need identification on either?" Walt asked. Beau cut his gaze to Addy.

She shook her head. "One is our employee, Leon Edwards, and the other is Rubin Hassler, a private guard from the royal Pavlovna family from Liechtenstein."

"Well, all righty, then. I'll see what I can

determine for you." Walt headed into the vault, his two employees on his heels.

"I need to go tell the princess and Edmond about Rubin Hassler and the theft. I'm sure there is a certain protocol for what needs to happen first in situations like this."

Beau couldn't even imagine the ramifications.

Raised voices echoed in the hallway outside the vault door. Beau turned to check out the commotion.

"This is my hotel, and I'll go where I see fit." Claude Pampalon, sternness etched deep into every line of his face, glared from the doorway to the vault room.

The repercussions were about to begin.

# 3

## DIMITRI

Dimitri spun at his father's words. Claude Pampalon barged past the young uniformed officer who had arrived and stood at the door to the vault.

Detective Savoie left Adelaide and blocked off his father. "Sir, this is a crime scene. You can't be in here."

Claude glared at Detective Savoie. "This is my hotel, and I'll go wherever I please," he repeated. He moved to sidestep the detective.

But Beauregard Savoie was too fast, effectively blocking him again. "No, sir. Not when there's a double homicide."

Claude glanced over to the open safe, then to Adelaide. "Ms. Fountaine, is there anything left in the safe?"

Adelaide shook her head. "No, sir."

Dimitri moved to the doorway. "Father, I've concluded my statement to the police, so why don't we go to your office, and I can give you the details of the incident?"

" 'Incident'?" Claude Pampalon was many things, but a kind and gentle man wasn't one of them. His parenting style left much to be desired as well. He glared at Adelaide and the police before turning on his heel and joining Dimitri back in the hallway. "This isn't an incident, Dimitri."

Just the way his father said his name would have made others balk. But not Dimitri. No, he'd had a lifetime of hearing the disappointment in his father's voice. It was the only way his father spoke to him as of late.

"No, Father, it isn't. Two men are dead." Dimitri looked over his shoulder at the officer who'd taken his statement. "My father and I will be in his office if you need us to answer any questions, Detective Taton."

Dimitri turned and took deliberate steps toward Claude's office, hearing his father's hard footfalls behind him. He could picture his father's face: flushed red tone, frontal vein bulging, and eyes hardened like set stone against the lines of his face. Dimitri quickened his pace and held open the door to the office, allowing Claude to precede him before he shut the door securely behind them.

Claude strode behind his desk and took a seat in his executive chair. Dimitri sat in one of the two wingbacks facing the desk. "Let me bring you up to speed, Father."

"Oh, please do." Claude's words themselves might have carried the perception of politeness, but his tone dripped with sarcasm.

Dimitri ignored the disdain of his father's tone and quickly explained about the room-service orders, the hack, and Adelaide and Sully finding the bodies and empty safe. He ended with the arrival of the police. "The cyber-crimes unit has already found the threads of code that the hacker used to access the system."

"Have they identified the hacker?"

"No, sir, but they're very sure they will be able to trace him."

"I see. Does anyone know how this hacker was able to penetrate our system?"

"Not yet. The police have begun their preliminary investigation and will start with all the employees here at the Darkwater who have access to the system."

"I see. And what is Lissette doing in regards to the . . . 'incident'?" Dimitri sat up straight in the chair.

"Obviously there's no way Adelaide or I would've thought to train her how to handle such an emergency, so she's following our lead."

"And what, exactly, is your and Ms. Fountaine's lead?" Claude tented his hands over his desk, a common gesture he used to indicate his displeasure in a conversation.

Resisting the urge to squirm under his father's scrutiny, Dimitri kept his posture straight. "First and foremost, we're following the directives of the police. As I've said, they've just begun their investigations. Their cyber-crimes unit will coordinate with the homicide department to work the simultaneous investigations. For right now, they're gathering statements and garnering insight, and we need to stay out of their way and let them do their jobs."

"Yes, I saw how effectively they were doing their jobs." Claude dropped his hands to his desk. "How effectively are you, Lissette, and Adelaide doing your jobs? Have you started a risk analysis? Have you pulled the employee files for everyone who had access to the security system?" He lifted a pen from the holder on his desk and flipped it through his fingers. "Have you even bothered to locate the princess to inform her of her guard's demise and her crown jewels being stolen?"

"Not yet, Father. I just gave my statement to the police. As soon as Adelaide has concluded hers, we'll visit the princess together with Lissette to inform her of the situation."

"This isn't a slumber party, Dimitri. The princess and Edmond don't need a group to inform them of the situation. You and Ms. Fountaine can do the announcing."

"But Lissette—"

"Will only be awkward and in the way. You yourself said she hadn't been trained in what to do. She's not needed."

"But the only way she'll learn is to be taught."

Claude's eyes narrowed into slits. "Then you

can tell her later. My business associate will not be a guinea pig on teaching your . . . Lissette how to manage a hotel."

"My sister, you mean?" Dimitri blurted it out before he could think that statement through.

"Your half sister." Claude's face was as devoid of emotional connection as it was lined with controlled rage. "I'm still not certain she belongs at this hotel in such a capacity."

Dimitri let out the breath he'd been holding. "We've been over this, Father. She's a legal heir. She has as much right to the hotel as I do."

"No, Dimitri, she doesn't. You are a legitimate child. A Pampalon. You were born and raised to conduct yourself as such, even though you often forget your upbringing." Claude shook his head.

"It's not Lissette's fault you abandoned her and her mother." Dimitri had already fought this battle last year—and won. But there had been little things his father had said over the last several months that made Dimitri wonder if maybe Adelaide had been right and Claude had given in too easily. Dimitri and Lissette had demanded that their father accept Lissette and allow her to be groomed to take over the management of the Darkwater Inn and let Dimitri follow his passion as a chef. Adelaide had warned that Claude was a man used to getting his way, and yet he'd accepted their arguments fairly easily . . .

"I owe neither you nor Lissette any explanation.

Despite the blood running through her veins, she isn't a Pampalon and was raised with voodoo and such nonsense—some of the very reasons I couldn't abide her mother's ways. While I've been generous in allowing you and her to be indulged, make no mistake that from a *legal* standpoint I'll soon owe her nothing."

Dimitri sat glued to the chair. He recognized his father's tone of voice. Claude had consulted with lawyers—some of the best, Dimitri would bet—and had learned that in some way Lissette's claims could be disregarded. Both of their positions at the Darkwater were at Claude's sole discretion.

His father smiled that smile of his that held no humor. "Yes, you understand. See, Dimitri, that's why you're a Pampalon. You can pick up little nuances and manners and know when it's best to hold your tongue. You read people, which is valuable in the hotel business."

"What are you going to do, Father?"

"Nothing, at the moment. Once this murder and burglary business is concluded, I'll decide what to do about Lissette, you, and Ms. Fountaine. A lot depends on how this sticky situation is handled."

Meaning if they didn't have it solved and wrapped up before the princess and her fiancé left, heads would roll. Dimitri didn't care so much about his own future, but he cared greatly about what happened to Adelaide and Lissette. He was, as his father loved to remind him, a Pampalon and had many options because of the weight his last name carried. He would be okay, but Lissette and Adelaide? They needed their jobs. They needed the Darkwater.

"I see we understand one another, yes, Dimitri?" His father's expression had morphed into one of a cat toying with a mouse. The hunter having his prey exactly where he wanted it.

No sense arguing. At least not while he didn't know his father's hand, or his own play. He'd have to consult with a legal specialist to find out where his and Lissette's legal standings were. That didn't even take into consideration Adelaide, who was, in his father's eyes, just an employee who worked for him. A dispensable employee at that.

"Yes, sir." Dimitri stood. "I'll get Adelaide, and we'll go speak with the princess immediately."

"Good boy." Claude kept that infuriating smile in place as the condescending tone rolled off his words. "And Dimitri, do keep me updated."

Jaw locked, Dimitri nodded and strode from the office. His father was the most infuriating, irritating, frustrating man—

He turned onto the main hallway behind the offices and ran right into Detective Taton.

"Whoa!" The tall African American detective steadied him. "Dimitri." He dropped his hands.

"Sorry. I wasn't paying attention. What are you doing back here?" The offices were off limits as a general rule.

"Addy told Beau that your dad had some personal items in the safe but didn't know what exactly. I need to get an inventory for the report, and he'll need that for the insurance claim. Unless you know what he had in the safe?"

Great. Something else his father would blame Adelaide or Lissette for. Dimitri shook his head. "I know he often keeps a wide range of items in the safe, even more over the course of the last several months, but I have no idea what he had in there as of today."

Claude had been furious last year to learn that Lissette—although they didn't know it was her at the time—had been able to enter the house several times without their knowledge. He'd since updated their security system but still felt vulnerable at home. Now he'd probably feel that way about the safe here at the Darkwater, which meant a preventive upgrade would be forthcoming. Along with many more updated security measures Claude would deem necessary.

The detective pointed at the door to Claude's office. "That's your dad's office, right?"

Dimitri nodded. Maybe he should warn Detective Taton about his father's mood. He hesitated. It wasn't a secret that his father could be quite . . . Well, he was just difficult. Which led Dimitri to tilt his head at the detective, then just walk away. The man had a badge and the authority behind it. Maybe he could bring Claude Pampalon down a few much-needed notches.

He cleared the lobby, then spied Adelaide and Lissette behind the front counter. He made a line for them.

Adelaide looked up as he approached, and for a split second her eyes softened as she looked at him. Then, just as quickly, they focused back into work. "Records show the princess is still in her room. We're on our way there now."

Dimitri placed his hand on Adelaide's shoulder. "Perhaps you and I should go speak to the princess alone."

Lissette's eyes widened. "Why shouldn't I go? I'm going to need to handle such situations." Confusion and hurt marched across her face.

He licked his lips, hating his father for putting him in this position. "I understand, and normally I would agree with you entirely." He sighed. "In this case, because of international protocol that I'm not even totally sure of myself, I think the fewer people who show up at her door to give her such news the better."

"Then why don't I go with Adelaide and you check in with the cyber-crimes unit?" Lissette put her hands on her hips.

"Because this one is a little dicey, Lissette.

Let's not forget who the princess's fiancé is and why she's here."

Adelaide caught his gaze, held it, then turned back to Lissette. "I think Dimitri might be right. Additionally, we need someone to keep tabs on what's happening with the investigation. I can't be in two places at once." She smiled at Lissette. "Since the crime scene unit is working in the vault, why don't you go back to security and see if there's anything happening with the cyber-crimes unit. I'm sure Sully will need guidance."

Lissette let her gaze dart between him and Adelaide before she let out a long breath and nodded. "Please come get me when you're done?" she asked Dimitri.

"Of course."

Adelaide smiled at Lissette before gesturing for Dimitri to walk with her toward the elevators. As soon as they were out of earshot of Lissette, she turned to him. "Claude demanded she not go to tell the princess?"

He nodded, grateful that she understood. "I know my father, and he's got something up his sleeve. I'll need to meet with our attorney again."

"Oh, Dimitri." She rested her hand on his forearm as they stepped into the elevator. "I'm so sorry," she whispered to him before she smiled at the elevator attendant. "The penthouse suite, please, Richard."

The Darkwater Inn boasted a history almost as

41

old and rich as the Big Easy itself. Records of the Darkwater dated from the 1840s, and several of the original structures had survived the ravages of time and hurricanes such as Isle Dernière in 1856, Audrey in 1957, Camille in 1969, and, most recently, Katrina in 2005. Dimitri knew how much Adelaide loved the history and nuances of the old building as well as the fact that it had endured so much yet still stood proudly. This was her home, in every sense of the word, and Dimitri would do whatever he could to allow her to stay.

The third floor of the hotel housed the penthouse suite along the side of the building, looking out over the courtyard, but the back and opposite side of the floor also held two executive apartments: one for the owners' use and one for the general manager. The elevator they rode now let out directly in front of the penthouse while the private elevator let out in front of the apartments.

The elevator dinged, and Richard held the door for Dimitri and Adelaide. They stepped into the hall and headed toward the penthouse suite. Adelaide sucked in air and squared her shoulders. "Come on. Let's do this."

Dimitri had never admired her more.

# 4

## ADDY

"I'm Adelaide Fountaine, the general manager of the hotel. I need to speak with Princess Katerina von Pavlovna." The muscular man with the handgun on his hip didn't seem to understand . . . or care. "It's very important."

A young blonde woman crossed the room behind him and smiled at Adelaide. "Luca does not speak or understand English." It was easy to tell German was her native language as she spoke rapidly to her guard.

The bulk of a man stepped aside, allowing them into the room. He grunted as he shut the door behind them, then stood with his back to the door, barring an escape.

"Please, come sit." The princess waved them to the sitting area of the penthouse suite. "Luca is doing his job. He is protecting me. I told Edmond I do not need to have a guard here in the room, but they insist." Although German was the official language of Liechtenstein, the princess's English was very good. Probably the royal tutor's doing.

Addy had done her homework as soon as Mr. Pampalon had informed her the princess and entourage would be guests of the Darkwater Inn. Despite her years in college, she had to admit she hadn't a clue about Liechtenstein. Her research taught her that Liechtenstein was a doubly landlocked country—one of only two in the world—in Central Europe, located in the Upper Rhine Valley of the European Alps. Austria bordered the country to the east while Switzerland bordered the south and west. Liechtenstein was also one of the few countries in the world that maintained no military. Also, interestingly enough, in the US all consular affairs for Liechtenstein were handled by Switzerland.

She'd also learned that the princess wasn't merely a courtesy title, it was an official office. The country was a constitutional monarchy headed by the prince of Liechtenstein. Although all members of the royal family, no matter how distant, were named princes or princesses, because of Princess Katerina von Pavlovna's birth into the royal family, she was a legitimate princess. As such, she lived in one of the castles deemed to be royal residences, even if it wasn't the famous Vaduz castle that overlooked the capital of the country.

Addy now considered the woman who plopped down on the chair across from where she and Dimitri sat on the couch. Naturally blonde, mid-twenties, with the lightest blue eyes, the princess looked more like a sorority girl than a royal. Except for the manner in which she carried herself. No slouching, no bad posture, no lack of grace. Her privilege showed with her every movement.

Addy caught sight of the table, still covered in plates of food from an obvious room service order. "I'm sorry to disturb your dinner."

"It is no problem. I had finished my meal already. The food here is quite remarkable." The princess's smile revealed perfectly straight and stunningly white teeth.

"Thank you," Dimitri spoke, almost automatically.

The princess gave a slight dip of her head. "Now, what may I do for you?"

Addy took a deep breath. "Princess—"

"Please, call me Katerina. *Princess* is too formal among friends."

"Katerina," Addy corrected, "there's been an incident at the hotel this evening." She swallowed, choosing her words carefully. "A robbery."

The princess gasped and put her hand to her neck. "A robbery?"

"Yes. I'm . . ." Adelaide hesitated, then squared her shoulders and continued. "I'm so very sorry to tell you that your guard was killed during this robbery."

Katerina's eyes widened and filled with

moisture. "Rubin? Dead?" She looked over Addy and Dimitri's head to her bodyguard at the door. "It cannot be."

"I'm so very sorry. The police are here now." Addy could only imagine how she'd feel if she were in Katerina's position.

Luca had obviously been alerted by the princess's reaction that something was wrong. He began moving in their direction, and the princess stood as he came to support her with his hand under her elbow, whispering to her in a thick German dialect.

Addy and Dimitri stood as well. Might as well get it all out. "I'm also very sorry to tell you that your tiara was one of the items stolen in the robbery." Addy lifted her chin, determined not to sob along with the royal.

The princess dropped back down to her chair. "My crown? Is stolen?"

The suite door clicked, then opened. Luca rushed toward it, hand on his handgun, as Edmond Jansen entered.

Edmond took a split second to register Luca's demeanor and that of his fiancée and brushed past the bodyguard to be at the princess's side. "What is going on here?" His stern stare hit Dimitri and Addy dead in the face.

"Rubin is dead. My crown is gone." Tears spilled out of the princess's eyes, silently sliding down her cheeks before she ducked her head.

Luca once again held vigil at the door to the suite, but stood even more rigidly if that was possible.

"Rubin? The crown? What?" Edmond kept his arm around the princess as he sat on the arm of the chair, but looked at Dimitri. "What is going on here?"

"We had a robbery this afternoon. During the course of that crime, your guard, Rubin, was killed. One of the items stolen was the princess's tiara that was stored in our safe." The back of Addy's throat burned as she pushed the words out.

"Stolen? That is unacceptable." Edmond's face flushed a deep red.

Addy sunk back down on the couch, and Dimitri eased beside her. She leaned forward, closer to the princess. "I'm so sorry, Mr. Jansen . . . Princess. The police are here now, starting their investigation. They'll most likely need to speak to you soon. I wanted to let you know as quickly as possible as I'm sure there are certain protocols that need to be followed."

"Yes. We will need to contact the Swiss embassy, as my crown belongs to my country, not me personally." The princess leaned against Edmond. "I cannot believe Rubin is dead. He was a good man. Loyal."

"What happened?" Edmond asked.

Addy shook her head. "I haven't received the

details just yet. We're waiting on the report from the police for the official cause of death."

"Is there a chance he might still be alive?" The princess shifted just slightly out of her fiancé's embrace to look at Addy.

"I'm so sorry, but no. He's dead, as is one of the hotel's security guards as well."

"How did this happen, Dimitri?" Edmond ignored Addy.

"As Ms. Fountaine said, the police are just beginning their investigation, so it's too early to be sure. But from our best estimation, a hacker gained access to our security system to release the locks on our vault room and the safe." Dimitri's tone came out evenly, and once again Addy felt a surge of gratitude that he was with her.

"A hacker killed two people as well?" Edmond pushed.

"Again, the police are just starting their investigation, so it wouldn't be prudent to guess." Dimitri spoke slowly, his tone devoid of any emotion. "I'm sure the police will let you know as soon as they're able."

"How could this have happened? We were told storing the crown in your vault would keep it safe while we were here." Edmond's voice lifted an octave.

"We will know more as the police investigation gains traction and we are given information."

Dimitri's voice might have remained even, but he tensed on the couch alongside Addy.

She pressed her leg against Dimitri's, hoping it would give him a measure of comfort as he had provided to her so many times before. "I understand how upset you must be, both of you. But I assure you that our local police detectives are very good at their jobs." Beau was the best, and she didn't think she was just being biased. Everyone who knew him sang his praises. He'd just been promoted to a higher-grade detective in the last year. The New Orleans police didn't promote those who were unworthy. "We will find out what happened and see justice served."

Edmond's frown pinned her to the couch. "But you can't guarantee that, can you?"

"I'm pretty certain." She demanded her voice not waver under his judgment.

"What about Katerina's tiara? Will that be recovered? That's irreplaceable."

Her mouth went drier than dry. "The hotel carries very good insurance, Mr. Jansen. We will be sure to file a claim on your behalf and work with whatever authorities that protocol demands."

"No amount of money can replace this particular tiara. Most of the current pieces worn today by members of the Princely House of Liechtenstein have been acquired by family

49

marriages and hail from Austria, Bavaria, and Russia."

Katerina sniffled against him, then straightened. "Do you know the story about Tsar Nicholas Romanov, the Romanov dynasty, and the missing Russian crown jewels?"

Addy let out a slow breath, trying to remember what she'd read. "A little. Something about certain pieces having been claimed to be in the collection of the crown jewels but never fully documented. They supposedly went missing along with the Romanov daughter Anastasia."

Katerina gave a little smile. "That is the basic story most in the States have heard, but that is not the full story. The tales of the missing child Anastasia gained more interest than that of the missing crown jewels."

She sat ramrod straight in the chair and continued. "At a library here in the United States, a director perusing the rare books collection found a very large book with no title or identification information on the spine or cover. It was, in essence, an album. Upon further inspection, the researchers at the library found the title page hand drawn with an elaborate design and noted *Moscow, 1922*. The title was in Russian, and when they had it translated, it read *The Russian Diamond Fund*. This is the name that has been given to the imperial regalia for the Romanov family. The book contains eighty-eight photographs of the Romanov jewelry with descriptive captions, all in Russian."

Dimitri visibly relaxed. "The Romanov family were the rulers of Russia for more than three hundred years, yes?"

Katerina nodded. "Yes. Nicholas abdicated in 1917, and his entire family—except for his daughter Anastasia, or so it is believed—was executed in 1918. Even after the family's remains were tested in the late 1980s, there is a daughter missing." She inched forward to the edge of her chair. "The crown jewels are rumored to have been sewn into the hems and such of Nicholas's daughters' clothes. That is not proven or disproven, but it is a fact that in that 1922 book found in the library, there are photographs of what are known to be the Russian crown jewels, like the Orlov Diamond in the scepter and the grand crown, which has the huge stone at the top."

The princess's accent became thicker as she spoke faster. "The crown jewels were worn by the Romanov royal family until they were seized during the Russian Revolution, after the Romanov family was executed. The jewels were said to be secured in secret until 1922, when they were unpacked and a full inventory was taken. The *Russian Diamond Fund* dates to the same year, and the photographs appear to have been part of the initial inventory."

Edmond lost his attitude and picked up the story. "The Orlov Diamond is a 189-carat stone that is rumored to have been stolen from the eye of a statue of a Hindu deity in southern India. It is but one of the priceless pieces in the collection of the Diamond Fund."

Addy nodded, not entirely sure there was a connection to be made.

Katerina smiled at her fiancé. "Yes, many wondered the fate of the collection of jewels. Much of the collection was preserved by curators at the Kremlin in Moscow, and in 1925, the official photographs and documentation of the collection was published with the title *Russia's Treasure of Diamonds and Precious Stones.*"

Addy wrinkled her brow. "But you just said they found the album dated 1922 with photos of the crown jewels, which included these pieces."

Katerina's smile widened. "Yes. There are many in Russia who believe the 1922 book and its contents are not correct, but there is no denying that those photographs match, at least mostly, the photograph and details published in the official published collection in 1925."

"But there is a noted difference that has baffled many." Edmond stretched the full length of his legs out in front of him and crossed them at the ankles as he remained perched on the arm of the chair. "There are four pieces in the photograph in the 1922 album and also in the picture in the 1925 book, but those four specific pieces aren't actually documented in the 1925 book."

Katerina nodded. "A sapphire brooch, an emerald necklace, a sapphire and diamond bracelet, and a diadem. We know that the sapphire brooch in the 1922 book was sold at auction in London in 1927, as there are records even though it was not listed in the 1925 book, but the necklace, bracelet, and diadem have never been officially recorded, and the Kremlin refuses to acknowledge that there were ever such pieces in the Diamond Fund."

That made no sense. Addy raised a brow. "But they are pictured with the rest of the crown jewels in the photograph in both the 1922 album and the 1925 book?"

The princess nodded. "Yes, but officials claim they do not really exist. Or if they do, they are not part of the Diamond Fund. They are not recognized as being part of the Russian crown jewels."

Addy couldn't imagine a country denying the existence of such assets. "If those four pieces are in the photograph of the 1922 album, and later one of those *nonexistent* pieces is sold at auction and documentation proves as such, then wouldn't it stand to reason that the other three pieces must also exist and belong to the collection?"

Edmond nodded. "Exactly."

Fascinating story, truly, but Adelaide couldn't understand why they were telling her and Dimitri this right now, with two dead guards and a robbed safe.

"The diadem in the photographs of both the 1922 album and the 1925 book reflects a sapphire and briolette diamond *kokoshnik*-style tiara." Edmond sobered as he spoke. "*Kokoshnik* basically means a traditional Russian headdress worn by women that was made popular when the Romanov court ladies began wearing them in the nineteenth century. The original large *kokoshnik* headdresses, in the hands of the Romanovs, became smaller and more crescent shaped, looking more like halos. The Romanovs embellished the *kokoshniks* with jewels and sometimes with veils."

Edmond sighed. "The diadem photographed contained nine large sapphires and was covered in diamonds, including several drop diamonds."

Addy's heart beat so hard she could feel her pulse pounding in her eardrums. At the same time, waves of nausea crashed in the pit of her stomach.

Katerina's eyes filled with moisture again. "Identical to my tiara, which is listed as having been purchased from a Russian family in the early 1920s."

# 5

BEAU

"Well, Walt, what can you tell me?" Beau stood next to the older coroner as the other two men with the coroner's logo emblazoned on the backs of their jackets zipped black bags around the two fallen guards.

The CSU team closed their field cases, the snapping and latching echoing off the walls inside the vault.

"Cause of death to both was gunshot. My best guess without having them on my table is that they were shot with a .38 caliber." Walt pulled off the plastic gloves from his hands and shoved them into the pockets of his jacket. "Probably shot from about three or four feet away. From the entrance wounds and where the bodies were found, I'd say they were inside the vault when the shooter came from behind them. The hotel guard was shot first—once in the back that hit his heart. The other guard turned and was shot twice in the chest."

Beau glanced at Marcel. "Why would they be inside the vault?"

Walt shrugged. "Not my job to figure that out.

I'll do the autopsies tomorrow and get you my report as soon as I'm done."

"Thanks, Walt. I appreciate it."

"Yep." The coroner shrugged past Beau and Marcel.

"Maybe there was a click when the electronic lock disengaged and they stepped inside to check it out?" Marcel stared at the vault door.

"Maybe." Beau glanced at the outline on the floor of the bodies. "A .38 gunshot isn't exactly quiet, yet no one reported hearing the shots."

"Thinking a suppressor?"

Beau shrugged. "Something to muffle the sound."

Marcel stood over the outlines. "Okay, so let's play it out. The vault's electronic door disengages and clicks, which gets their attention."

"But why open the vault and enter?" Beau stared at the chairs set outside the vault's door. "If they're sitting there and they hear the door's lock disengage, why get up and come inside? It doesn't make sense."

"Maybe it's policy if the lock opens they have to check it out?" Marcel suggested.

"I'll ask Addy." Beau made a note in his notebook. "Okay, so for whatever reason, they came inside." He moved to stand in the outline of where Leon's body had been. "The hotel guard gets taken out with one shot to the back."

Marcel stepped into the outline of where the

Liechtenstein guard had been. "He's beside the hotel guard and hears the gunshot and sees the man fall." He pivoted toward the door. "He turns and takes two in the chest."

"We recovered two .38 bullets." Nolan returned to the vault. "We'll start running prelim tests and should have some info for you tomorrow. We're done with everything and are about to head out now, unless there's something else?"

"Not that I can see. Thanks, Nolan." Beau turned back to Marcel. "We can safely assume that the hack and the robbery are connected."

"And that these guys were in the wrong place at the wrong time. I doubt either was a target."

Beau shook his head at his partner. "We can't assume that. This might have been a deliberate hit all along, meticulously planned around the hack as a distraction, and the other guard was in the wrong place at the wrong time."

"You think that?" Marcel asked.

"Not really, but we can't just assume that's the case without investigating it." Beau turned away. *Marcel should know this*, and on some level he probably did. But lately, his partner had been quick to jump the gun on the way to investigate instead of letting the facts of the case lead where the investigation went. Beau didn't know what was going on with his partner, but he needed to figure it out so the younger man's career didn't take a shift downward.

"That would be a little over the top, don't you think?"

Beau shrugged and went back outside the vault, then walked back to where the body outlines lay. "Ten steps."

Marcel waited, studying Beau. "What's your scenario?"

"Maybe whoever shot them waited until the vault was unlocked, then pulled a gun on them and had them open the vault door."

"I thought cyber-crimes confirmed that the hack unlocked the vault and the safe."

"Maybe the shooter was smart and didn't want his prints on the door, which would indicate that he knew about police procedures and didn't want to take a chance on being identified. It would make sense why they were inside the vault instead of outside the door where they were posted."

Marcel nodded. "Yeah, I guess it does."

Beau made a note in his notebook. It was his experience that even in the most horrendous of crimes, logic played a role. It also played a very large part in solving the crime.

He glanced around the vault a final time before flipping the page in his notebook and scanning his notes. He didn't want to overlook anything. They had very little to go on at the moment, and he hoped the CSU team would have something useful for them.

He stepped into the hall and removed his shoe coverings.

"What next?" Marcel removed his shoe covers as well.

"When you spoke to Claude Pampalon, he said he didn't have anything of his in the safe?"

Marcel nodded. "That's right."

Beau shook his head. "If he had, I'd bet it wouldn't be worth half of what the princess of Liechtenstein's crown is worth."

"A real princess." Marcel shook his head. "Who brings a real princess in for a Mardi Gras parade? According to Pampalon senior, the princess always wanted to come to the States to visit, and this was a great opportunity." He snorted.

Beau loved the carnival season as much as the next native New Orleanian, but to bring in real royalty for the krewe was pushing it. "We know that the main reason he did was to line his own pocket. Inviting the princess and having her happy made her fiancé happy, who I'm sure let his father know how accommodating his business associate was."

"Oh, you got that right." Marcel sighed.

Beau stuffed his notebook back into his pocket. "And now there's the murders and robbery. We'll need to call the captain and let him know immediately before we have an international incident on top of everything else."

"I'll make the call if you'd like."

"No, I'll do it. The captain won't be thrilled about the after-hours call, or the situation." He grabbed the sign-in log that the NOPD had put in place from the chair outside the vault and scanned the scrawled writing. No one unauthorized had entered the vault after they'd arrived. "Why don't you holler at Zach and see if we can chat for a few minutes before I talk with Addy? I'll fill the captain in." He pulled out his cell phone and made the call.

As Beau had predicted, the captain wasn't happy about the situation. Or the call. But he gave Beau the green light to follow the investigation tonight and make the call to the embassy in the morning.

"Zach said he'll meet us in the lobby." Marcel slipped his cell back into his jacket pocket.

Beau nodded and led the way out of the hotel's labyrinth of hallways, past the front desk, and into the front of the hotel. A quick scan of the area didn't reveal anything out of the ordinary. The hotel seemed busy, but it usually did. Especially during Mardi Gras season.

The Darkwater Inn stood in the heart of the French Quarter, right in the middle of the hub of the city that breathed a life all of its own. Mardi Gras brought out the best, and worst, of New Orleans, who knew how to keep her secrets. Knew how to turn out the parades and festivals and how to adore her many krewes. New Orleans was unlike any other city in the United States, everyone who'd ever been there and experienced what she offered firsthand knew that.

"Detective Savoie." Zach Monet, a lead detective in the cyber-crimes unit, reached out his hand.

Beau shook it. "What's the latest?"

The dark-haired young man led them toward a small sitting area of four chairs, away from the crowding of the front desk. He was maybe twenty-two or twenty-three but already a lead detective in the cyber-crimes division. Technology experts were coming younger and younger these days. Made Beau feel like an old man at thirty-four.

"Most hackers have certain strings of codes that they use for identification. Kind of like a signature, but a way of showing off. This one doesn't have any identifiers like that. That's unusual in itself, but there's more."

Beau leaned against the back of his high-back chair, jotting notes in his notebook.

"Stranger is the hack code itself. It's the most basic I've ever seen in a hack job of this magnitude."

"What does that mean?" Marcel asked.

"The way he accessed the system was basically juvenile-level hacking."

Beau stopped writing and stared at the young

man. "You might need to explain it like you are explaining it to a juvenile."

Zach smiled. "I didn't want to insult."

"Neither Marcel nor I speak technology, so please, don't worry about insulting us."

Zach nodded. "Yes, sir. The hack is essentially no more than opening a back door into the system. It's like the back kitchen door was left unlatched so someone could sneak into the house and steal everything of value."

Beau looked up from his notebook. He must have misunderstood. "Are you telling me that this was an inside job?"

"Well, I can't say that just yet, but every indication we've seen tells us that whoever set this in motion had physical access to the system and knew which system the security programs ran on. As complex and updated as the computer system is here, it would be a hard press to hack it without access. That's all I'm saying."

Beau nodded as he wrote. "They had to have physical access to the system?" That would definitely mean an inside job. The Darkwater had a state-of-the-art security system, Beau had learned last year.

"For this level of entry, it would be nearly impossible not to have physical access to the system to create the back door. Right now, Hazel has shut down the access and is running a backward trace to pinpoint where the remote access linked from."

"I'm assuming your team is questioning everyone who had access?" Marcel asked.

Zach nodded. "Oh, yeah. Raphael has his list to run backgrounds on everyone who had access. He'll run those first thing in the morning. He's finishing up interviewing the security personnel here tonight, then will interview the other three tomorrow. I'm about to go speak to all management personnel who are still here." He pushed his glasses back up to the bridge of his nose. "I believe that's Mr. Pampalon senior and junior, Ms. Fountaine, and Ms. Bastien, unless Mr. Pampalon senior has already left, which we were told he might."

While they needed to speak to the princess regarding her tiara, Beau also wanted to be able to watch the reactions of those being interviewed by Zach. He also didn't want the young detective, no matter his rank, to have to face Pampalon alone. "Marcel, why don't you go interview the princess since you've already spoken to Mr. Pampalon?" Beau closed his notebook and looked at Zach. "If you don't mind, I'd like to go with you on your interviews this evening. It will help me to hear the conversations."

Zach smiled. "I don't mind at all, Detective. Let's start with Mr. Pampalon senior. I understand he doesn't live onsite."

Marcel tossed Beau a knowing grin before leaving them. Beau waited, willing to let Zach take the lead, but the young man didn't move. "Do you know where Mr. Pampalon is?"

"Oh. Yes. His office. This way." Zach meandered toward the hallway where Addy's office was housed. Claude's office was around the corner from Addy's. As they passed her office, Beau noticed no light shone from under the closed door. She did live onsite, but there was no way she'd be in her apartment already. More than likely, she'd be working the situation long after everyone from the police department left.

One of the many things that made Beau love her.

# 6

## DIMITRI

"I'm sure I don't need to spell it out for you how imperative it is for Katerina's tiara to be recovered and returned to her, posthaste." Edmond Jansen had lost all premise of politeness now that he had left his fiancée in the hotel room with Adelaide and stood in the hotel hallway facing Dimitri.

"Of course I understand the importance." Dimitri chose to ignore the man's accusing glare and tone. Edmond had every right to be upset. Dimitri couldn't help but put himself in Edmond's place if the situation were reversed and it was Adelaide who'd been robbed. Of course, he and Adelaide weren't engaged, weren't even a couple—yet—but he could understand Edmond's emotions all too plainly.

Edmond took a step closer, invading Dimitri's personal space. "I hope that you do, and quickly. I would hate for my father to arrive this weekend for your father's parade and the tiara still be missing. My father would be most displeased, and I'm certain his displeasure would be made clear to your father."

Dimitri straightened, reclaiming his personal

space. "There's no need for veiled threats, Edmond. We will continue to cooperate with the police in the investigation, as we would for any guest."

"That's just it, Dimitri. Katerina is not just any guest. She's a *princess*, a royal who deserves more than just your cooperation with the police. Her stature demands that the focus of the investigation and your efforts be centered on finding her tiara and returning it to her quickly."

*If it were Adelaide . . .* "Of course we are doing everything in our power to return the princess's property to her."

"As we explained, those jewels are priceless."

Dimitri nodded. "I understand." Although he couldn't understand why the royal family would allow such valuables out of their country.

"I hope that you do, Dimitri. I think our fathers have a very mutually beneficial business association. I would hate to see that connection severed." Edmond Jansen's eyes were as hard as the cutting edge of his words.

There was no response Dimitri could make that would smooth the man's ire, so it was best just to hold his tongue in check.

Edmond, however, still had plenty to say. Or perhaps he just needed to release his frustration. "I'm beyond disappointed in your ability to secure such valuable belongings. We were told the hotel's vault and safe were impenetrable, otherwise we would have never left Katerina's tiara in your custody."

Dimitri just nodded, not pointing out that even though their own armed guard and bodyguard accompanied the princess, the royal family hadn't seemed to put too much emphasis on security of their crown jewels.

Until they were stolen.

The anger in Edmond's eyes shimmered under the harsh lights of the hotel hallway. Dimitri could almost touch the man's emotions, and in spite of his frustration he empathized. How horrible to not be able to be in control when he was clearly accustomed to being so. How awful to not be able to protect the prize of the woman he loved. "We are doing—and will continue our efforts to do—whatever it takes to recover the princess's crown."

"See that you do, Dimitri."

The door to the hotel suite swung open, and Adelaide stepped into the hallway like the breath of fresh air she always was. Despite the circumstances, Dimitri couldn't stop the smile that instinctively slipped across his face. "Are you finished?"

She nodded at him but moved her gaze to Edmond. "Again, Mr. Jansen, on behalf of the Darkwater Inn, I apologize. Please know that we will do all that we can to rectify this awful situation. As I told Katerina, the police will be here soon to interview you both. While their questions might seem redundant, please understand they must gather as much information as possible, no matter how minute it might seem to you, in order to do their best on the investigation."

Dimitri stood at the ready, just in case Edmond decided to give Adelaide any of the rudeness he'd displayed a few moments earlier. It looked like he just might when he opened his mouth, eyes still hard. But then he glanced at Dimitri and paused for a moment before he spoke to Adelaide.

"Thank you for coming to tell us in person, Ms. Fountaine. Katerina and I will await the police's arrival."

She smiled her response, then headed toward the elevator. Dimitri gave Edmond a curt nod before following her. As soon as they were safely in the elevator, Adelaide told the attendant they were going to the main floor, then leaned her head against the wall and closed her eyes.

Dimitri sent up a silent prayer for her as he reached out and took her hand. Her eyes shot open and she stood straight.

He didn't release her hand, instead caressing her knuckles with his thumb. "It's been a long day."

She smiled. "For all of us. It isn't going to be over anytime soon, either, I'm afraid."

The elevator door opened, and she pulled her

hand gently from his. "Thank you," she said to the attendant as she stepped out of the car.

Dimitri fell into step alongside her as they crossed the polished marble floors of the lobby. She stopped just before she reached the front desk, her gaze wandering over the massive space. He could almost hear her assessment: good traffic flow for the guests. The location made for easy entrance to the streets of the French Quarter, yet the Darkwater provided a private courtyard for quiet evenings. There was just something special about the hotel that pulled Adelaide to her. Dimitri would forever be grateful for that.

Adelaide slowly started toward her office. Dimitri moved with her, sensing the enormous weight making her shoulders sag. He pulled out his cell, sent a quick text to his sous chef, then followed Adelaide into her office.

"What do you make of that story about the missing jewels of the Romanov family?" She stood, grabbing notes from her desk, scanning them then absently sorting them into different piles across the desktop.

Dimitri took a seat at the little sitting area in front of the windows of her office. "If it's true, I can't help but wonder why the royal family would allow the diadem to leave the country."

She nodded, still sorting. "That's what I was thinking. And if I were Katerina, there'd be no way I'd wear something so valuable."

If she only knew how valuable he found her, Adelaide, to be. She'd asked for space and he'd given it, but that had been nearly a year ago, and his feelings hadn't lessened or changed. If anything, they'd only grown stronger.

"They did bring a guard to watch over the crown, but still . . ." Adelaide tossed the last scrap of notes onto the desk and came to sit on the little loveseat across from him. She kicked off her heels and curled her legs under her, making her look more like a young college student than the woman of almost thirty years that he knew her to be. "Katerina said they would take care of notifying the royal authorities, but I can't stop thinking that we should also call the embassy in the morning. Just to cover our bases. And we'll need to call our insurance agent as well to start a claim."

She leaned her head back against the loveseat, closing her eyes and pinching the bridge of her nose. "There's so much that we'll need to start on. And I need to go visit Leon's family in the morning after the police notify them of his death. It's almost overwhelming."

It was, and Adelaide wouldn't delegate any of the responsibility of any of it. That wasn't who she was. She would bear the weight of it all.

"We'll go to Leon's home first thing in the morning. The hotel will, of course, provide all the financial support they need for the funeral.

I'll have Lissette get with HR to assist Leon's wife in processing his life-insurance claim." Dimitri moved to sit beside her and gently pulled her feet into his lap, where he kneaded the heel, the pressure point for the lower back. "Relax, *mon chaton.*"

She sighed and closed her eyes again. "That's heavenly." She rested her head back once more. "Did your father say what he had in the safe?"

He didn't want to talk about his father, but he also didn't want anything to interrupt her allowing him to comfort her. "He said he had nothing in there."

Her eyes shot open. "He did have something in there. It was like a tube in a black velvet bag in the bottom of the drawer."

"You must be mistaken. He said there was nothing of his in there."

She shifted to sit up. "There was. I saw it myself when I put the princess's tiara in the drawer. It was a black velvet pouch, about, oh, maybe a couple of feet tall, kind of tube shaped, that was maybe three or four inches thick. I'm positive it was in there."

Dimitri rubbed the ball of her foot a little more forcefully, trying to ease her into relaxing. "Well, it must not have been too important if he forgot."

She eased back against the sofa again. "It was important enough to have in the safe, so it had to have some value. I'll speak with him tomorrow

71

before we contact the hotel's insurance agent. I'm not sure how we'll file the claim for the princess's crown."

"I'm sure the embassy will instruct us." He moved the pressure up her foot to the outer sides of the heel, the reflexology point for her sciatic nerve.

The signs of tension on her face lessened as he kneaded. "Yes. Did Marcel give you any indication of how the investigation would be handled?"

"From what I gathered from listening to the detectives and the cyber-crimes officers, they have jurisdiction over the investigation, and the embassy personnel would be more supportive than active on the case."

"Good. I know Beau doesn't appreciate when other agencies interfere in his investigation."

Dimitri didn't reply, just kept rubbing her feet. He really didn't have anything against Beauregard Savoie. The man was honest, hard-working, dependable, and very much ethical and honorable.

But he was also in love with Adelaide and shared a common past with her that Dimitri could never compete with.

Not that she ever made him feel like she compared the two, but how could she not? Both he and Beauregard had declared their feelings for her, albeit at an inconvenient time for her, and stated their interest in furthering their relationship. Talk about overwhelming. With everything she'd been dealing with then, she'd needed space and told them both she couldn't think about a romance with either at the time. But now . . .

A gentle knock rapped against the office door.

Adelaide's eyes popped open, and she shot upright, then to her feet. "Come in."

One of the room-service attendants rolled a cart into the office. He smiled at Adelaide, then straightened as he spied Dimitri. He carefully lifted the plate covers from the steaming food. "Tonight we are serving red beans and rice with handmade biscuits and house-made butter."

The enticing aroma filled the office, and Dimitri smiled to himself, allowing that brief moment of ego to fill him with pride. While his father had groomed him from birth to take over the operations of the hotel, learning every aspect of the business, his heart had led him into the kitchen and hadn't let him go yet.

He was a good chef. Excellent, actually, and he wasn't just being vain. He had a natural bent to adding just the right mix of unusual spices to create masterpieces. Food critics agreed he not only knew how to prepare exotic and savory meals guaranteed to make taste buds stand up and take notice, but he knew the history of the cuisine he made as well.

The Crescent City teemed with culinary

wonders, but one of her most intriguing assets was the inviting and delectable Cajun cuisine as well as that of the Creole foods. Although both types of cooking were suffused in French tradition, the two were not the same. Creole, derived from the Spanish word *criollo*, was more of a reflection of the area's multicultural heritage—a combination from France, Spain, West Africa, and the Caribbean. On the other hand, Cajun delights were more connected to the French Acadians who, after being expelled from Nova Scotia in the mid-eighteenth century, had found sanctuary in southwest Louisiana.

Dimitri knew the differences between the two types that would forever be entwined with New Orleans and had perfected his ability to cook within the boundaries of both. Eating at the hotel restaurant to sample his culinary creations was a big draw for the Darkwater Inn.

He stood and crossed Adelaide's office. "Thank you." He grabbed the ticket, scrawled his name, then handed it back to the young man, who took it and made a hasty retreat.

"Yes, thank you, Dimitri." Adelaide's face had lit up, and the worry lines seemed to have smoothed.

Dimitri smiled. The woman so appreciated food, which spoke directly to his very heart. They were, for many reasons, perfect for one another. "I figured you'd forget to eat." He wheeled the cart closer to the sitting area and then moved the platters to the little glass table between the available seats.

"I shouldn't be able to eat with everything going on, but oh, this looks and smells divine." She took a seat in front of where he'd set one of the platters.

He sent up a silent grace as he finished setting their food and drinks on the table.

Adelaide took a bite and smiled behind her pressed lips before she chewed, then swallowed. "Oh, this is perfection on a spoon, Dimitri."

He nodded, then lifted his own spoon. They ate in comfortable silence. He couldn't help but wonder if their life would ever get uncomplicated enough that they could enjoy simple evenings of eating alone.

Another knock on the door dispelled that notion.

Adelaide stood as Lissette stuck her head around the door. "I wondered where you two went." She stepped inside. "That smells great."

"Have some," Adelaide offered.

"I'll get some later." Dimitri's sister glanced at him, accusations beaming in her eyes. "How did it go with the princess? I've been waiting for an update."

He should've called her. He stood. "I'm sorry. We were—"

"It went fine." Adelaide cut him off, taking

control of the situation as she filled Lissette in on what they'd learned from the princess. He observed quietly. There was still a level of distrust from Adelaide toward Lissette. He couldn't really blame her. Lissette had, after all, put voodoo curses and hexes on both him and his father, not that he believed in any of that nonsense. Maybe he should be flattered that Adelaide cared enough about him to be cautious around his sister because of her actions toward him.

Then again, Lissette seemed a bit resentful of Adelaide, almost jealous at times, for the way she'd had to claw her way into the Darkwater while Adelaide was already established.

Once Adelaide finished bringing Lissette up to speed, she grabbed her water bottle and took a long drink.

Lissette nodded. "Well, at least that's that. The cyber-crimes unit finished speaking with Claude, who said we should call him at home with any updates. The detectives need to speak with each of us but have asked to do so separately." She turned to Dimitri. "They've requested to speak to you first. They're waiting in my office."

Of course they had. Beauregard would save Adelaide for last—out of deference, of course, but also so he could spend more time with her. Nothing he could do about it, though.

With a nod, he left Adelaide and walked with

Lissette toward the office that had once been his. Lissette stopped him in the hall with her hand on his arm. "Look, I'm not real sure what they've already found out because they aren't giving me all the information, so if you can get them to tell you, please do."

"Why do you think they know more than they're telling you?" Police normally didn't disclose more than required, but if Lissette knew something . . .

She shrugged. "Gut feeling, I guess."

Dimitri stared into his half sister's eyes. Maybe Adelaide's caution and wariness was justified. "You aren't talking about voodoo or hoodoo, are you, Lissette? You said you were done with all that."

"I am. I am." She flushed. "Mostly. Look, I can't help if the spirits can't accept I've changed."

Detective Savoie stepped into the hallway. "Am I interrupting?"

In more ways than he knew. Dimitri whispered to Lissette, "We'll finish this discussion later," before smiling at Beauregard. "I'm sorry to have kept you waiting. I was having dinner with Adelaide."

The look on Beauregard's face was as priceless as Princess Katerina's tiara.

# 7

## ADDY

"So, you were completely unaware of the threat to the hotel's security system until Lissette came and informed you?" Marcel stared at her from his chair in front of her desk.

"That's correct." Addy spared a peek at Beau, sitting beside his partner. He'd been quiet through most of their interview, just making notes in his notebook as he usually did, letting Marcel ask most of the questions. "Here at the Darkwater, everyone knows their job and does it well. I don't have much use for needing to run any security protocols."

She shouldn't be offended—he was just doing his job like she had to do hers, but she sometimes wished they could just talk like they usually did, as friends.

"Tell us about the hotel's employees in the security department." Addy nodded. "Well, since Geoff's imprisonment, Sully Clements has been the acting head of security. He's very thorough and a very hard worker." He just wasn't as instinctively good as Geoff. Man, she really missed Geoff. Only a few more months and he'd be released and able to come back to work, even if he couldn't carry a gun again.

"Trustworthy?" Beau looked up from his notebook.

"Yes. I don't have his employee file on me at the moment, but I know his employee record is stellar since we verified everything in his file last year before we promoted him to acting chief."

"What can you tell me about Leon? Do you know if he had any problems with anyone?" Marcel probed.

She shook her head. "Not that I'm aware of. I'm sorry to say I didn't know him as well as I do Sully or Hixson. Leon was always very respectful to me, and as far as I know, he did his job satisfactorily."

"And what about Hixson Albertson?" Beau asked.

"Hixson is probably one of the youngest in the hotel, but he's scary smart when it comes to everything technical. We hired him right out of high school. He takes online computer programming and coding classes."

"He *is* young. And very smart with the programs. Someone who would be able to hack the system very easily, as well as cover his tracks."

Addy pinned Marcel with her stare. "Are you saying you think Hixson had something to do with what happened?" She couldn't imagine the young man being involved in anything so illegal.

Marcel shrugged. "He's young, like you said. The young guns always think they're infallible, don't they? You just told us that he has the smarts to pull this off. He clearly had the means and opportunity to do it."

"But why? There's no motive."

Beau looked up from his notebook. "How do you know he had no motive?"

"Well . . ." He had her there. "I mean, I don't know for sure, but I just can't imagine him being involved."

Marcel chuckled. "You do know that most people are shocked after serial killers are revealed. Next-door neighbors, work associates, even spouses are often fooled by duplicitous people. Happens every single day."

Sure, but Hixson? No way. "I guess, but you'd be wrong about Hixson. He's just a kid. Albeit a very smart kid, but still just a kid."

"You'd be amazed at what the right bit of motivation can do to move people to do things you'd never think they would. A debt over his head that he couldn't see a way to break free of. A threat to his ego if he couldn't. Drowning realization of pending doom. People are threatened on so many different levels by so many different things. Who's to say this kid doesn't have a mountain of debt?"

"Does he?" If he did, he could have come to the hotel. All the employees knew that the hotel—at least per her and Dimitri's policy, anyway—took care of their own. Then again, she had been gone for six months . . .

"We won't know until we get the backgrounds back on everyone, but that just goes to show you don't know." Beau's smile took a little of the sting out of his words.

She smiled back instinctively. "I guess not."

"What about Claude Pampalon?"

Addy turned her attention to Marcel. "What about him?"

"He said he didn't have anything in the safe at the time of the robbery. Is that correct?"

She shook her head. "I could have sworn he had a black velvet pouch in there, but I must have been mistaken since he isn't claiming anything of his was stolen. It *is* his hotel, so he needn't report to me when and what he puts in and takes out at his leisure." He could have taken the pouch out, of course, but if that were the case, why didn't he just say so? It really bothered her, and she didn't quite know why. "But the fifty thousand dollars in cash, while technically belonging to the hotel, would actually belong to Claude—at least the way he usually sees it."

"What about Dimitri Pampalon?" Beau's question was loaded at best. Weighted at worst.

She let out a slow breath. "I'm unaware of anything he had stored in the safe."

"But he knows the combination, yes?" Beau pushed.

She nodded.

"Who all does know the combination?" Marcel asked.

"Claude, Dimitri, me, and Lissette. If anyone else knows it, they were told by one of the other three, and I have no knowledge of that." But it didn't make sense for any of them to be suspect. "Although the hack is what opened the vault and the safe, so the person didn't know the combination."

"We don't know that to be true. The hack's unlocking could just be to throw us off the truth and make us not suspect someone who actually had a combination."

She considered that, chewing her bottom lip. "That would be a lot of covering up involved. A double murder isn't easily disregarded, I would think."

"No, nor is knowing there was fifty thousand dollars in cash sitting in that safe." Marcel gave a slight tilt of his head.

"There would've been a double murder either way, since the vault was guarded constantly by the Liechtenstein guard." Beau held up a finger. "But the hotel doesn't have a posted guard at the vault all the time, does it?"

She shook her head. "Almost never. The only reason Leon was guarding the vault today was because of the princess's crown."

"Who all knew the crown was in the safe in the vault?" Beau asked.

"Claude, Dimitri, me, Lissette. Everyone in the security department: Sully, Leon, Hixson, and Jackson. The princess, obviously, and her guard who was killed. Her other guard, Luca." Addy ran through people's faces in her mind. "Her fiancé, Edmond Jansen, and I'm sure his father, Edward Jansen. I'd say others in her country would have known to ensure the crown's safety, but I wouldn't know who exactly."

"Has she taken it out of the safe since she's been here?" Beau continued.

Addy shook her head again. "No. I put it in once she arrived Monday night about seven thirty, and she told us she wouldn't need it again until the parade on Saturday at noon."

"So it was understood by all in the know that the crown would be in the safe until Saturday, yes?" Marcel confirmed.

"Yes." Addy understood exactly what Marcel was really asking.

"Before the princess arrived, did they send anyone ahead to inspect the security setup? Call and ask for video? Anything?" Beau asked.

"No. Nothing like that happened that I'm aware of." Which, now that she knew the story of the tiara, seemed rather odd. If those jewels were really believed to have been some of the missing crown jewels of the Romanov family, then she couldn't imagine the royal family letting them be so vulnerable. Unless . . . "But I don't know what Claude might have told Edmond or his father. He might have given them detailed information." She could clearly see Claude doing that. She could almost hear him telling his business associate not to worry about security for the crown because of the state-of-the-art, brilliant security system the Darkwater Inn had.

He wouldn't really be lying. A few years ago, Claude had invested a lot of money in the security system at the hotel. Security video that was monitored twenty-four hours a day, seven days a week. The elaborate electronic safes in each room, the old bank vault door, the safe. Everything was top of the line and updated regularly.

As Addy considered everything, she realized it wouldn't have been arrogance for Claude to have assured the crown's safety. She would have done the same herself. "I can understand if Mr. Pampalon guaranteed such security. There is absolutely no reason to think that the crown wouldn't have been one hundred percent secure here."

"Yet it wasn't."

She opened her mouth to give Marcel a piece

of her mind, then clamped it shut before uttering a word. He had a point. No matter the security system, the crown had been stolen. From her hotel. Under her watch.

Beau shifted in his chair beside Marcel, facing her desk. "In looking at the notes I've taken of the timeline, I just need to verify something. In Dimitri's statement he has documentation that the first signs of the hack—the room service orders—came at precisely 5:08 this evening. The call to our cyber-crimes unit was recorded at 6:42, and a team was dispatched shortly after. The 911 call was logged in at 7:08, and our cyber-crimes team arrived at 7:12. Marcel and I arrived a few minutes behind them at 7:19 p.m."

He glanced up from his notes and met her gaze. "I'm wondering a couple of things. First, why did it take so long after the initial incident at 5:08 for anything to be reported to the cyber-crimes unit at 6:42? That's an hour and thirty-four minutes, about an hour more than is customary to call in our teams. Why the delay?"

Addy did her best not to feel personally judged, but it was hard.

Yes, Beau was just doing his job, but he *knew* her. Knew how she would follow protocol and procedure as best she could. She licked her lips. "At first they thought it was just a glitch. It took them a little while to realize the system had been compromised."

"*They?* Not you?" Beau pressed. "Who are *they?*"

Addy detested putting anyone else in the hot spot with the police, but she couldn't lie to them. She'd learned her lesson on that the hard way last year and had no intention of repeating the mistake. "Dimitri was the one who initially realized the problem, of course, because of the room-service orders."

"So he made the decision to delay notifying the police?" Beau asked.

She most despised pitting Beau against Dimitri. The unspoken animosity between them wasn't a secret to anyone. "It's not that simple. He had to eliminate the possibility that it was just a glitch in the system. He had Hixson look at the system to see what was causing the problem. Once it was established there was a problem, he told Lissette who told me. I also spoke with Hixson before I told Lissette to call the cyber-crimes unit."

"Ultimately it was you who made the determination to call the police, yes?" Beau asked.

"Yes. I probably should have made that decision as soon as Lissette told me we'd been hacked, but I needed to talk with Hixson and verify first."

Marcel rubbed the stubble on his chin, looking more like Taye Diggs than ever. "You're the general manager of the hotel here, right?"

"Yes."

"Claude is the owner," Marcel continued.

She nodded.

"And Dimitri is also an owner, right?"

"Well, yes and no."

Marcel's brows shot up.

"Yes, Dimitri is Claude's son and was being molded to take over as CEO of the hotel, but he hated it. He's brilliant in the kitchen and wanted to be our chef. Last year, during all the craziness with Kevin Muller's murder, Lissette was determined to be Claude's illegitimate daughter. She and Dimitri went to Claude and worked out the arrangement that Dimitri would continue as chef and Lissette would be trained to take over as CEO."

"I'm still having a hard time buying that Claude Pampalon agreed to that." Beau tapped his pen against his notebook. "Just knowing how big his ego is, I can't imagine him letting his son, the bearer of the Pampalon name, step aside in favor of a woman."

She thought the same thing most times, too, but wouldn't give her opinion when they were working an investigation, so remained silent.

"So neither Dimitri nor Lissette thought to call the cyber-crimes unit until you told them to?" Marcel asked.

"Lissette is in training, so she looks to me and Dimitri to make the decisions."

"Which brings me to my next question." Beau flipped through pages in his notebook. "What time were you notified of the situation? Doesn't have to be the exact time, just a ballpark figure is fine."

She'd looked at her phone right after Lissette had barged into her office. "Six thirteen. I'd checked the time."

Beau wrote, then held the pen over the notebook. "Dimitri and Lissette realized there was an issue a little after five. They check on it themselves, taking over an hour before they tell you. Once they do tell you, it takes you only twenty-something minutes to realize the situation requires police attention and instruct Lissette to call cyber-crimes. Is that about right?"

She nodded.

"I'm wondering . . ." Beau closed his notebook and met her stare with his own. ". . . why it took Dimitri and Lissette twice as long to realize there was a problem and to tell someone than it did you."

Addy knew Beau would do his job and not allow personal bias to interfere in the investigation, but he would also jump on any mistake of Dimitri's. "I can't answer that. Maybe it took longer for Hixson to identify there was a hack and not just a glitch."

"I see." Beau and Marcel exchanged looks, then they both stood.

Addy stood as well. "Is there anything we need to do at this point?"

Marcel shook his head. "We'll be continuing our investigation, so we might need to ask you for more information."

"Most certainly." She stepped around her desk.

"And we'll need to speak to various employees as well." Beau slipped his notebook into his pocket. "So we'll be around the hotel over the next couple of days or so. Of course, we'll do our best to be discreet and unobtrusive."

"I appreciate that." She walked them to her office door.

"Thank you for your time and cooperation, Addy." Marcel smiled at her.

She still didn't like the man's cocky attitude, but over the last year she'd at least come to appreciate his frankness. And his loyalty to Beau. Addy appreciated that more than she cared to analyze at the moment. "Of course."

He opened the office door and started down the hall.

Beau hesitated. "Are you okay, *sha*? Really?" His tone softened with the lowering of his voice.

She smiled and nodded. "I'll be okay."

He reached out and ran a hand down her arm. "I know this has to be tough on you, for a myriad of reasons."

"You, too, I'm sure."

He drew her into a quick hug. "We'll get through this case too. At least you aren't a suspect." He grinned and squeezed her to him.

"Well, there is that." She nudged him with her hip. His teasing eased the tightness in her gut. "Daddy said he invited you to join us tomorrow night. Are you going to make it? We're having BBQ."

"As long as you aren't the one cooking it." He chuckled. "I mean, I don't think I've recovered from the gumbo fiasco of last month."

"Hey, now. It's not my fault Daddy burned the roux." But the gumbo hadn't been edible, and they'd had to speed to the pizza joint before it closed.

"Sure, it was all his fault." Beau stopped laughing and hugged her again. "It's going to be okay, Addy. We'll find who did this."

She nodded, but tears burned her eyes, so she dropped her head.

Beau used a single finger to lift her chin so that he could look her in the eye. "I promise you, Addy, I'll catch whoever killed them." He leaned over and gently kissed the tip of her nose. "I'll catch them and see that justice is served."

She had no doubt he'd do just that. What she didn't know was if it was that fact or his sweet and innocent kiss that warmed her all the way to her toes.

# 8

## BEAU

The February morning dawned brighter than usual over Crescent City. The cooler air carried a crispness, an edge to it. Beau stood at the edge of Jackson Square, facing the majestic St. Louis Cathedral, and cooled down from his jog. The statue of Andrew Jackson on horseback stood proudly before the cathedral, the sun casting shadows around the military officer who was regaled as *The Hero of New Orleans* for defending the city against the invasions of the British in 1815.

Beau loved the city's rich history, colorful as it often was. New Orleans had her flaws, certainly, but she was regal and graceful at the same time, and unlike anywhere else on earth. Those who were lucky enough to call her home enjoyed her vibrant culture, cuisine, and heritage. Beau took it even a step further in that he felt an obligation to defend her, to keep her streets safe for his fellow New Orleanians. Being a cop was more than a job to him—it was his legacy and his duty, but also part of who he was. He related to Andrew Jackson in that way, being a defender of New Orleans.

His cell phone vibrated, and he pulled it from his arm's sleeve band. He checked the display before he tapped the screen to answer the call. "Hey, Marcel." He automatically turned to head back to his car.

"Just heard from Sully Clements at the Darkwater Inn. The security officer who was off yesterday, Jackson Larder, was due in this morning at eight. I'll give you three guesses who didn't show up, and the first two don't count."

Beau unlocked the car's door and slipped behind the wheel, making a note of the time illuminated on the dashboard clock: eight eighteen. "Give me fifteen minutes and I'll pick you up. Get Larder's address while you're waiting."

"Already got it. See you."

Fourteen minutes and a shower later, Beau pulled up in front of Marcel's apartment. His partner stood waiting with a cup of coffee, leaning against the side of the old brick building. He pushed off and slipped into the passenger's side of the cruiser. The smell of rich chicory wafted from the open cup and filled the car's cabin.

"Where are we going?" Beau asked as he eased away from the curb back into the flow of traffic.

Marcel rattled off the address, which wasn't very far from where they were. "Here's the rundown on what we know about Larder, according to Sully Clements. He's forty-two. Retired from the navy after having served two tours. Honorable discharge. Held a couple of security jobs for various local businesses before coming to the Darkwater about nine months ago. Never married, no significant other. No children. Parents are both deceased. No siblings."

Marcel paused to take a sip of his coffee before continuing. "Clements reports that Larder has been a good enough employee. Was easy to train. Kept to himself. Did his job. Has never called in and only took two days off in nine months for doctor check-ups. Never been late before. Clements says they've called him several times with no response. The calls go straight to voice mail."

"Well, isn't it peculiar that the first time he decides to either be late or not show is the day after a major robbery where cyber thinks it's an inside job."

Marcel didn't answer, just took another sip of his coffee.

Beau turned onto the street his partner had given. "Zach called this morning. The hacker definitely used a back-door-style hack, which he says he's about ninety-nine percent certain had to be an inside job."

"The only people who had access to the system are the Pampalons—including Lissette—Addy, and the security department employees."

"I can't imagine the Pampalons or Addy being involved since it's very bad for business." Beau took a sharp left. "Although, I have to admit, the delay in notifying the police was a bit of a shocker. They all should know better."

"Maybe, but remember, Pampalon junior and Addy are training Lissette, who couldn't know procedure on such an event. I think it was just bad timing, nothing to make too much out of."

"Probably." Still . . . Beau pulled the car in front of the small house and parked.

The yard was meticulously manicured, unlike the neighbors' up and down the street. The house itself appeared maintained—no peeling paint, rotting boards, or obvious cries for repair were visible. A Chevy sedan about six years old sat alone in the driveway. No spots of leaked fluids pooled underneath.

The walkway to the front door had a smattering of leaves, but not too many, indicative of having been kept swept pretty often. The steps didn't even creak as they climbed them. Marcel rang the doorbell, and the somber tone echoed to the front porch. No other sound came from inside.

Marcel knocked on the front door. "New Orleans police." Still no response.

"Let's check around back." Beau stepped off the porch and moved into the fenceless backyard, which was just as methodically cared for as the front. The back patio held a small gas grill and an electronic smoker, of which the lids of both were shut, and both were anchored to the metal poles with chains. The neighborhood wasn't the best part of the city, so the setup was understandable. Many homeowners, or even renters, took the small extra steps to secure their property.

Beau opened the screen door and raised his hand to knock on the back door, then realized it wasn't closed. He nodded at his partner as he pulled his handgun from its holster. Marcel did the same.

"New Orleans police. We're coming in." Beau eased the door open and stepped inside. Marcel moved behind him, his own gun drawn as well.

The kitchen was clean, held a two-chair dinette set, and was small and empty. Beau pointed to one of the rooms off to the side of the kitchen where they'd entered.

Marcel nodded and moved in that direction. "New Orleans police."

Beau headed toward the front of the house. He could see the front door, deadbolt engaged, as he stepped into the den. Two chairs and a well-worn sofa faced a television on a stand. The carpet showed signs of wear, but the room was clean and tidy, even the bookshelves on either side of the pedestal TV stand.

He turned to head down the hall.

"Beau. In here."

Following the sound of Marcel's voice, Beau

entered the master bedroom with his gun at the ready.

There was no need. Marcel stood over a lifeless body on the threadbare rug over the scuffed hardwood floors. There was no sign of a struggle, no sign of anything out of the ordinary, in fact.

Except for the dead body with what looked like a gunshot wound.

Beau holstered his gun and looked at his partner. "Larder?"

Marcel shrugged. "I'm guessing. I'll call it in." He stepped into the hall, cell to his ear.

Beau carefully bent over the body. Shirtless, wearing sweatpants. He was about the right age to be Larder. The familiar navy anchor insignia was tattooed on the right shoulder blade. Looked like it'd been there for some time.

"CSU and the coroner are both on the way. Nolan's team is on call, but Walt's already working on autopsies, so one of his juniors will be coming." Marcel stayed in the hallway.

Beau made his way to join his partner. "At least we'll have Nolan's team. We'll need the best to make sure nothing is overlooked."

"We'll need to notify Addy as soon as identification is confirmed." Marcel glanced into the room. "Whoever did this sure got in and out without disturbing much."

"They didn't give Larder a chance to put up

much of a fight either." Which told Beau that the plan was to kill Larder all along.

That brought the body count up to three. Not a lot, by New Orleans standards, but in relation to the hotel robbery it stood out.

They were dealing with someone ruthless and determined. A very deadly combination.

After CSU and the coroner arrived a few minutes later, Beau and Marcel went directly to the precinct.

"I'll call the embassy and fill them in if you'll bring the captain up to speed." Beau plopped down at his desk and looked up the number for the embassy. He made the call, and as the captain had advised, they merely wanted to be kept informed regarding the investigation. He breathed a heavy sigh. At least there wouldn't be international officials mucking up his case.

The phone on his desk rang. "Detective Savoie."

"This is Allison Williams with WDSU, Channel 6."

A reporter. Great. "What can I help you with, Ms. Williams?" Beau struggled to keep his overall disdain for reporters out of his voice. His captain had been on his case for months to play nice with the press, especially since his promotion.

"I'm following up on a report about a theft and

murder at the Darkwater Inn. Would you care to comment?"

How did she know already? For some time there had been rumors about a leak in either the coroner's office or in the police department. Seemed likely at this point.

"We have no comment at this time." Beau rested his elbows on his desk and noticed the file from Walt. Autopsy reports.

"So you can only verify there has been a murder?"

The woman was clever, he'd give her that. "No comment." He really wanted to tell her to bug off, but was pretty sure his captain would flip.

"Come on, Detective, we know that you and your partner were dispatched to the hotel yesterday, as well as the coroner and CSU. The story will break on our noon broadcast. Is there anything you'd like the public to know about the theft and murder?"

It hurt that her information was as accurate as it was. "I'm sorry, Ms. Williams. You understand that the police can't comment on things such as this."

"Because it's an open investigation?"

Beau ground his teeth, locking his jaw. "No comment, Ms. Williams." He hung up the phone, pretty sure Captain Istre would consider it rude, but knew that was the most polite he could be at the moment.

If the reporter was hounding him, she most likely had already contacted Addy. Their "No comment" remarks wouldn't be presented in a flattering way, and there was no way the story would be stopped. He could only hope that Ms. Allison Williams didn't yet have the information about the princess or her crown being stolen. The international repercussions could be devastating to the Darkwater Inn, and Addy would bear the brunt of any of those.

Beau scanned the contents of the autopsy reports on the men killed at the hotel. Nothing unusual reported.

"Captain said to keep him in the loop." Marcel returned to their work space, carrying a fresh cup of coffee. Well, not that anyone would call the precinct coffee fresh.

"Same with the embassy."

Marcel sat at his desk and took a sip from his steaming mug. He nodded at the file Beau still had open. "Anything useful?"

Beau passed the folder to his partner. "Nothing more than what Walt already surmised yesterday at the scene. He's releasing the bodies today. Only new detail is time of death—Walt's report puts both men's time of death between five thirty and six yesterday." He stared at the timeline he'd written. "If they had acted earlier when the initial hack happened, the murders might have been prevented."

"You think so?"

"The initial sign of the hack is reported at five-oh-eight. Time of death is between five thirty and six. That's an overlap."

"But they didn't realize it wasn't just a glitch. They didn't inform Addy until six thirteen, right?" Marcel's memory was as sharp as ever.

"Had Lissette and Dimitri brought Addy in from the start, she would've made the call and brought the police earlier."

Marcel took another sip of coffee. "Hold up, though, partner. It took Addy herself over half an hour to make the call to the police, and that was after she was informed it was a hack."

He had him there.

"And," Marcel continued, "it might seem fishy that one of her first instincts after calling cyber was to check the vault. Almost like she knew something would be up with that."

"Oh, come on." Addy Fountaine was no more involved or aware of what happened than Beau was. "You can't even go there, man."

"No, I don't think any of them over at the hotel were involved. I'm just pointing out that a case could be made for any of them. I don't think we should waste our time going down that trail—unless you have reason to think differently?"

"I don't." Beau was impressed with his partner's thought process on this one. Just when he'd thought Marcel was heading in the wrong direction in his own career, he about-faced and really shined.

"What's your gut telling you?" It had taken Marcel many months and almost as many cases before he came to realize that while he might have the gift of total memory recall, Beau's gift was his hunches and instincts. They were usually right on target, and Marcel had come to respect them.

"That's just it—I don't have an indication either way just yet. There's something off that I'm not seeing yet." Which was bugging Beau like crazy. He'd tried to work it out on his jog this morning, but nothing had clicked. "I think maybe I need to speak to the princess myself, and Claude. A follow-up interview might give us more information too."

"Then what are we waiting for?" Marcel slurped his mug empty. "We won't get any forensics reports from yesterday until later since Nolan's team is still at Larder's house. Might as well start shaking the bushes." He stood.

Beau grinned and stood as well, reaching into his drawer for his gun. His partner said the funniest things sometimes, outdated and cheesy, but he was a good partner. Marcel might be a lot of things, but Beau knew he could always count on him to have his six, and at the end of the day, that's what mattered most between partners.

# 9

## DIMITRI

"You're doing great, by the way." Dimitri stared at his half sister sitting behind the desk that had once been his own.

Lissette glanced over the computer monitor at him. "I feel like I'm doing everything wrong. We both know Claude doesn't think I should be here. And now, with everything, I think Addy might have the same opinion."

"Don't be silly. Adelaide thinks nothing of the sort." Although she had been reluctant to bring Lissette into the company at such a high level initially, Adelaide's first responsibility had always been to the Darkwater Inn. It was one of her traits that made her so valuable as the general manager.

"I often wonder if she's setting me up to fail." Lissette sounded dangerously close to a whining child with her jealousy showing.

"Adelaide isn't that type of person, Lissette. She wants everything to go smoothly and knows the best way for you to learn the hotel business is like I did, from the ground up and working in every department."

"She didn't."

Dimitri smiled. "No, but she went to college and got her degree in hotel services and management before she came to work here. Even so, once she was hired, she spent time in each department, learning protocol, policy, and procedures."

"Still, it feels like she gives me the most mundane of tasks."

"Like what, exactly?" Dimitri didn't mind indulging his sister's complaints most of the time, mainly because he recognized what she'd gone through to get to where she was now. She'd never had an easy life. As the illegitimate child of Claude Pampalon, she was kept hidden away by Claude and her own mother. When her mother died, Lissette had had to fight for her place in the family empire. Dimitri respected that about her, even if she sometimes seemed resentful—albeit misguidedly—toward Adelaide's position.

"Like calling the embassy to notify them that we needed the official appraisal of the princess's tiara to fill out the insurance claim and then filling out this insurance form. Her assistant could easily have done either. Or both. Or Addy herself could have done them. They're menial tasks, not something the CEO would need to do personally."

Dimitri wouldn't allow Lissette's jealousy of Adelaide to run rampant. Adelaide, too, had had to overcome the death of a mother and personal hardships to get to where she was today. He would not allow anyone to diminish her strength or accomplishments. Especially not when she held his heart captive. "Oh, quite the opposite, dear sister. Calling an embassy is not something an underling should or could do. It's an official inquiry. One that, if it isn't dealt with properly, could incite an international incident. Filing an insurance claim for a theft such as this must surely be done by a Pampalon. Adelaide has provided you the means to show our father that you are indeed acting as a Pampalon and taking care of business. She could have made the call and filed the claim herself, yes, and shown that she is doing her job. But instead, she's allowing you to show off your knowledge and ability to our father."

Lissette's unique eyes, so much like Claude's, widened a little. "Oh, I guess I didn't think about it that way."

Dimitri softened his tone. "Why would you? No one has ever stood by and let you take the limelight before. You're not accustomed to that." He grinned. "But you should get used to it more. Adelaide is like that. I've found that she will often give credit to others, even to her own detriment." It was part of who she was and why she meant so much to him.

"Well, I've gotten all the basic information filled out. All I need are details about Princess Katerina's crown."

"Where should you go from here?" Walking Lissette through the processes he'd taken for granted all his life made Dimitri appreciate all that Adelaide did.

His sister tapped her fingernails lightly on the computer keys. "I spoke with the ambassador's assistant and explained why I needed the official appraisal of her tiara. They took my information and said someone would get back with me. I suppose I could just ask the princess herself, yes?"

Dimitri tilted his head. "Katerina von Pavlovna is young, only twenty-four. I doubt she knows the legal description and value of her crown. That information will likely come from a representative of the royal family." He glanced at the copper steampunk-style clock with the oversized gears hanging over the credenza behind her desk. It was one of the many things Lissette had changed out since taking over his office. The clock, in particular, suited her personality. "Liechtenstein is seven hours ahead of us. It's eleven thirty here now, which means it's after six thirty there. I'm betting that most of the royals' official offices are closed for the day."

"Right."

"I'm guessing the embassy will get back in touch with you later today or tomorrow."

Lissette nodded. "So, I should wait?"

"I think that'd be wise. However, it might be prudent to update Father."

"Now?"

Even though she'd gone after Claude last year like a scrapper boxer, once she'd been accepted—in large part to Dimitri siding with her against their father—she'd lost some of her backbone when dealing with Claude. Dimitri understood she wanted to gain their father's approval, and despite what she claimed, it wasn't only to step into the CEO position at the hotel. Didn't every little girl want her daddy's approval?

Lissette so wanted her father's attention and affection. Having been denied it all her life, his sister didn't even realize how much she wanted it. It was clear to Dimitri how she craved Claude's approval, and it saddened him to know she'd probably never receive it, not because she didn't deserve it—she most certainly did—but because Claude Pampalon was incapable of giving affection. Not real affection. Not love.

Dimitri knew this. Had known it all his life. At one time, he'd longed for it just like Lissette. Luckily, his mother had known how Claude was, and she had compensated with Dimitri. Some would say she overcompensated, but Dimitri had grown up not needing Claude's love and approval to be happy. Perhaps that was another reason he stood up for and beside Lissette. He knew the struggle she faced and wanted to overcompensate a little on her behalf.

Lissette continued. "You know, Addy seems pretty adamant that Claude had something in the safe. Maybe I should double-check with Claude about that."

Dimitri shook his head. "I think Adelaide is mistaken. Trust me, if Father had something in the safe, he would be telling everyone."

Lissette chuckled. "You're right on that." She stood. "Then I'll go update him."

Claude's last conversation with Dimitri replayed itself over and over in his mind. "Why don't I go with you? I want to feel Father out to see if he's still going to go forward with his silly Mardi Gras krewe parade this weekend." Dimitri stood and waited on Lissette to come from behind the desk.

"Do you think he will with everything that has happened?" Dimitri grabbed a notepad and pen from her desk before opening the office door for her. He handed her the items. "It wouldn't surprise me in the least. He started that krewe because of his own vanity. Krewe of Aion, the Greek god of eternity. Father's attempt at immortality. Making sure the Pampalon name lives on and on."

Lissette chuckled as she stepped into the hall and took the few steps to Claude's office. "And here I thought that's what you were for."

"Cute." He paused at Claude's closed door, giving her a little nod.

She knocked, her hesitation showing in the timid way she rapped on the door. Dimitri didn't wait for a response, just opened the door and basically pushed her inside. Claude respected someone taking authority, even if he didn't appreciate it against him.

His expression masked as Lissette entered before Dimitri. "What is it, Lissette?" His tone was that of a bored superior.

"I contacted . . . um, our insurance agent. Uh, as soon as I get the . . . um, appraisal on the princess's crown, I'll . . . uh, I'll complete the claim." Her broken speech pattern reflected her intimidation.

Dimitri wanted to confront their father on her behalf, but it would only give Claude's reservations about the situation more ammunition. Instead, he stood beside Lissette, silently praying for her fortitude.

"Is that all, Lissette?" Condescension dripped even from the way he pronounced her name.

She licked her lips and drew up her shoulders. "Um, Addy, I mean, Adelaide, I mean Ms. Fountaine—"

"I know who you are referring to. What about her?"

Claude's impatience was a clink against Lissette's bravado, but only for a moment before she straightened her posture and jutted out her chin. "Well, she is quite adamant that you did, in fact, have something in the safe. Something of yours. In a black pouch, so she claims. Is it possible you just forgot?"

She'd pushed too far. Their father's face went to stone. "As I have explained, I did have something in there—nothing of great value, of course, more sentimental than valuable. I removed it prior to the robbery." He glared at Lissette.

"I was wondering if you were still planning on Princess Katerina riding on your float this weekend." Dimitri hoped he would deflect Claude's irritation.

"Of course. Why would I not?" Claude shook his head as if Dimitri had asked the stupidest of questions.

"Considering her crown has been stolen and her guard murdered, I thought perhaps you might think it in poor taste."

Claude's eyes narrowed, looking very much like Lissette's had earlier. "Your thoughts are too linear, my son. A celebration is needed to lift the spirits of all." He smirked at Dimitri. "Besides, Ms. Fountaine is quick to sing the praises of the detectives on the case. Perhaps the crown will be recovered before this weekend. Truly a time to celebrate then."

Of course his father would refer to Detective

Savoie and Adelaide's relationship just to goad him. Claude had learned of Dimitri's feelings for Adelaide last year and in his true narcissist form had done a background check on her, learning of her close friendship with Beauregard. Claude enjoyed rubbing it in Dimitri's face when he himself felt threatened.

"I'll get you a copy of the insurance claim as soon as I turn it in."

"See that you do." Claude didn't even look at Lissette.

She and Dimitri turned and headed to the door. "Dimitri, I need to speak to you for a moment alone."

Sighing, Dimitri forced a smile at his sister. She left and he turned back to face his father, but remained by the door. "Yes?"

"I take it you recall our last conversation regarding the importance of how this situation is handled?"

How could he forget? "I do."

"Then you understand how important it is to recover the stolen items, yes?"

Dimitri nodded. "We're cooperating with the police in every way, Father."

"Perhaps the police are confined in their investigation by their rules and policies. Maybe an independent source could be of assistance."

Wait, what? "Are you suggesting that we hire a private investigator?" His father had done so on occasion before, but always without consulting Dimitri, or anyone else, for that matter.

"It might be in the best interest of recovering such a valuable item quickly." Claude pinned Dimitri to the spot with his stare.

What was his father up to? Had to be something. Or was it possible he was trying to teach Dimitri like Dimitri was trying to teach Lissette? To guide him in hopes that Dimitri would, for whatever reason, opt to take on what Claude felt was his rightful role as CEO to the Darkwater Inn? It sounded like a plan his father would come up with.

"Dimitri?"

Even if he never intended to become CEO, acting on his father's suggestion could only be a bonus in building trust between Claude and Lissette. And Adelaide. "I'll look into it, Father."

"Smart decision, son."

Dimitri paused. "Do you have any suggestions, Father?"

"Me? No, of course not. I don't associate with such people." Sure he didn't. "Perhaps someone in our security department could make a suggestion."

Dimitri nodded. "Of course. I'll see to it, Father."

"Oh, and Dimitri?"

He stood, hand on the door, and stared at Claude.

"Something of this nature is usually best kept quiet, if you know what I mean."

Hire a private investigator to try and recover the crown, but don't tell anyone. Yeah, he knew exactly what his father meant. But with Claude holding Lissette and Adelaide's future in his hands, what choice did Dimitri have but to play along?

He nodded, then stepped out of his father's office. In the hallway he gulped in air. Claude had the ability to suck the life right out of most people, Dimitri included. He couldn't allow that to happen to his sister.

Or Adelaide.

# 10

## BEAU

"We really appreciate you coming with us to speak to the princess." Beau shortened his stride to match hers.

"Of course." Addy smiled as they made their way across the lobby. She looked as fresh as the morning to the outward observer, but Beau knew her better than most and he could detect the puffiness under her eyes that said she hadn't gotten much sleep last night. Yet here she was, putting her best foot forward because that's who she was.

"Her fiancé asked again when Rubin's body would be released. He's anxious to make arrangements to have the guard taken back to Liechtenstein."

Beau nodded. "I imagine. That's one of the reasons we need to speak with them. The coroner has released the body, and I have the contact information for them." He always carried a couple of the coroner's informational cards with him. Over the years, he'd found it was much easier to hand a card with instructions on who and how to contact regarding the remains of a loved one to the grieving family than to try to verbally give them the information.

"And now we have to deal with Jackson Larder's murder." Addy smiled at the elevator attendant as they stepped into the car. "Penthouse suite, please."

"Yes, ma'am." The respect the young employee had for Addy was apparent in the way he addressed her. Beau liked that. So many of the young people today lacked respect for those in supervisory positions.

"When I spoke to the ambassador's office at the embassy this morning, they seemed a little surprised by my call." That was putting it mildly. While the ambassador had seemed polite and reserved, he hadn't hidden his surprise very well over being told that the crown had been stolen. That had struck Beau as unusual.

"Really? That's odd." Addy nodded at the attendant as the elevator door opened and they stepped out of the car.

"Yeah. It was." Beau rang the bell at the penthouse suite's door, which still baffled him. A hotel room with a doorbell? Definitely above his pay grade.

The large bulk of the princess's bodyguard opened the door, his shoulders so wide they nearly wedged into the doorway.

Addy smiled at the man. "Hello, Luca." She lifted her voice. "Princess Katerina? It's Adelaide

Fountaine here with Detectives Savoie and Taton. They need to speak to you again." She glanced at Beau and Marcel. "Luca doesn't speak English."

The woman spoke quietly in German, and Luca shifted so they could enter.

The princess sat on the couch with her fiancé, tears streaming down her face. Edmond Jansen jumped to his feet as they approached.

"What's happened, Katerina?" Addy went automatically to sit beside the princess and put her arm around her. Her natural response was to comfort. Beau recognized it easily as he had been on the receiving end of Addy's care many times over.

"I am in such—how do you say it?—big, big trouble." Her shoulders shook as she sobbed.

Addy patted her back. "What's wrong, Katerina? How can we help?"

"You can help by finding her crown and returning it to her." Edmond Jansen's face twisted with anger and . . . fear?

"We're working on that, Mr. Jansen." Marcel moved to stand shoulder to shoulder with Beau.

"Are you? Because I don't see you doing anything at the moment but standing here bothering the princess. Why aren't you out there finding who did this? Scouring the streets to recover the tiara before it's dismantled and the jewels scattered?"

Katerina's sobs increased.

Beau's internal radar was off the scales. Something was very wrong here. Without being invited to, he sat on the sofa across from Katerina, Jansen, and Addy. He pulled out one of the coroner's cards and laid it on the coffee table between the two sofas. "Here is the information for Rubin's remains. The coroner has concluded his examination."

Katerina lifted her head and dabbed at her eyes with a tissue she'd balled up. "Thank you, Detective. I know his family will want to see to his proper burial."

Beau's research into the country had taught him that the predominate religion in Liechtenstein was Roman Catholic. Naturally the family would be anxious to have his remains properly buried as to their religious beliefs and customs.

He nodded. "I hate to bother you, Princess, when I can only imagine how distraught you are, but there are a few follow-up questions I need to ask for our investigation."

As she nodded, he pulled out his notebook and pen.

"Prior to your arrival, who knew your itinerary here in the States?"

"Luca, Rubin, my assistant Giulia, Edmond, and Edmond's father. That is all I can think of who knew the details of our trip."

A very limited number. "Who knew of your trip, just not the details?"

"Oh." Katerina's eyes widened. "Many people. Most all of my staff knew I would be coming to the United States. Several in my family. I suppose I could have Giulia compile a list."

"I would appreciate that. Thank you." It might be a waste of time, but it might come in handy later in the investigation. "I've read your initial statement, but could you walk me through your arrival procedure again?"

"Is this really necessary? Wouldn't your time be better spent actually looking for the crown?" Her fiancé was too small to be acting like such a bully.

"Mr. Jansen, I need to speak with you regarding a few details as well." Marcel stood, winked at Addy, and waited. "Could we please go into another room?"

"Please, use the study," Katerina volunteered.

"But I don't want to leave you, dear." Edmond's voice softened as he wove his arm around her waist and scooted her closer to him. He kissed her temple.

She smiled. "I am fine, my love. We must assist the police as best we can in order to help their investigation."

"Of course." He kissed her temple again, then stood. He didn't bother to hide the mask of animosity covering his face as he stood and motioned Marcel with his arm. "This way."

Once they left, Beau turned his attention back

to Princess Katerina von Pavlovna. "Please, I know it's redundant, but walk me through your arrival."

"Yes. Our private plane landed Monday evening. About seven your time. The hotel had a car waiting to bring us here. We met with Ms. Fountaine and Mr. Pampalon and Ms. Bastien. They took us to the vault, where we placed my tiara in their safe. Bottom drawer. They secured the safe and the vault door. Rubin was assigned guarding the crown first. We left Rubin outside the vault, and we were brought to this suite."

Beau held up a finger. "So, Luca would relieve Rubin?"

The princess nodded. "Luca and Rubin scheduled the times they would stand guard outside the vault. Let me ask Luca how many hours they would stay at the vault before they switched out." She spoke to the guard in her native tongue.

"*Neun*," Luca replied.

She nodded. "Each would be there nine hours. They usually sleep for about five hours, then spend the rest of their waking hours watching over me before their next time guarding the crown."

"It was the plan for the vault to always be guarded, then?"

She nodded again. "Yes. The tiara is always guarded. It is only customary for me to have a guard when I am out in public. If I am wearing the tiara, I have at least two guards with me."

Something didn't seem right with that to Beau. "Wouldn't it have been easier to have brought an extra guard—or two—to relieve Luca and Rubin and still have both you and the crown guarded all the time?"

Her face reddened, and tears filled her eyes. "We should have. I should have known better. Now I am in such trouble." She ducked her face into her hands and wept.

Addy patted her back but shot Beau a confused look that matched his own.

"I'm sorry, Princess, but I have to ask what you mean by that."

"My uncle is—how do I say this?—very mad . . . furious. He is demanding I return home immediately."

Beau flipped his pen through his fingers. "He's probably just worried about your safety, Princess."

She shook her head. "No. That is not it. He is angry that I let the tiara be stolen."

Well, Beau could certainly understand that. Still, it wasn't the princess's fault. "Of course he's upset, just as you are, as Ms. Fountaine is, as we all are, but he can't be angry with you. It's not your fault the tiara was stolen."

Tears streaked down her face, leaving wet tracks in her makeup. "It is. If I had not wanted to come to the States so badly, my tiara would not have been at risk."

"Accidents happen, Katerina. You couldn't have known this would happen."

Addy's soft tone only seemed to intensify the princess's cries. "But my uncle, he does not see it as an accident."

"I'm sure you followed the customary security measures of your country, yes?" Beau couldn't help but feel like he was missing something.

"Yes and no."

"What do you mean?" Addy asked.

"I followed the protocols as usual."

"See? You did what you were supposed to." Addy rubbed the princess's shoulders. "You can't be held responsible."

"But I am to blame. My uncle is furious. The ambassador called this morning after he was informed." The princess stared at Beau. "I do not blame you for phoning him. I know you were doing your job."

Blame him? Why on earth would that be a consideration?

"Of course, everyone is working to solve the case and recover your crown. Your family and the ambassador have to know that. They're just upset."

The princess shook her head. "No, they are accurate. I should not have come."

Addy wore her confused look again, which

Beau was pretty sure matched his own. "Katerina, did you not follow protocol in some way?" Addy asked.

The princess stared at Addy. "I followed the protocols as best I could." She dabbed at the fresh tears pooling in her eyes. "But they are mad because the tiara was exposed. It could not have been stolen had it not been here."

Beau tapped his pen against his notebook. "I'm sorry, I don't know such policies and procedures, but I'm not following what you're saying here."

Her big blue eyes glimmered with moisture. "I did not have permission to bring the tiara."

"What?" The one word question was out before he could stop it.

The princess's waterworks were back in full force as she spoke between sobs. "I know. I did not ask to bring the tiara . . . because I knew my uncle . . . would not allow it."

Beau dropped his pen.

"I took it." She sniffled. "I should have brought at least two more guards . . . but then . . . I would have had to . . . explain why I needed them."

Beau met Addy's wide-eyed stare.

"My uncle is sending one of the court jewelers here. If the tiara is recovered, we will require an inspection from someone who is most familiar with the pieces."

"What?" Addy shifted to stare into the princess's face. "Who? When?"

"Our plane returned today to my country to collect the court jeweler."

Addy's expression told Beau that no one had bothered to tell her of the arrivals. Was it a trait of the Liechtenstein royals to not keep others informed? No wonder the ambassador had been so surprised. No wonder the princess was beyond upset—more that her tiara was missing than that men had died.

This opened a whole new can of worms for Beau's investigation.

# 11

## ADDY

"Trace, thank you for meeting me for lunch. I needed to get out of the hotel." Addy swung her legs from the metal stool at the tall table and smiled at her best friend, Tracey Glapion. She'd really needed to get out once the story broke and her father called. He was only concerned, of course, but his intensity sometimes made Addy feel a bit like she was incapable of handling her job. That was one of the things she'd thought she'd left in Europe—her feeling of not being in control—yet here it was, back again to pay a visit.

Tracey smiled. "Girl, you know I'm always up for good food. Unlike you, I don't get to eat gourmet every day." She took another bite and made smacking noises. "I do love me some hot boudin."

Addy chuckled and shook her head. "I don't get to eat gourmet every day."

"You could if you wanted. Dimitri would cook you up anything you wanted, anytime you wanted. You know that."

Addy glanced around the restaurant. Cochon Butcher Restaurant sat nestled next to Cochon's in the Warehouse District of the city. It was a sandwich and butcher shop with a wine bar that specialized in house-made meats. Not as delectable as the culinary creations Dimitri whipped up back in the Darkwater Inn kitchen, but Addy was quite partial to Cochon Butcher's smoked turkey sandwich. The spicy meat was served on grain bread with avocado, sprouts, and basil aioli. Perfect for a lunch out of the hotel.

"Hey," Tracey tapped Addy's hand. "I saw the noon news. I'm so sorry this business was leaked to the news. I can't even imagine how they get their information. How're you doing? Especially since you really just got back and into the swing of things again."

"It's so frustrating because it's all factual, so we can't dispute the report, but we can't tell the whole truth either." Addy shrugged, running her finger along the rim of her glass of tea. "Beau's leading the investigation, and I have no doubt he and Marcel will eventually solve the case, but that won't bring back Leon or Rubin. And who knows about the princess's crown."

"Okay, that whole deal is just crazy. I can't fathom that they were able to leave her country with it without anyone knowing."

"I know. You'd think they'd have a checkout policy or something." Addy still couldn't believe Katerina had, in essence, pilfered the crown jewels. And now they'd been stolen under Addy's watch. What a mess.

"I kinda respect her."

Addy's eyes widened.

Tracey laughed. "Come on, Ads, you have to admit, that's a pretty gutsy move on her part. To have such gumption . . . I'm impressed."

Addy chuckled. "Okay, okay. I'll admit that I think it took a lot of guts for her to take it and leave, but I also think that says a lot about the security of her country. I told you what the rumor is about that tiara. Who in their right mind would risk it? Forget the possibility of it being stolen—a stone could have come loose and gotten lost." She shook her head and wiped her mouth. "A gazillion things could've happened to it. Something did happen to it."

"I'm sorry, sweetie. What happens now?" Tracey took a swig of her sweet tea and balled up her napkin and tossed it on her empty plate.

"Lissette will file the insurance claim as soon as we get the paperwork. The royal family's court jeweler, according to the princess, will be bringing the appraisal of the crown. We wait and see what our insurance policy will cover." Addy let out a heavy sigh. "I did a little research about the missing crown jewels of the Romanov family. I have to tell you, Trace, I've got a gut feeling that Katerina's tiara is the undocumented diadem in the picture. I saw it with my own eyes. Hey,

I'm the one who actually put it in the drawer in the safe."

"What if it is?"

"Then our insurance policy isn't going to be enough to cover what the tiara is worth."

Tracey finished off her tea with a final swig. The ice cubes rattled against the glass. "You said it wasn't considered part of the Russian crown jewels."

"The Kremlin doesn't recognize it as being so."

"Then the value of the tiara can't be based on it being part of the collection, right?"

"That's what makes sense, but still." She finished off her own glass of tea. "Even if it's not considered part of the Russian crown jewels, it's still extremely valuable. I mean, they're sending the court jeweler with the appraisal."

"I don't even know what a court jeweler is, but it sounds pretty impressive to me." Tracey gave Addy's hand a gentle shove over the table. "Come on, Ads. I know this is bad for you right now, but you have to admit, it's intriguing as all get-out too."

Her bestie always did know how to just lay everything out in the open. "It is, and just the story behind the tiara would be enough to have me in total awe if it hadn't been stolen from my hotel."

"Okay. So, Beau's working the case, right? He and Marcel are awesome at their jobs, yes?"

Addy nodded. "They're very good. Beau's so good that he was promoted not too long ago by his captain."

"See. Then stop stressing. Let Beau and Marcel do their jobs." Tracey threw some bills on the table before standing. "You need to get your mind on other things."

Also standing, Addy added a five to the table. "Unfortunately, I don't have time to think of anything else. And now our other security guard was found dead at his home this morning. Murdered."

"I hate this for you, girl, I really do, but again, that's a police matter. Let Beau and Marcel do their jobs."

Tracey linked her arm through Addy's as they stepped out onto Tchoupitoulas Street. The early afternoon sun beat down on the Big Easy, but the crispness in the air kept the temperature cool. "Tell me how you're feeling toward Dimitri and Beau, now that you've had several weeks to get back into your routine," Tracey said as they turned toward the parking lot.

"There's not much to tell. I've been busy getting back up to speed on what's been happening at the hotel, preparing for the carnival season, then all this happened."

Tracey stopped and spun, facing her. "Adelaide Fountaine! Both of those men let you know they had romantic feelings for you almost a year ago. Both of them asked you out."

"I know. I know." Addy shook her head. "I told them I needed time to figure out what I wanted."

"Again, this was almost a year ago, before you decided to head off to Europe."

"I needed to get away. To think. To clear my head. And the opportunity to study at that hotel was awesome."

"Yes, but you're back now." Tracey gave her a little shove. "You can't just leave them hanging. I've seen the way both of them look at you. It isn't fair to them. You need to do whatever it takes to decide if you want to be with either of them."

"How do I do that, exactly?" Addy hated to think of hurting either man—they were both so important to her. "It's so very complicated."

Tracey started walking slowly toward the parking lot again. "Life is complicated, Ads. It's never going to be simple. You should decide what you want in the midst of chaos, because that's when you realize who you really want on your side."

Addy strolled alongside her best friend. "I hate the thought of hurting either one of them."

"Or do you hate the idea of giving either of them up?"

Oh, her best friend did have a way of cutting to the heart of the matter. "I don't really know." Tears burned her eyes. "I don't know what to do, Trace."

"Oh, honey." Tracey pulled her into a tight hug. "Look, I'm by no means a love guru, but here's my simple advice: be up front and honest with both of them about how you feel, but let them know you want to see how the romance between you goes."

"Both of them?"

"Honey," Tracey grinned, "that's called dating. People date to get to know one another on a romantic level to decide if they want to get serious. You date more than one person to decide who you want to pursue a monogamous relationship with."

"You're suggesting I date both of them, at the same time?"

Tracey looped her arm through Addy's again and gently tugged her toward the parking lot. "Yes. People do it all the time. That's what dating is."

"With our history . . . I mean, I know them both so well . . ."

"Not romantically, Ads. Knowing a man as a friend, coworker, whatever is totally different than knowing him romantically."

Addy's heart raced just to think about Beau and Dimitri romantically. "But won't it be more complicated to date them both?"

"How ever will you know who you should be with, or if you should even be with one of them, if you don't date them?"

True, but still . . . "I guess."

"Look, just let each of them know that you would be willing to go out on a real date, then let them decide. If they're still interested, they'll ask you out."

Sounded almost too simple. "But there are two of them."

"Yep, you let them both know. Dating is your business, so you don't have to announce that you're seeing the other one too. But be honest. If asked, tell him. Don't let either of them believe you're only dating him unless that's the truth."

Tracey made it sound so easy, but it wasn't. Addy knew how convoluted the situation could be. "I'll think about it."

Tracey laughed as they headed to their cars parked side by side. "You need to do more than think, Ads. You need to decide."

Addy pulled out her keys and shook her head.

"Ms. Fountaine!" Addy turned to see the dreaded older woman with curly hair and face devoid of makeup. "I don't know if you remember me. I'm Allison Williams from WDSU Channel 6. I'm following up on a report of the murder this morning of another of the Darkwater Inn's employees, Jackson Larder. Would you care to comment?"

What? Addy scrambled to cover her surprise that the woman knew details so quickly. "I remember you, Ms. Williams."

The woman smiled. "Good. Do you have a comment about Jackson Larder's murder?"

That it was awful and horrible that another man was dead? "Perhaps you should share with me what you already know, Ms. Williams."

"New Orleans crime scene unit and coroner are currently at Mr. Larder's residence. My sources tell me that Mr. Larder was shot. Would you care to comment on the connection between his murder and that of the other two men at the Darkwater Inn?"

How did the woman have such accurate information? "I'm sorry, Ms. Williams, I can't comment at this time."

The woman frowned. "That all three people were associated with the hotel is more than mere coincidence, Ms. Fountaine. What is the hotel's statement regarding the safety of everyone connected to the hotel?"

"Statement? We have no statement. No comment." She turned back to her car, unlocking it with the remote fob.

"Surely you can spare a word or two, Ms. Fountaine. To put the public's mind at ease."

Intent on ignoring the reporter, Addy opened the driver's door.

"She told you she had no comment." Tracey's tone left no doubt that the conversation was done.

"We're running the story with or without a

131

comment from the hotel." Allison lifted her voice.

Addy slipped behind the steering wheel.

"It'll be without a comment." Tracey winked at Addy, then shut the door to Addy's car.

Addy started the car and jammed it in reverse. She couldn't get out of the parking lot and heading toward the Quarter fast enough. Her thoughts raced as fast as she could drive.

How did the press know so quickly that Jackson Larder had been murdered?

# 12

## Dimitri

"Have you hired a private investigator?"

Dimitri looked up from the *macque choux* he was preparing for dinner tonight in the Darkwater Inn's restaurant. He didn't know whether he was more shocked that his father had lowered himself to enter the hotel's kitchen or that he'd sought out Dimitri to ask for an update. Neither were common actions of Claude Pampalon.

He set aside the corn he'd removed from the cob and reached for the onions and bell peppers to chop. "Not yet. I've spoken with a couple, but haven't hired one."

"Why not?" Claude's face tinged red, but he kept his voice lowered.

"Because I didn't think either of the ones I spoke with were right for this particular job." To be honest, Dimitri didn't know exactly what he was looking for but knew he needed to hire someone who wouldn't step on the police's toes nor cause an international incident. His chopping was automatic, but his father didn't take the hint and leave.

"Then you should be searching for the right

person instead of—" Claude waved his hand over the kitchen prep island. "—whatever it is you're playing at here."

Dimitri resisted the urge to sigh and slam the knife into the butcher block counter. They'd gone round and round with his being a chef and with his father's unwillingness to accept that fact, and he'd thought he'd finally gotten his father's acceptance with Lissette wanting to take over the CEO position. Apparently not.

"I'm cooking, Father. That's what chefs do."

"You're no more a chef than I am a pauper, Dimitri. I've indulged your whim, but I warn you, you're on the edge of my generosity."

Dimitri mixed the chopped bell peppers and onions with the corn and dumped it into the stock pot simmering on the stove. He eased the wooden spoon around the pot before placing the lid on slightly askew and facing his father. "You should ask Lissette to hire someone. I'm sure she's got more contacts and probably a much better gut feeling."

Claude's face turned a deeper red. "Come with me." He turned and headed out of the kitchen.

Dimitri let out a sigh and followed.

His father, scowling as usual, stood in the hallway near the delivery door. "That girl is incapable of hiring a private investigator. I thought you understood that her time here at the Darkwater is short."

"She's your daughter, Father."

Claude's eyes narrowed into slits. "I told her mother to abort her fetus when she told me she was pregnant. I even gave her the money for the procedure. She refused. A man should not be expected to support a child that he never wanted. As a man, you should understand that."

How did the man live with himself? Dimitri had never been more ashamed of his father than he was at that moment, yet he reined in his emotions. "Not taking into consideration the moral obligation, you know there is the legal one."

Claude smiled that humorless smile of his. "Ah, yes. The forced-heirship governing laws only in the state of Louisiana."

Just what Dimitri's attorney had told him and Lissette about last year before they confronted Claude. Even though Claude might want to cut Lissette out of his will, Louisiana operated under a unique system of laws set forth to prevent a person like Claude from disinheriting his legal children. These laws, which were derived from the Louisiana Constitution, placed restrictions on a person's ability to leave his property to someone other than their legal children.

"That's right, Father. Like it or not, you're legally obligated to include Lissette because of the forced-heirship laws."

Claude grinned wider. "Did your second-rate

lawyer inform you that the laws only cover offspring through the age of twenty-three? That once a person turns twenty-four, they are no longer considered covered under the silly forced-heirship laws?"

Dimitri felt sick. Lissette had turned twenty-three a few months ago. That meant she'd turn twenty-four before the end of the year.

Claude chuckled. "Ah, yes. I see you've done the math. That girl's time at the Darkwater is limited, and there isn't a thing she or you or any attorney in the state can do about it."

How could his father look at himself in the mirror every day? The man had no heart. Certainly no conscience. "Be that as it may, Father, I'm not turning my back on Lissette."

"The issue you should be worrying about, Dimitri, is getting back into my good graces in hopes that I forgive and forget this little whim of yours I've allowed you to indulge."

He would not go back to being miserable.

"You may think you care about what happens to the little witch, but you should care about what happens to you."

Dimitri squared his shoulders. "I'm not like you, Father. I won't put myself before others."

"Really? How about putting one person ahead of another?" Claude crossed his arms over his chest, looking as if he were truly enjoying himself. "What about Ms. Fountaine?"

"What about Adelaide?" But Dimitri's pulse had already begun to race.

"Are you willing to put the little witch before Ms. Fountaine?" Claude ran a finger along the side of his nose. "I wonder, dear boy, who would you fight to keep? Your half-mix *sister* or Ms. Adelaide Fountaine?"

Surely his father wasn't that cruel . . .

Claude chuckled. "Ah, I see you have a dilemma." He stopped laughing. "It would be in your best interest, *son*, to do as I wish and do so well. Lissette is already on the way out, whether you want to accept that or not. Your actions from now on determine if Ms. Adelaide Fountaine is on her way out as well."

Dimitri couldn't even think with the blood rushing in his head and ringing in his ears. He couldn't pick one over the other, but by what his father was saying, Lissette was already gone, but he still had a chance to save Adelaide.

If he did as his father instructed without complaint. There was always a rub with his father. Always.

"Ah, perhaps you are more like me than you care to admit, my son. That a woman can get under your skin and make you do things you abhor."

"Adelaide doesn't make me do anything. You're the one trying to make me do things I detest."

"Either way, a woman is a weakness. Don't worry, you'll learn soon enough." Claude straightened and met Dimitri's disgust-filled stare. "See to it that you hire an investigator soon, Dimitri. They stand a much better chance of finding who hacked our system and robbed us." Claude gave him a final glare before turning and striding down the hall, away from the kitchen.

He couldn't seem to make his legs obey his command to move. His father had put him in the worst spot, and Dimitri didn't know what to do.

"So, you'll do as Claude says, or Addy will lose her job—is that it?" His sister's voice was filled with raw emotion.

Dimitri spun to face her leaning in the doorway. "Lissette!"

Her hands were balled into fists on her hips. "No, I want to know where I stand with you."

"How long have you been there?" The pain on her smooth mocha complexion was enough of a sign to know she'd heard enough.

"Apparently long enough to hear Claude demand you betray me."

"It's not that simple." How could he explain? He didn't want her to think he was giving up on their plan.

"He didn't mince words, Dimitri. He said I was already gone, basically."

"Because you're going to turn twenty-four soon."

"What does my age have to do with anything?" She crossed her arms over her chest and raised her chin.

"Because as the law is written, the forced-heirship mandates of the state don't apply to anyone over the age of twenty-three."

She shifted her weight from one leg to the other. "Is that absolute?"

"I'm not sure. I put in a call to Mr. Kidel's office this morning because of the way Claude was acting regarding you. I figured he was up to something, so I just wanted to get confirmation of our legal standing like what we were told last year."

"What did the attorney say?"

Dimitri shook his head. "Xavier's been in court, according to his assistant, with a big trial and will be for the rest of the week. She took a message to have him call me when he comes back to the office next week." He closed the distance between them and took her hand in his. "But don't worry. We'll figure something out."

She jerked her hand free of his. "It sounds to me like Claude's already figured out how to get what he wants. He can get rid of me as soon as my birthday rolls around, and he can get you to do his bidding by threatening to fire Addy." Tears filled her eyes. "The great Claude Pampalon wins again."

"No, don't say that, Lissette. We'll figure something out after we talk to Xavier and see what the law really says."

"Who did we think we were kidding, Dimitri?" She shook her head. "Seriously, who are we to go up against Claude Pampalon? You've been his puppet all your life, whether you want to admit that or not. I stepped into the play willingly. Wanting to be accepted. Wanting to please." Her eyes glistened even as her voice cracked. "I should have known that I could never be enough for Claude. That he never wanted me to begin with. I didn't know, though, that he'd asked her to get rid of me before I was born. That's a whole new level of hurt."

Dimitri's heart and gut flipped places. "No, Lissette, don't go there. Claude is a callous narcissist who will lie and say anything to hurt those he considers threats. Don't believe him."

"Why wouldn't I? He might be the biggest, most pompous jerk I've ever met, but he hasn't lied to me. He told me he didn't want me, and he never has, apparently. Seems to me he's been consistent in wanting me to just disappear."

The defeat in her voice was Dimitri's undoing. He pulled her into a hug. She resisted for a second, then leaned into him. "Shh, *cher*. If you give up, he wins. He wants to destroy our plans, but we won't let him. I won't."

"But he'll fire Addy, and I know how you feel about her . . ."

"I'll figure something out, Lissette. Please know that I will." He didn't know what, but he'd do everything in his power to make sure both Lissette and Adelaide were taken care of.

Dimitri would do whatever it took. No matter what.

# Beau

"Well, lookie here, it's the forensics report back from the Darkwater's vault." Marcel waved the file folder at Beau as he plopped down on the edge of his desk.

Beau glanced over to his partner. "Anything surprising?"

Marcel opened the folder and read. "Let's see . . . one set of fingerprints on the vault door was identified, belonging to Leon Edwards."

Expected and didn't help their case. "What else?"

Marcel went back to the report. "Two sets of fingerprints on the safe itself. One set belonging to Claude Pampalon, and the others are Addy's." He read more, then stopped and grinned over at Beau. "There are three sets of prints on the drawer in the safe. Claude and Addy's, but the last set belongs to Jackson Larder."

"Really?"

Marcel's words spilled out on top of each other. "Also, got the report back from Raphael in cyber on all the security guards at the Darkwater. Guess what Larder did in the navy?" Marcel didn't wait for Beau to guess. "Virtual intel. Cyber counter-intelligence."

"Bingo!"

"Yep. A hack would be no problem for Larder. I guess you were right that Larder had gotten Leon to open the door to the vault and probably the safe, then shot Leon and Rubin. But why didn't he have Leon open the drawer too?"

"He might not have gotten that close to the safe to see that there was a drawer that would need to be opened. Think about it. He's standing a few feet away from them. Tells Leon to open the safe. Leon does. For whatever reason, Larder doesn't check the safe, just sees that the door's open, so he thinks it's safe to shoot them."

Marcel nodded.

"Or," Beau continued, "maybe something spooked him so he shot and hurried to grab the crown to get out."

"Could be either."

"But with the prints there, that's evidence that he was in that vault and in the safe. I doubt any of the security guards are given access to the safe itself." Beau lifted a pen and rolled it through his fingers. "Addy said the only ones with the code are the two Pampalons, herself, and Lissette."

"Right."

Beau's cell rang. He smiled at the display photo

of him and Addy at one of last year's Mardi Gras balls. "Hey."

"How does the press know Jackson was murdered?"

"I'm just as unhappy as you are, Addy. And my captain is furious." Beau leaned back in his chair. "We're doing everything we can on this end to see if we can find how the information is getting out there."

"That Allison Williams woman nearly accosted me leaving lunch."

"I'm so sorry. Are you okay?" The reporter reminded him too much of a bulldog— determined and focused, with little regard for anything else.

Addy laughed. "I'm fine, but you might want to check on her. When I drove off, Tracey was giving her an earful."

"Oh, my!" Addy's best friend, while beautiful and with a heart of gold, was very defensive when it came to Addy. Beau loved that about her.

"Anyway, just thought you might want a heads-up that she's sniffing around for comments."

"I appreciate that." He sat up and ran a finger over his bottom lip. "Hey, do you think it's possible that she's getting her information from someone at the hotel?"

"What?"

"I mean, like a housekeeper or somebody like

that? It just seems that as soon as information is available at the hotel, the reporter seems to know it too."

"I doubt it, but I guess anything is possible. I'll see what I can find out."

"Thanks, Addy." He lifted his notes. "Hey, in Jackson Larder's file at the hotel, do you have what he did in the navy?"

"Hang on just a second. All of security's personnel files are on my desk." The sound of papers rattling filled the background of the connection. "Um, no. He just has down here that he was in the navy for five years and was honorably discharged. Why?"

He shouldn't give her such information, but this was Addy, and she was pretty good at reading people too. "Off the record?"

"Okay."

"He dealt with cyber details. A computer hack would be nothing for him to pull off. Would that surprise you?"

She hesitated. "I didn't know him well, but now that you ask, there was a little something that seemed, I don't know, reserved about him. I thought perhaps all ex-military were reserved. Is he a suspect?"

"Right now he's the best suspect I've got for the hack at your hotel, but then that begs the question of who killed him."

"This is getting really complicated, Beau."

"Don't stress. We're still working the investigation. I guess I'll see you at your dad's tonight for dinner. Still BBQ?"

"Yeah. See you then."

Beau hung up the phone, but he couldn't deny the surge of happiness that rushed through him over knowing he'd get to spend some time with Addy in a relaxed setting. Away from the case. Away from the hotel.

And away from Dimitri Pampalon.

# 13

## ADDY

"Here are the video files you requested, Ms. Fountaine." Hixson handed Addy a USB stick across her desk. "They're titled for the day they were recorded. I included Monday, Tuesday, and Wednesday until the system went down."

"That was fast." She smiled at the young man. No matter what Beau and Marcel might consider, she knew—she *knew*—Hixson was not involved in any way. He was barely more than a kid, and a kid who wanted to please.

"It was easy." A blush crept over his cheeks, and he diverted his gaze to the floor. "We had already isolated the files for the police's cyber-crimes review." He shifted his weight from one leg to the other and jiggled his keys in his pants pocket. "I've gone over the files myself several times with the police cyber investigator. Is there something specific you're looking for, Ms. Fountaine? I might be able to save you some time."

She couldn't very well announce that she thought the hotel owner was lying about taking something out of the safe, but she really didn't have a lot of time to waste either. She popped the

USB stick into her computer and accessed the drive. "Did you happen to document everyone going in and out of the vault?"

His head bobbed, his too-long bangs falling into his eyes. "Yes, ma'am. The police asked for an index, too. It's right there on the file. The one named *Index*. I also cross referenced that with the people who are on the video entering and exiting the vault who corresponded correctly with the electronic code used to disarm and open the vault door. Also, on the videos, twice a day, housekeeping service came by and cleaned the outer door and the floor in that hallway. I didn't document those times or who was there because they never disarmed the door. If you need that information, I can track it down for you."

He'd given her exactly what she needed. She double clicked on the file name. "That's not necessary. This is perfect. Thank you, Hixson." She smiled at him again.

His blush deepened. "Yes, ma'am. If you need anything else, well . . . you know where to find me, Ms. Fountaine."

He turned so fast that he nearly tripped over his own feet rushing from her office. She shook her head, smiling as he stumbled out her door like a kid racing out of the principal's office. Once the door clicked shut behind him, she lowered her gaze and read the list of files on the index:

Monday: 0800: Sully Clements enters the vault—exits 0805 Monday: 0932: Claude Pampalon enters the vault—exits 0944 Monday: 1941: Adelaide Fountaine enters the vault with Lissette Bastien, Claude and Dimitri Pampalon. Accompanied by Princess Katerina von Pavlovna, Liechtenstein royal guards Rubin Hassler and Luca Banzer, and Edmond Jansen—all exit 1958 Monday: 2001: Leon Edwards enters the vault—exits 2005 Tuesday: 0758: Sully Clements enters the vault—exits 0804 Tuesday: 1958: Jackson Larder enters the vault—exits 2011 Wednesday: 0801: Leon Edwards enters the vault—exits 0805

Addy read that the file noted the recording ceased at ten after five on Wednesday afternoon. She sat back in her chair. Claude Pampalon had definitely lied. He had never taken anything out after they put the princess's tiara in the safe. He'd never even logged going back into the vault after Monday evening.

She clicked on the video file for Claude's visit to the vault on Monday morning and narrowed her eyes as Claude's figure filled the screen. His salt-and-pepper hair glistened under the hotel's chandelier in the hall.

Gripped in his left hand was the black pouch she recognized from the drawer in the safe. It was tubular shaped, about four inches in diameter, and about two feet or so long. She watched as the on-screen Claude disappeared into the vault with the pouch, leaving the heavy door ajar. He stepped out again and locked the vault door behind him at nine forty-four, according to the video's timestamp.

He had nothing in his hands.

Had she not seen the black pouch in the safe's drawer, she would assume from this video that he put it somewhere other than the safe. But she *had* seen it. Her fingers had grazed the velvet when she set Katerina's tiara in the drawer in front of it. She wasn't crazy.

What had he put in the drawer? Why did he keep saying nothing of his was stolen when something clearly was? That was so out of character for him. Claude was the type to scream from the rooftops if someone stole anything from him. Ever.

Addy closed the file and ejected the USB drive, the possibilities racing in her head. Did Claude know whoever had broken into the safe? Oh, mercy, had he been in on it? Had whatever was in the black pouch been payment to someone for breaking in?

Surely not. But . . . he claimed nothing of his had been stolen, which was clearly a lie. Even if he knew who'd done it, that wouldn't stop him from claiming his belonging had been stolen. And the stolen fifty thousand dollars in cash was no small chump change.

Addy's gut knotted. Was his denial of anything being stolen because he'd orchestrated the whole robbery? To what avail? For the tiara? Considering what Edmond and Katerina had told her about the history of the tiara, she could understand the significance of the crown. But would Claude really steal it? To what—just own it? He couldn't ever display it. Just to know that he had it? That thought made her want to hurl.

Yet it seemed the most logical answer, and that terrified her.

She needed to talk to somebody. Tell somebody so they could laugh at her and tell her she was being crazy. Someone who would poke gaping holes in her theory.

Addy's gaze settled on the framed photo on the corner of her desk. It was one of her favorite pictures of her and her father, taken years ago during Mardi Gras. They'd been to a parade, and Beau had snapped the candid shot of them with piles of big beaded necklaces around their necks. Both of them wore their identical smiles. It was a rare photo of them out in public together. Ever since Vincent Fountaine had become The Master of Suspense in the literary world under the pen name of R. C. Steele, he'd avoided the public arena almost entirely.

Immensely proud of her father, Addy did miss the anonymity that had allowed them to go out to eat or to the movies or just about anything. But he'd been too visible in the public eye years ago, garnering some of the most unwanted attention. When a younger version of herself had been threatened by Vincent's "fans," he'd pulled out of the public awareness completely. Hiding away in their very private cabin just outside of New Orleans, her father had tightened the circle around them, letting very few in.

Vincent had loosened a little over time, as Addy had gotten older and built her own life, but he'd never forgotten and wouldn't let his guard entirely down. Maybe that's why the photo of them together at the carnival was one of her favorites.

That her father was a thriller writer meant he created suspense out of nothing—not the best feature for the talk she needed to have. She tried to call Tracey, but got her voicemail. No wonder—it was the time that Tracey usually started getting ready for her evening. She ran a business that provided evening cemetery tours so wouldn't be available to talk until tomorrow.

Beau's face filled her mind. He would be at dinner tonight at her father's, and perhaps he'd be a good sounding board on this. He always did seem to understand her. Or would at least tell her she was just being crazy.

Some days she wondered if there was ever any question of that not being the case.

She unlocked her bottom desk drawer and

jerked it open, dangling the USB drive. She started to drop it inside, but stopped. Her old Bible lay in the drawer.

Surprising herself, Addy lifted it and set it on her desk, the worn leather soft under her touch. She'd brought it to the office and locked it in her desk soon after starting work at the Darkwater, unable to bear looking at it in the house. It had been more or less ignored ever since.

She gently opened it and waited for the rush of emotions to hit her like they normally did, but this time . . . This time no anger nearly suffocated her. No resentment threatened to unhinge her.

The intercom on her desk buzzed. She dropped the Bible and USB into the drawer and locked it back as she answered the phone.

## DIMITRI

"Rodney Ardoin, pleasure to meet ya." Dimitri shook the hand of the middle-aged man with the hippy hairstyle. His bland facial features were ones that would allow him to make inquiries without notice. To move about many people and remain unremarkable. Unrememberable.

He was nothing like Dimitri had expected and yet everything he needed in a private investigator.

"What can I do you for?"

Dimitri quickly explained who he was and what he needed. Rodney nodded as Dimitri spoke, never breaking eye contact, but not writing anything down either.

"Just to be clear, your main priority is the return of the diadem and apprehension of the person who stole it and murdered three people, yes?"

Dimitri nodded. Put so bluntly, he couldn't imagine someone willing to take the job.

"Sounds simple enough." Rodney didn't so much as blink that three people had been killed over the tiara. He rattled off his rates, which were on the high end of the going rate, but he had the references and success rate to justify the expense.

"I'm not sure anything about this is simple." Dimitri provided more details about Princess Katerina and the value of the jewels according to what Edmond and the princess had told him and Adelaide.

"I hear ya, man, I do. No worries. I'll start on this immediately and should have an initial report ready in the morning. How about I call you around ten and give you an update?"

Really? "That fast?"

Rodney smiled. "I said an initial report. Just what I can find out in my starting-point queries and look-see."

"Oh. Okay." That made more sense. "I just need to stress again how critical discretion is on this matter."

Rodney nodded. "I understand completely, and

153

I assure you, I'm the epitome of discretion. I've never had a complaint yet in that regard."

"Good because . . . Well, you understand."

"I do." Rodney ran a hand through his almost shoulder-length hair. "Let me get through my questions now."

"Okay." Dimitri sat back in his chair, allowing himself to relax a little. Ever since he'd walked into the gritty little office on the backside of the Viavant-Venetian Isles neighborhood, about twenty or so minutes from the Darkwater Inn, his gut had been twisted into knots. Now he felt like he could breathe somewhat.

"Chances are slim that I'll be able to recover the cash, but I'm sure you know that."

Dimitri nodded. He'd figured that fifty grand was gone forever. "Aside from the cash and the tiara, there was nothing else inside the safe, correct?"

He started to nod, but hesitated. Adelaide had been so adamant . . . "There's a chance that there was something else in the drawer itself, but I don't know what." Dimitri scrambled to remember what Adelaide had described. "Something tubular in a black pouch."

"Interesting. No idea what it could be?"

Dimitri shook his head. "I'm not even sure there was something else in there. One person says there was, another says there wasn't. We know for sure the diadem and the cash were in

154

there, though. There's no question on those."

Rodney nodded. "I'll keep my eyes open for anything that might could have been in the safe that would be tubular that would fit in the drawer." He flipped through the papers Dimitri had provided him. "The 200EH safe's drawer, if I remember correctly, is about fifteen or so inches deep and somewhere about two and a half feet wide. That would easily hold a small-to-medium-sized tube and the tiara."

Dimitri nodded.

"And the cash was not in the drawer, yes?"

"Right. The cash was on the shelves in the safe." Dimitri knew this to be true. They always kept it there and had for years.

Rodney nodded, as if he were mentally cataloguing all the details. He pointed at one of the pages. "These are all the people who were inside the vault within the last week and knew what was inside the safe, correct?"

"Yes. That's everyone."

He glanced over the list, tilting his head from side to side. "Not too many people on your list."

"Not many people knew what was in the safe."

"Limits suspects. Makes my job easier." Rodney looked up from the papers. "And three of those are now dead."

"Yes." Dimitri still had a hard time accepting the murders. Three men, gone . . . and for what? Money? Jewels?

"Okay. Well, I'll see what I can dig up and figure out." Rodney stood.

That was it? Dimitri pushed to his feet. "You don't have any more questions for me?"

Rodney grinned. "Not right now. I'm sure once I start digging into the case I'll have more."

Dimitri handed the man a check that should cover quite a chunk of the fee. Rodney glanced at the amount and nodded. "This will get me started."

"Okay, then. I guess I'll just wait to hear from you tomorrow morning." Dimitri extended his hand.

Rodney shook it. "Yes, I'll call you around ten."

Dimitri let the older man lead him out of the back office and onto the street. Several people— the unsavory types—stared at him as he returned to his car.

As he drove off he sent up a silent prayer that he'd done the right thing. Even if it wasn't, at least in doing his father's bidding he'd bought himself a little time to figure out what to do to save Lissette's position at the Darkwater Inn.

And Adelaide's.

# 14

## BEAU

"Blue Oak never disappoints." Vincent Fountaine swiped a napkin across his mouth. "I don't think I could ever get tired of the Doobin' Lubin. Ever."

Beau chuckled, but Addy's dad had a point. The hearty sandwich from the BBQ joint was a masterpiece of pulled brisket, smoked sausage, coleslaw mixed with pickles, onions, and a signature BBQ sauce stuffed on a bun. It was melt-in-your-mouth delicious.

Addy stuffed empty take-out containers into the trash. "You should try something else from the menu, Daddy. Everything is amazing."

"You try everything. I'll stick with what I love." Addy grinned at Beau as she shook her head.

He grinned back and carried silverware to the sink. He was as comfortable in Vincent's home as he was his own. No wonder—the Fountaine house was practically his second home. After his father died in the line of duty when he was a boy, Vincent had taken Beau under his wing. Taken him hunting and fishing, showered him with fatherly praise, and made sure Beau always had a remarkable male role model.

Beau had never forgotten how Vincent had

stepped into the part of parent after Beau's mother was killed by a drunk driver when Beau was just a teen. He didn't know what he would've done, who he would have become, had it not been for Vincent Fountaine. So, naturally, when the best-selling thriller author had asked Beau to be his crime investigation source, Beau had been only too happy to agree.

That had been a decade ago, and the bond between the two men had only grown, even when last year Beau had finally revealed the secret he'd kept for fifteen years: that he'd been a match as a living-kidney donor to Addy's alcoholic mother and hadn't donated. Both Vincent and Addy had understood, which made Beau know the Fountaine family was his own. Being with them . . . Beau was home.

Addy finished folding the dishtowel and laid it over the sink separator.

"Okay, Addybear, out with it. What's on your mind?"

She grinned and went to stand behind her father, wrapping her arms around his neck and placing a kiss on his cheek. "You've always been able to read people, Daddy."

He guffawed. "Not all people, but definitely you. So spit it out. What's bugging you?"

She sat down and motioned for Beau to sit as well. "It's about Claude Pampalon."

Beau's gut tightened into a wad. "I can't

discuss an ongoing investigation with you, Addy. You know that." But boy did he want to talk it over with Vincent. Yet that would mean asking the man he respected most in the world to keep something from his daughter, which would break Vincent. Beau wouldn't put him in that position.

"No, I actually have something I need to tell you. Officially, I guess."

"Oh. Okay." He pulled out his ever-present notebook and pen.

"I know Claude Pampalon told you and Marcel that there was nothing in the safe except the cash and the princess's tiara, but he's lying."

That snapped Beau's head up to look at her. "Maybe one of you are just mistaken?"

She shook her head. "No. I checked."

"How?"

Addy held out her hands. "Let me explain." She took a drink of her root beer in the Blue Oak cup. "The video surveillance from Monday morning showed Claude carrying a cylinder-shaped item in a black pouch into the vault. I saw it in the safe's drawer Monday evening when I put Katerina's tiara in there. I touched it. The black pouch was velvet and sat in the back of the drawer. I put the tiara in front of it, shut the drawer, then locked the safe." Her eyes were steady as they held his stare. "I know this, Beau. I'm one hundred percent positive."

"Okay." But . . . that didn't make sense. "Is it

159

possible that he maybe got it out after you put in the tiara?"

She shook her head. "That's what he said he did, but he didn't."

"How do you know?" Vincent asked.

"Because of the video surveillance. From the time we left after putting the tiara in there, he never went back into the vault. Not once. So there was no way for him to take anything out. It would've been impossible for him to have gotten into the vault without being caught on camera, and he never went back in." She turned back to Beau. "He said that what he'd had in there wasn't valuable and he'd had it in the safe for sentimental reasons. Does that sound like Claude Pampalon to you?"

Beau snorted. "Not even close." He glanced back over his notes. "But, Addy, that doesn't make any sense."

"I agree, it's not logical. Unless . . ."

"Unless what?"

Her gaze darted between Beau and her father. "Okay, this is going to sound crazy, I know."

"Go ahead, honey." Vincent leaned back in the kitchen chair and considered his daughter intently. "Give me your theory, no matter how outlandish."

She let out a puff of air. "Okay. What if Claude was in on the robbery?"

She couldn't be serious. "Addy—"

"No, hear her out." Vincent nodded at her. "Go on."

She took another drink of her root beer. "Think about it. He arranged to have the princess come. He knew when she arrived and where the tiara would be kept."

"Yes, but he couldn't be sure she'd bring the tiara. After all, if she had asked permission, she would have been denied."

"What better way to get her to bring the tiara at any risk than to tell her she'd be queen of his Mardi Gras krewe and get to ride on a float in a real parade?"

All of that was true, of course, but still . . . "Are you saying he's a hacker?" That was a reach at best.

She shook her head. "Of course not, but he could have hired someone. He could have given someone access and set up the whole hack as a distraction."

Zach *had* said someone most likely had to have physical access to the server to set up the hack.

"I'm not saying Claude went into the vault himself, but I can see him hiring someone to do it."

Pampalon was just the type to hire someone to do his dirty work. "But there would be a money trail. He'd have to pay the hacker, and the actual thief."

She nodded. "Fifty thousand cash is a hefty

161

sum for one, and whatever was in the black pouch could have been payment for the other."

Ahh . . . now he saw where it all came together. Possibly.

What Addy suggested wasn't as farfetched as he'd initially concluded. But the implications were horrific. "That's an awful lot for a man to orchestrate just to get some jewels." He held up his hand when she opened her mouth. "Yes, I know about the possibility that Princess Katerina's tiara is part of the Romanov family jewels. I realize that would make it invaluable, but that would also make it impossible to sell without fear of being caught." Even for Pampalon, that was a huge risk.

"Unless they remove the jewels and sell them off in pieces." Vincent's low voice turned both Beau's and Addy's head. "When I was researching for one of my books, I spoke with a gemologist who told me that often in the black market, if there is a hot piece that the thief can't move, they'll pull the jewels out and sell them in pieces. Then later, sometimes years and years later, once the investigation dies down, the thief will collect and put the original jewels back in the original setting to sell to a private collector." Vincent shrugged. "Or, as in my book, after the insurance company paid the claim and enough time had lapsed, the owner was able to reconstruct her necklace and wear it. The ultimate version of having your cake and eating it too."

Beau nodded slowly and looked at his notes. It was possible. Plausible. Could even be likely. He didn't like Pampalon even a little bit, but he didn't consider the man to be a murderer either. Then again, maybe that hadn't been part of an original plan.

He stood and pocketed his notebook. He needed to look over the evidence again. Maybe pull some info on what Mr. Pampalon had been doing in the days leading up to the robbery. "I appreciate you telling me this, Addy. I'll look over the evidence to see if your theory will fit."

"I'm not saying I know Claude did anything wrong because I don't." Addy stood and pushed the chair under the kitchen table. "I'm just saying that there was a black velvet pouch with something in it inside the safe's drawer when the tiara was taken."

"Okay." He clapped Vincent's shoulder. "Thank you for dinner. As always, I've enjoyed our visit."

"Anytime, Beau. You know that."

"I do." He did, too, and the sincerity warmed him.

Addy smiled at him. "May I walk you out?" Her voice seemed softer, lower, as if she were unsure of herself with him, which was silly.

"Of course." He gave Vincent a final pat on his shoulder and opened the kitchen door, letting

Addy precede him around the porch. She clearly had something on her mind that she wanted to tell him but didn't want to discuss in front of her father. Since she'd had no qualms about discussing Claude and the robbery in front of him, what else could it be?

Nerves filled him as he followed her into the darkness. She always found a way to keep him off balance.


## ADDY

What was she doing? She'd lost her mind, that's what was happening.

Addy hugged herself, wishing her father's driveway would just open up and swallow her whole.

"Are you cold?" Beau moved beside her. Close enough that she could smell his spicy cologne.

Oh, mercy. "No. No. I'm fine." She was insane. Why had she ever listened to Tracey? This was crazy. Just the idea of telling Beau she was interested in him . . . It was asinine. She couldn't be that bold. Not like Tracey.

"Are you okay, *sha*?"

Oh, merciful heavens, her hormones must be in overdrive or something, because the softness of his voice nearly made her swoon. Dadnap Tracey!

"Addy?"

Heart racing. Pulse pounding. Knees literally shaking. She turned and faced Beau.

Sweet, kind Beau. The boy who had always been there for her when her mother was drunk and embarrassing. He'd never let any of the other kids tease her about her mother's drunkenness and let them get away without a busted nose or black eye.

The teen who'd taken up for her when her first boyfriend cheated on her and broke her heart. Beau had listened to her rant at the unfairness, let her cry on his shoulder, then gone and beat the snot out of Rusty Pitts. Broken one of his ribs and everything.

Loyal and honest Beau. The man who had loved his own mother to distraction and done everything he ever could for her. A perfect son. The man who had done so much for Addy's father, filling in the shoes of a son Vincent had never had.

Beautiful Beau with the expressive eyes that could undo Addy's anger with just a glance. His smile that warmed her all the way to her toes. His arms that made her feel safe and protected when he danced with her. Walked with her. Held her.

Kissed her.

"Addy?" Those eyes of his locked on hers, and for a moment—that single, time-standing-still moment under the February full moon—she felt at home.

"I like you."

Beau chuckled. "Is that a surprise?"

Her heartbeat echoed in her head, deafening. Words wouldn't form as she stared at him.

"Oh." He stared at her and stopped laughing. "Oh." Her inability to speak cemented her to the spot.

"I like you too." He took a step toward her.

She put her hand on his chest. His heart thumped against her palm. She had to be honest. Had to play fair. "But there's also Dimitri."

He froze. The moonlight reflected the pain in his eyes. "I see."

"I don't know what I'm supposed to tell you right now." She really just wanted to curl up in bed and pull the covers over her head. Or vomit.

"What am I supposed to say to that, Addy?"

"I don't know. I just . . ." She was going to slap Tracey across the face or punch her in the gut the next time she saw her for putting these crazy ideas in her head. "It's very awkward, and I know I've been putting you both off for a year, but going to Europe allowed me to really analyze my past and move past the hurt and fear of a relationship, and I did that, or at least I'm pretty sure I did, and I want to have a full life complete with someone to love me and someone for me to love, but I don't know how to make that decision, and I don't know what I'm supposed to do or feel or even think, but I know that it's all so crazy, and it's driving me nuts and—" She ran out of breath and gulped in air, staring at the ground.

Beau's soft chuckle jerked her head up.

"Addy Fountaine, are you trying to tell me that if I asked you on a date, you'd agree to go with me?"

Relief filled every muscle in her body, and she thought she might collapse. "Yes. Yes, I think I am."

"Then how about we go out to dinner on Saturday night? Does that sound good?"

She nodded. "Yes."

"Then I'll pick you up at six, okay?"

The parade for Claude's krewe was scheduled for noon. Six would be plenty of time to handle everything after the conclusion and still have time to get ready. She nodded again, not trusting herself to speak.

Without warning, Beau moved and had her in his arms, hugging her. He kissed the side of her neck with the gentleness of the evening breeze, then released her. "I'll see you Saturday if I don't talk to you before."

Addy nodded like a silly schoolgirl before turning back toward her father's house. It was all she could do not to skip all the way back inside. She did manage to resist the urge to turn and wave as she heard Beau start his car and back out of the gravel driveway onto the street.

She could kiss Tracey Glapion!

# 15

## DIMITRI

"Good morning, Dimitri."

He smiled automatically at the sound of her voice. "Good morning, Adelaide. You look as fresh as these flowers this morning." He handed her one of the daisies from the bouquet he'd brought in to the hotel on his way to work.

Her returning smile tightened his chest. "Thank you. Vicky said you needed to see me?" She smelled the flower, closing her eyes as she did. Even her eyelashes were delicate and feminine against her smooth skin.

Dimitri swallowed back his emotions, just as he had for many, many months. *Many* months. "Yes, on a couple of issues. First is my new breakfast plate for the menu. You haven't eaten, have you?" Without waiting for an answer, he began laying out the plate. "It's a twist on the usual *pain perdu*, also referred to as French toast. As some of the earliest Cajun recipes I've found dictated, I've added brandy and orange flower water to the egg and milk mixture." He added a dollop of Creole cream cheese, then topped it off with berries and sprinkled it with sugar. "Tell me

168

what you think." He pushed the plate in front of her and handed her a spoon.

She settled on one of the stools across the workstation from him and took a bite, closing her eyes as she chewed. "Oh, Dimitri, this is divine."

He chuckled, loving how she always appreciated good food. She was an honest critic, fair in her assessment, but when she liked it, she loved it. This was one of those times, apparently, as she took another big bite. "Yes, this goes on the menu immediately. Today. This morning." She scooped up another bite.

Dimitri poured her a glass of the satsuma juice he'd squeezed fresh just moments ago. Adelaide took a sip. "Oh, that's really complimentary to the recipe."

He grinned and nodded. Not many people outside of the kitchen grasped the importance of the perfect blending of food and drink to be a pleasure to the palate. Adelaide understood it perfectly, naturally. She was a delight to cook for, always taking such pleasure in tasting new recipes, and he coveted her instinctive reactions.

She finished the last bite, then swallowed the last of the juice. "That was excellent, Dimitri. Seriously, there's nothing you should change on it."

"You don't think it needs any syrup?" Her

expression of horror said it all, and he laughed. "Okay, no syrup. Maybe serve with a side of bacon and grits?"

She smiled. "That could be an option to consider, but truly, it's perfection just the way you prepared it."

He gave a mock bow. "Thank you kindly, ma'am."

She stood, taking the daisy in her hand. "Was there something else besides feeding me?" Her smile could warm the iciest of emotions.

"Actually, there is." He moved to take her elbow and gently led her into the private area behind the kitchen where they kept the paperwork for produce and food orders. "I wanted you to hear this from me."

"What?" Her eyes went wide.

"I know what Claude's doing."

"You do?"

He nodded. "He's biding his time until Lissette's birthday."

"What?" Confusion settled over her expression.

"She turns twenty-four this year. The forced-heirship laws only go through age twenty-three." He ran a hand over his hair. "We'd thought once she proved herself, he'd accept her. That isn't the case. He's just waiting until her birthday, and then plans to oust her."

"Oh, Dimitri." She laid a hand on his forearm. His skin tingled at her touch. "I'm so sorry. I know how much you wanted this to work out for her. What are you going to do?"

"I don't know yet. I've got a call in to the lawyer and should hear something back next week. Until then, I'm just trying not to irritate Father too much."

She nodded. "Dimitri, I think he's hiding something serious. I'm positive he had something in the safe that he's denying. That alone should make us suspicious."

He shook his head. "It doesn't make sense for him not to own up to having something stolen, Adelaide."

"Unless he's involved in some way."

"You think my father is responsible for the hack? For the murders? Why? To steal from his own safe?"

She took a step closer to him. "Think about it, Dimitri. As you said, why on earth would he lie about having something stolen? The only thing I can think of that makes sense is that he wanted Katerina's tiara. Maybe he believes the lore that it's part of the Romanov family jewels."

He shook his head. "Father is many horrible things, I'll give you that, but this just isn't logical, Adelaide."

"Isn't it? He's the one who arranged to have Katerina here. He ensured she would bring her crown by letting her be the queen and ride on his krewe's float during a Mardi Gras parade."

"Okay, I'll buy that, but what does any of this have to do with him having something stolen that he claims wasn't?" She was adamant, he'd give her that, but it just didn't make sense.

"What if he arranged to have Katerina's tiara stolen, and whatever he had in that black pouch was payment? Either to the person who actually went into the vault and safe and stole the tiara, or to the person who set up the hack, if it's not the same person? Consider that the police's cyber-crimes unit believes the hacker originated the infiltration physically with the server. Claude could have made that happen."

What? "Wait a minute. You're saying you think my father hired a hacker and/or additionally a thief to hack the system and steal the princess's crown?" He shook his head. "If that were the case, why wouldn't he just make it easier and give the thief the codes to open the vault and safe?"

"There are only a few people who have the codes. He'd be suspect. All of us with the codes would be. With the hack, anybody could be behind the robbery and subsequent murders."

In a very warped and roundabout way, her theory was plausible. But his father a murderer? Ruthless and determined, yes, but he'd never known Claude to be willing to kill someone.

Except he *had* wanted Lissette's mother to abort her. Wasn't that the most ruthless act of all?

"I don't know any of this to be fact, of course. It's just an idea. I do know that whatever Claude had in that black pouch in the drawer of the safe was taken when the crown and the cash was taken."

On that she was consistent.

"I guess we'll see once the police conclude their investigation."

The police. Beauregard. "I suppose so." He hated the feelings of jealousy he had whenever he saw the other man who took up space in Adelaide's life, but his attempts to ignore them went unheeded.

"How is Lissette taking it all?"

He shook his head. "Not very well. She's upset, naturally. It's like being rejected by her father all over again."

"I'm so sorry. Would you like me to try and talk with her?" Considering that his sister harbored her own jealousy against Adelaide, that probably wasn't the best idea, especially since she'd been acting more bitter since Adelaide had returned from Europe and settled back into her position of general manager. "I appreciate the offer, I do, but right now I think Lissette's feelings are too raw."

"I understand." Adelaide's hand rested on his forearm again. "Let me know if there's anything I can do. I just hate this for you."

"Me too."

He started to tell her about hiring Rodney, but

173

something made him stop. What if she assumed he'd hired someone privately because he thought the police couldn't do the job to his satisfaction? What if, heaven forbid, she felt the need to defend Beauregard? Or worse, thought he might be trying to cover anything his father might have done wrong?

No, she wouldn't think that. She knew him better. At least he hoped she did.

"I need to tell you something, Dimitri."

Something about her tone . . . His heart plummeted to his toes. "What's wrong?"

## ADDY

"Nothing's wrong. Well, not really. I mean, I don't think so." Mercy, was she always going to be so awkward in the dating scene? It was as if she couldn't coherently string two words together anymore. Her cheeks burned.

Maybe it was a sign that she shouldn't be dating. Shouldn't be putting herself out there to Dimitri and Beau, regardless of what Tracey said.

"Adelaide, what is it?" Dimitri's eyes were so filled with concern, it made her legs feel like they were jelly.

"I . . . um." *Come on, Addy, get it together.* "I like you, Dimitri."

His easy smile released the butterflies to swarm her stomach. "I like you, too, Adelaide."

The strong sense of déjà vu washed over her, but she shook it off. Tracey had been right: she owed it to herself, and to Dimitri and Beau, to figure out what she wanted romantically.

"I mean, I really like you, Dimitri."

His eyes widened, and she knew he understood. She needed to make sure he really understood. She wouldn't be one to play games. "I really like you, but I really like Beau too."

He froze, his expression like stone. "I see."

She was going to make a mess of everything. "I don't want to have secrets or play games. Right now, I'm just starting to let myself feel the emotions I've been trying to analyze for a year. I did a lot of soul searching in Europe and realized I want to have opportunities to let myself fall in love, if that's what my heart wants. I want to explore all the emotions, and I'm just trying to be as upfront and honest as I can." She bit her bottom lip and held her breath.

His expression softened, as did his voice. "Adelaide, I want nothing more than for you to be happy. Really happy."

Her heart beat so hard, as if it were trying to escape her chest.

"I truly believe I'm the man to make you as happy as you make me, and I'd like the chance to prove that."

She exhaled slowly, the blood rushing in her head.

"I won't push you or rush you, but you will know the depth of my emotions for you. I will not allow you to ever doubt how I feel."

Oh, swoon time!

"Why don't we start by going out tomorrow night? I'll cook a special meal, just for us."

Tomorrow. Saturday. Date with Beau. "Um, I can't tomorrow. Maybe Sunday?"

His smile and nod put her at ease. "I return from church services at noon. Lunch about one, then?"

She nodded. "That would be lovely."

He reached out and took her hand, then turned it over and kissed her palm. Little bolts of tingles shot up her arm and she felt . . . gooey.

"I look forward to our *date* then."

*Speak, Addy!* "Me too." Of course, she could've come up with something a little more intelligent, but she was grateful she'd gotten anything out. This was going to be complicated, she could feel it.

He took a step toward her.

"Am I interrupting?" Lissette's harsh glare at Addy let her know immediately that Dimitri's sister knew she was interrupting and was doing so on purpose.

Dimitri released Addy's hand, but he still stood close to her. "Of course not, Lissette. Who did you need, me or Adelaide?"

"You, Dimitri. I wanted to go over this week's

produce budget." She gave Addy a look that women used between themselves all the time. The one that said *I know you two are into each other, and I don't like it one little bit.*

Addy didn't know what to make of that. She'd never done anything to Lissette to incite the animosity she felt from her right now. Sure, she was wary of Dimitri's half sister, but only because of her voodoo background and how she'd tried to cast hexes and spells on Dimitri. That said, Lissette had always been more than a little standoffish toward her, but lately it'd been more like she didn't want to heed Addy's advice or instruction.

"We'll talk later, yes?" Dimitri asked her now.

She nodded at him, unable to stay perplexed with him smiling at her like he did. "Of course." She gave Lissette a curt nod, then headed out of the kitchen.

It made no sense for Lissette to act as she did toward Addy. Unless she was just jealous that Dimitri's attention was on a woman—not that it mattered which woman. Lissette might think if Dimitri and Addy began dating, his relationship with Lissette would take a back seat, and that would probably upset her. Addy could somewhat understand. Lissette had never experienced a loving family relation until she and Dimitri connected. That had only been a year ago, so she probably didn't realize Dimitri was so incredibly, fiercely loyal. He was kind and gentle and sincere—all the things that Addy could ever ask for in a man. It was one of the many things that drew Addy to him.

She strode into her office, happy but also conflicted. Her feelings for Dimitri were just as strong as her feelings for Beau. Addy had the surest sense that her love life was about to get as complicated as her work life. She didn't know whether to be excited or terrified.

Maybe she was a little of both.

# 16

"Nothing really remarkable on Walt's autopsy report of Larder except the man showed signs of steroid abuse." Marcel tossed the folder on Beau's desk, sat down at his own desk, and then took a sip of coffee.

Beau opened the file and flipped through the notes. "Interesting. Time of death was between five and five thirty Thursday morning."

"The morning after he robbed the hotel."

"If he was, in fact, the thief." Beau nodded as he closed the file, his mind recalling what they knew.

"Which I know you think he is, and I do too." Marcel stayed silent for a minute, studying him from across their desks. "Okay, what're you thinking?"

They were missing something. Something big. "Going on the supposition that Larder is our hacker and thief, let's consider him as a person. Larder wasn't a street thug. He's ex-military. Think about it. He was smart enough to orchestrate the hack at a time he wasn't at work so he could get into the vault unseen. He knew to have Leon open the vault and safe doors so

179

his prints wouldn't be on the doors, even though he messed up and touched the drawer. But he probably thought he hadn't left any there."

Marcel nodded and took a sip from his mug. "It took some serious planning to make sure his timing was perfect."

"By all accounts, according to the report of Zach's audit of the Darkwater Inn's system, there wasn't a test to see if he'd coded everything correctly. That means he had to be sure he knew what he was doing." Beau stared at his partner. "One mistake and his plan would have failed."

"So, what're you saying?"

"It bugs me to think that someone who planned this so carefully, who was so meticulous in the details, whose house was clearly in order, would just take the tiara to a fence or a pawnshop. And breaking it apart to sell the individual jewels? It's worth much more money intact." Beau shook his head, remembering what Vincent had told him. "And waiting until the hype dies down to sell it doesn't fit with his characterization."

Marcel wrinkled his forehead. "I get your point, and I agree, but then what do you think he did with it?"

Beau ran his thumb and forefinger along his jaw, on either side of his chin, his mind settling on what had been bugging him. "He's already got fifty big ones in cash, free and clear. Fencing such a specific item would raise quite a few eyebrows if he tried to go through regular channels. So what's the quickest and easiest way to move it for a big enough profit?"

"Private collector?" Marcel chewed the end of his pencil. "Maybe, but then he'd have to go through having someone look it over and attest to its value. That would have too many people knowing he had it in his possession."

Marcel nodded. "His smartest bet would be to sell it back to the owner."

Beau grinned and nodded. "The princess hasn't reported that anyone's contacted her with the offer. Of course, it'd be hard to gain easy access to a visiting royal."

"One would have to figure out a way to get a message to her in order to let her know she could buy back her crown."

Beau's grin spread. "Since Larder knew who all was in her entourage, and who was closest to her, it'd be easy for him to realize the easiest person to give him the access he needed would be Edmond Jansen."

"Why aren't we talking to Jansen right now?" Marcel set down his coffee mug.

Beau held up a finger. "Oh, we'll talk with him, but hang tight for a second."

Marcel tilted his head. "Where're you going now, man?"

"If Larder did go to the princess via Edmond to sell the tiara back to her, where is he keeping it? It wasn't located at his house where CSU inventoried the crime scene. It hasn't popped up on any of the street reps' radar." Beau tapped his notebook. "We know Larder was methodical. A planner. He would have a place ready for holding the crown before he ever took it. Someplace safe. Secure. That only he had access to."

Marcel snapped his fingers and pointed at Beau. "A safety deposit box."

Beau shook his head. "Not enough time to get it there. It was stolen Wednesday evening after the banks had closed, and he was killed before the banks opened on Thursday."

"So where else?"

"That's my question." Beau opened the file on Larder's autopsy and stared at the lifeless man's face. "I think maybe we should go back and visit his house again, this time looking for the crown. There has to be some place he felt he could put it that would be safe until he could sell it."

"Let's do it." Marcel shuffled to his feet, grabbing a cutter to get through the police tape sealing Jackson Larder's door.

Beau stared at the photo once again. He'd bet his bottom dollar that the crown was someplace safe, all in one piece, at Larder's.

And he intended to find it.

He followed his partner out of the precinct and to their cruiser.

Beau tossed the keys over to Marcel. "You drive."

His mind tried to focus on the case, but being honest, he had to admit that it was hard not to think about his and Addy's conversation last night. And their date tomorrow. Where was he going to take her? He really couldn't compete in the meal department since Dimitri was a chef.

"What're you thinking, man?" Marcel steered the car toward Jackson Larder's address.

Beau realized his partner certainly never had any issues getting dates with a gaggle of ladies. Maybe he might have suggestions. "I have a date tomorrow night." That he blurted it out surprised him almost as much as it surprised his partner.

"Do tell." Marcel split his attention between the road and Beau. "With who?"

"It's whom, and Addy, of course."

"Hey, you say that like there's no other possibility, but she's kept you at arm's length for almost a year. What changed?"

Beau lifted a shoulder and considered his answer. "She was out of the country for half of that time, you know. She said she did a lot of thinking while she was gone, and now she feels ready."

Marcel made a humming noise.

"What?" Of course his partner would have reservations.

"Look, you know I like Addy and think she's a heckuva woman, but I just want to make sure you aren't being set up to get hurt."

"Addy's not like that."

"Yeah, not on purpose. What about Pampalon? You can't deny there's something between them." Marcel turned into Larder's subdivision.

"I know." The admission nearly scorched Beau's tongue. "But Addy's been very honest about that. She told me she liked me but also liked him. She's not playing games."

"She told you that?" At a stop sign, Marcel spared a stare at Beau.

"She did. I told you, Addy's not one to play games." If he got hurt, it wouldn't be because she hadn't been honest with him.

"Well, I know how you feel about her, so best of luck." Marcel whipped the cruiser into Larder's driveway, parking behind the Chevy sedan. "Where are you taking her?"

Beau released his seatbelt and stepped out of the car. "I have no idea. I mean, Pampalon is a chef . . ."

"Yeah, you need something really special." He led the way up the stairs to the front door, pulling the cutter out of his pocket and making quick work of the crime-scene tape.

"Any suggestions?" Beau followed his partner through the door, slipping on latex gloves as he did.

Marcel jabbed his hands into his own gloves. "For dinner? Let me think. I'll start here in the living room if you want to take the bedroom."

"Fine by me, and yes, dinner." Beau headed to the bedroom. CSU had inventoried most things in the room, but this time he'd actually look in places they hadn't. In the closet, under the bed, in all the drawers. Any place a tiara and fifty thousand in cash could be hidden. CSU usually only looked for physical evidence of a homicide, so they wouldn't have dug into things. "Remember to check vents this time."

Marcel laughed from the living room. "Sure, let me forget one time to check the air vents three years ago, and you have to remind me every time."

"Well . . ." Beau chuckled and again thought about how far Marcel had come and how their trust of each other had grown.

"Hey, how about Commander's Palace for dinner? It's really romantic," Marcel called out from the other room.

"Too crowded on a Saturday night during carnival season." Beau opened the first drawer in the chest. Underwear and socks. "I want something a little more intimate."

"August's?"

Beau moved on to the next drawer. T-shirts. "Same thing."

"Well, if you really want to make an impression,

185

make her a picnic and take her somewhere special."

Beau shut the last drawer, which housed sweat pants and gym shorts. "Hey, now that's a good idea." Using his flashlight, he peered through the grate of the air vent. Nothing.

"I've been known to have them. Moving on to the dining room."

"I could grab some takeout from Broussard's. Addy loves their bread pudding." Beau felt along the walls in the closet to make sure there were no hidden recesses.

"They make the best. Where will you take her for your picnic?"

Beau slid his hand between the mattress and box spring. "I have no idea. It'll be nice and cool out. Someplace away from the hubbub of the Quarter."

"City Park?"

"Still too busy. It's Mardi Gras season. Moving on to the bathroom." Not many places to hide a tiara or fifty grand in cash here, but Beau checked the linen closet and vent thoroughly, even checked in the exhaust-fan housing. Nada.

"You're gonna be limited then, bro. Dining room is cleared. Heading to the study . . . office . . . whatever."

"Yeah." So many people filled the city during the carnival season. While it was wonderful for the local economy, it was often hard on the locals.

Beau wanted someplace quieter. More remote, but not out in the middle of nowhere. Somewhere romantic but not run of the mill. Somewhere like . . . "Hey, what about the Fly?"

The Fly was a secret kept among the locals—a strip of frontage along the Mississippi River behind Audubon Zoo. The sun set right over the river, providing a truly spectacular sight. Natural romantic ambience.

"Oh, that's good, man. Good call. This time of year, it'll be pretty perfect."

Beau nodded as he turned off the bathroom light and headed down the hall. He stopped and checked the HVAC's return-air vent but again found nothing.

Addy would love a sunset picnic along the river. Broussard's and the Fly . . . He had a plan. He stuck his head into the room where his partner dug through a desk. "I'll check out the kitchen." Although he didn't have much hope. So far, the trip had been a big bust. Still, the kitchen might hold a perfect hiding spot. Decades ago, the coolest hiding place was in a freezer. Maybe he'd get lucky.

"Beau!"

He rushed back down the hall to the second bedroom Larder had used as an office. "Whatcha got?" He stepped into the room.

Marcel sat in front of the desk, the bottom right-hand drawer opened. Inside were five stacks of money, each with a ten-thousand-dollar label around it. Each label had the Darkwater Inn logo stamped on it. "I had to jimmy the lock, but this looks an awful lot like almost fifty grand, doesn't it?"

Excitement zinged through Beau as he pulled an evidence bag from his inside jacket pocket and passed it to his partner. He used his cell phone to take several photos of the stacks of money inside the drawer.

Marcel filled out the label on the bag, then began pulling the stacks of money out and counted them. Beau counted along with him, making notes in his notebook. Each stack had ten thousand dollars. After Marcel counted each stack, he dropped it into the evidence bag.

"All here and accounted for." Marcel closed and sealed the evidence bag. "He didn't take as much as a hundred."

"Probably didn't have time." Beau flipped through his notebook and read. "The hack and robbery hit a little after five on Wednesday afternoon. Walt said the guys' time of death was about five thirty to six. Let's say that it was closer to six."

"Larder kills them at six, grabs the stuff from the vault, then has to get out. At best, that would probably have him leaving the Darkwater around six fifteen-ish." Marcel signed the label on the evidence bag.

Beau slipped his notebook back into his pocket. "If Larder drove straight home, staying within the speed limit so as to not get pulled over, considering traffic at that time of day and it being carnival season with so many tourists here, he'd arrive about six forty-five to seven."

Marcel set the evidence bag on the desk. "Walt put Larder's time of death between five and five thirty on Thursday morning. That means Larder only had the money here in his possession for about ten hours before he was killed."

"Not a lot of time to spend any money." Beau watched as his partner checked the rest of the desk. No tiara. "I suppose he could have stopped somewhere else and hid the tiara."

"We didn't go through his car." Marcel stood. "I'm done in here, so I'll check it."

Beau nodded. "I'll go back to the kitchen." He didn't want to be discouraged. At least they'd found the money, which would make Addy happy. But he really wanted to find the tiara to get it back to the princess. Especially since she'd taken it out of the country without permission.

The kitchen looked as pristine as when they were here before. Beau didn't have much hope that he'd find the tiara there, but he checked inside the freezer first . . . just in case. Nothing but frozen pizzas. He opened the refrigerator and shifted things around. No crown. He couldn't swallow back the disappointment as he rummaged through cabinets, finding nothing more exciting than mismatched dishes.

Maybe Marcel was having better luck in the car. Beau went through the drawers. Silverware. Junk drawer. Takeout menus. He shut them all.

On the counter sat a fruit bowl with what looked like the sad and dried up remains of a couple of oranges, a rusted wrench, an almost empty roll of trash bags, and a roll of duct tape. Time to check on Marcel. He took a step, then stopped. Looked back at the fruit bowl.

What bugged him?

The wrench was rusted, indicating it had been left outside. Now it was inside. In the fruit bowl? Duct tape. The junk drawer was literally right under where the bowl sat on the counter. The half roll of electrical tape was in the drawer, so why was the duct tape in the fruit bowl? The end of a roll of trash bags? A box of them sat in the cabinet under the kitchen sink.

It made no sense. Larder was pretty meticulous. The kitchen was immaculate. Beau had noticed it when they found the body. So these odd items, out of place, didn't sit well with him. His detective senses were screaming not to ignore his gut instinct to pay attention.

He glanced around the kitchen. What would Larder have needed the wrench for? The stove/oven combo was electric, not gas, so no tightening a connection bolt.

Gas.

Beau glanced out the window over the sink to the back patio. The grill was a gas grill. He opened the kitchen door and stepped out onto the concrete. A breeze swept across the space, cool and fresh. He lifted the lid of the smoker. Nothing but the rack sat inside.

Yeah, a bit of a stretch he'd find something, but still, he had to check. He replaced the lid back on the smoker, then flipped up the hinged lid to the grill. The rack was empty. Beau let out a breath.

Another breeze shot across the yard. Something in the grill waved. Something wrapped in a trash bag and duct taped to the lid. "Marcel!" Heart thudding excitedly in his chest, Beau pulled out his cell phone and snapped several photos.

"Marcel!" He slipped the phone back into his pocket and headed to the side of the house. "Marcel!"

His partner straightened, having been bent over the trunk of the sedan. "I found a box of stuff back here."

"Come here." Beau moved back to the grill, his spidey sense going crazy. This was the crown. He knew it. *Knew* it.

"What did you find?" Marcel appeared from around the side of the house, carrying a cardboard box about two feet squared. "This was in the trunk. One of the file folders has the Darkwater Inn logo on it, so I figured we'd better take it all into evidence." He set it on the little table on the patio. "What've you got?"

Beau pointed at the lid of the grill.

Marcel let out a long, slow whistle. He pulled out his cell and opened the video app.

"I've already photographed as is." Beau gently pulled the trash bag from the lid, then tore off the duct tape.

He ripped open the plastic trash bag to reveal a very shiny, very sparkly, very bejeweled tiara.

# 17

## DIMITRI

"In summation, according to all of my sources, Jackson Larder was the hacker and the person responsible for stealing the belongings from the safe. The stolen items, I'm sure, are still at his home. Once the police clear the scene tape from his residence, I'll see what I can find."

Dimitri was impressed. The PI had gotten a lot done in a short time.

"I've not yet been able to trace who killed Mr. Larder, but I do have a couple of leads I'm following up on. For now, that's where I'm at on the case." Rodney Ardoin had been clear and concise since he called four minutes ago with his update. He'd been punctual, calling at ten o'clock on the dot, just as promised.

Dimitri appreciated his attention to detail. "Good work."

Rodney chuckled over the connection. "I haven't done much yet, but I've gathered the information I needed to dive in. I'll call you at ten tomorrow morning, unless I find out something that I believe you'd want to know immediately."

"Yes. That would be great." He smiled as

Addy stepped into the kitchen's private little office. "Thank you. Talk to you soon." Dimitri disconnected the call and stood. "Hello, Adelaide. To what do I owe the pleasure of seeing you twice in one morning?"

"Hi, again." The tips of her ears brightened and she averted her gaze. "The Liechtenstein court jeweler landed a little while ago, and the car is on the way here. From what I was told, while he is originally from Moscow, he speaks fluent English." Her cheeks were flushed, and a couple of strands of her long, dark hair had escaped the braid trailing midway down her back.

Completely how Dimitri could picture her looking if he had her in his arms like he wanted to have her, kissing her breathless.

"I'm going to meet him in the lobby and take him up to his room. I put him in a junior suite. Do you think that's okay?"

Dimitri forced himself to focus on what she said. "Yes. That's fine. Would you like me to go with you?"

"Yes. I called for Lissette, but she's not answering my calls. I left her a message."

That was odd. "Let me try her." His call went straight to voice mail. "Hmm. I guess she'll return our calls shortly when she realizes she missed them." He followed Adelaide down the hall of the backside of the kitchen.

"Should I take him directly to the princess, or

should I call Katerina first? I'm afraid I don't know the correct protocol."

"I would say to call the princess and let her know he's almost here. I would bet she'll tell you what needs to be done."

"Right." He hadn't seen her this flustered since . . . Well, it'd been a while since he'd seen her flustered over work issues.

"Let me call her suite." Adelaide stopped at the hostess's station and lifted the house phone. "This is Adelaide Fountaine, general manager of the Darkwater Inn. May I please speak with Princess Katerina von Pavlovna?"

Dimitri turned to see his father striding across the lobby, Lissette practically running to keep up with him, looking more than a little uncomfortable in her dress and heels. Claude marched right up to Dimitri, ignoring Lissette. "I'm told the Liechtenstein gemologist is in route?"

"Yes. Adelaide and I came to the lobby to meet him and show him to his room. Adelaide has made sure he has proper accommodations."

"The driver said they would be here soon." Lissette sounded almost out of breath. She kept her head ducked and her eyes averted.

Dimitri's gaze danced between his father and his sister. Something wasn't quite right.

Adelaide joined them. "The princess requested that we ask Mr. Orlov to ring her room when he's settled in and ready to see her." She smiled at Lissette's bent head, then Claude.

Dimitri's father scowled at her in response. "Ms. Fountaine, Lissette informs me that you've been telling people, specifically your *friend* on the police force, that I had something in the safe that was taken, despite my statement to the contrary. Just what are you trying to imply, Ms. Fountaine?"

"I'm not implying anything, Mr. Pampalon." Adelaide squared her shoulders and lifted her chin.

Dimitri swallowed, recognizing her stance.

"I'm stating that I saw a black velvet pouch of yours in the safe's drawer on Monday when we put the crown there. That's a fact." Adelaide held Claude's stare.

"How do you know such an item belonged to me, if it was even there?" Claude made sure to look down his nose at Adelaide.

She raised her chin a little higher. "Fair point, sir. I don't know that it was your item."

Dimitri's father smiled.

"I do, however, know that you carried that item into the vault earlier that very morning." Adelaide maintained eye contact with his father.

Claude stopped smiling. "What makes you so sure of that?"

Adelaide shifted her weight back to her left heel, leaning back just a little. "Because video

196

surveillance confirms you going into the vault on Monday morning with the black pouch item and leaving minutes later without it."

The vein in the center of Claude's forehead bulged. "I don't remember dates, so I must have removed it sometime after that." He made a waving motion of dismissal.

But Adelaide wasn't going to let it go. She shook her head. "Not according to the videos. It doesn't show you going back into the vault at all."

"Are you calling me a liar?" Claude's eyes were wide, and his neck turned red.

"I'm sure this is all just a misunderstanding." Dimitri stepped between his father and Adelaide, his face toward his father. "I hear the gemologist is Russian, from Moscow, but speaks English fluently." He noticed that Lissette wore the slightest smile as Claude continued to glare at Adelaide.

*Brrring.*

"Excuse me." Adelaide turned away, sticking her cell phone to her ear. She took a few steps from their group and spoke in a hushed tone.

"Lissette, I was looking for you earlier. You didn't answer my call." Dimitri stared at his sister but monitored his father's expression from the corner of his eye. Claude Pampalon could, and would, blow, and Adelaide was in line to take a direct hit.

"I'm sorry. Claude and I were discussing some hotel business." Something about her posture . . .

Dimitri's disappointment in his sister was second only to his concern for Adelaide's faring against his father. He could understand Lissette wanting to get into Claude's good graces, but throwing Adelaide under the bus was dirty pool at best. As soon as he was able, he'd certainly discuss the situation with Lissette and let her know this was *not* acceptable.

"Yes, *Lissette* seems most interested in putting this hotel first. Before personal feelings." Claude seethed.

Dimitri recognized the signs all too well of his father's fury. He was riled up good. Loaded for bear, as their housekeeper, Tilda, liked to say. Speaking of Tilda . . . "Father, Tilda asked if we had any openings here that we could consider for Elise. I was wondering if you could use another assistant in your office." Claude had always liked their housekeeper's niece.

"Perhaps Elise might be better suited to work in a different area." His father spoke in a level tone. His anger was still there, but was subsiding.

Dimitri just needed to continue to deflect Claude's attention.

"She's enrolled in the community college, taking several accounting courses. Perhaps we could use her in payroll?"

"Fine."

Before Claude could say anything else, the lobby door opened, and the driver preceded an older gentleman. The man stood about six feet tall, but his suit hung off of his frame like limp pasta off a spoon. His face carried deeply etched lines that weighted down the sagging skin, his cheeks wilting to hide behind a long, scruffy white beard.

Dimitri crossed the lobby to meet the man, extending his hand. "You must be Mr. Orlov. I'm Dimitri Pampalon. Welcome."

The man shook his hand, his skin as thin as parchment to the touch. "Yaromir. My pleasure to meet you."

Claude extended his hand. "Claude Pampalon, owner of the Darkwater Inn."

Yaromir shook his hand and nodded.

Lissette followed Claude in extending her hand. "Lissette Bastien. Welcome to the Darkwater Inn."

"Is Her Highness, Princess Katerina von Pavlovna, ready to speak with me?"

Dimitri nodded. "Yes, sir. She asked that we notify her when you are settled in your room and ready to meet her."

"I will speak with her now, please."

Adelaide stepped up beside Dimitri and took Yaromir's hand between hers. "Hello, Mr. Orlov. I'm Adelaide Fountaine, general manager at the Darkwater Inn. It is our pleasure to have you here, no matter the circumstances." She could charm a cobra.

Yaromir smiled at her like she was the only person in the world and patted her hand holding his. "Thank you, Ms. Fountaine. You are very kind." Dimitri understood how he felt. Adelaide had that way about her that made you feel like you were royalty yourself.

Adelaide smiled and included everyone in her gaze, even Claude, while not letting go of Yaromir's hands. "Wonderful news too. I just now got off the phone with the police. They have recovered the tiara." She smiled at Dimitri. "And the cash that was taken out of the safe." She looked back at Yaromir. "The police would normally have the princess come to the station and claim her property once the case is concluded, but because of the extraordinary circumstances, they will bring it here today, to the hotel, for you to inspect and to return to the princess."

The tiara was recovered? This was amazing. Dimitri wanted to scream and shout for joy. The money had been recovered and the tiara. This would certainly make his father happy. He glanced at Claude's face.

He didn't look very happy. His expression hadn't really changed. "This is magnificent news. We must tell Her Highness, Princess Katerina von Pavlovna, immediately." Yaromir finally released Adelaide's hand. "When will your police bring the diadem? I need to set up to inspect."

"Of course. Whatever you need, we'll have set up in your suite. Let me take you there now, and you can tell me what you need."

"Yes. Thank you. Let us go now."

Adelaide waved over a bellhop. "Bring Mr. Orlov's bags from the car out front to suite 113, please." The young man rushed to do her bidding as she placed a hand under Yaromir's elbow and looked at Dimitri. "I'll be back directly." She turned the Russian toward the elevator, speaking as they walked.

"Well, I guess that's that. Good police work has won out." Dimitri almost choked saying the last sentence but couldn't understand why his father wasn't more relieved. "Your fifty thousand will be returned, Father."

"Yes." He turned to look at Lissette. "You should contact our insurance and cancel the claim. We don't want a fraud case brought up against us." Claude's disdainful expression settled on Dimitri. "Did you take care of the matter we discussed?"

The matter they—oh, the PI. "I did, but I guess it's not needed now." He'd need to call Rodney.

"It most certainly is." Claude cut his eyes to Lissette, then back to Dimitri. "Come see me when you're done here." Without any parting remarks to Lissette, he marched down the hall toward his office.

"I guess I'd better call our insurance agent." Lissette's voice was barely above a whisper as she moved to follow Claude.

"Just a moment." He took her gently by the forearm and drew her off from the main lobby. "What you did, what you told Claude to get Adelaide in trouble—that was uncalled for, Lissette. I'm disappointed in you."

Her face hardened. "Disappointed? You were more than willing to have me axed if it meant saving your precious Addy. Don't blame me for taking up for myself."

"Taking up for yourself? Is that what you call it?" He didn't want to believe his sister would continue to act such a way toward Adelaide, but he'd noticed an increase in her animosity ever since Adelaide had returned from Europe.

"I only told him what Addy has been telling everyone who would listen: you, me, the police." Her stare hardened even more, if that was even possible. "It's not like I made anything up. You seem quite fine with her taking up for herself against Claude. I guess it's okay for her to do it, just not me, right?"

"You told Claude, knowing he'd be furious that anyone dare to defy him."

"They both seemed pretty adamant. Guess it doesn't matter now anyway, does it, if he had something in there or not? If the police recovered the crown and the money, anything else that might've been taken was probably recovered as well." She shrugged. "I'm going to my office to call the insurance agent like Claude asked me to."

"You mean ordered you to." He knew that would get under her skin. Lissette had a thing about people ordering her about. Yeah, he knew he was being petty and hated it, but he'd spoken before he could stop himself.

He hadn't been wrong. Lissette's brow furrowed. "You would see it that way because it wasn't in regards to your precious Addy." She shrugged, but her eyes had gone icy. "Whatever. I have work to do."

Dimitri didn't say anything or follow after her, reluctant to let his emotions cause him to say something he'd regret later.

# 18

ADDY

Yaromir Orlov closed the jeweler's loupe, slipping it into his pocket. He adjusted his bowtie and settled his glasses on the bridge of his nose. "Your Highness—"

Katerina held up her hand. "Yaromir, I've asked you several times to just call me Katerina."

He didn't flinch, didn't blink. "Your Highness, most of the jewels are intact as before you came to these United States."

She gave a little shake of her head and snuggled next to her fiancé on the loveseat. Everyone— Addy, Dimitri, Beau and Marcel, the princess and her fiancé—had settled in the gemologist's suite for his inspection of the princess's tiara. Her formidable guard, Luca, stood in front of the closed and locked door, even though Beau and Marcel both had their guns in the holsters at their sides. Addy and Beau sat across from the princess while Dimitri was off to the side and Marcel just hovered. The gemologist had everyone's attention at the moment.

"All of the gems are as they should be except for the largest sapphire. The twenty-five-carat one is not the original sapphire from Mother Russia.

It is an imitation, and not even a good one."

"What?!" Beau, Marcel, Dimitri, and even Addy herself all spoke in unison. Katerina gasped, and Edmond's mouth went slack.

"All of the other jewels are the same as when I inspected last year for the royal appraisals, but not the large sapphire. It is not even a cheap sapphire replacing the original beauty. It is colored glass."

"That can't be." Edmond finally found his voice.

"Are you sure?" Marcel asked.

The gemologist ignored the princess's fiancé and cut Marcel a smoldering look that would have put Claude Pampalon to shame. "I have inspected the royal jewels acquired from Russia every year for the past twenty years. I know each of the gems like they are my own. I am sure." He gestured to the tiara. "This imitation sapphire has no inclusions."

"An inclusion?" Beau had his notebook and pen out.

Yaromir sighed. "An inclusion in the gemology world means that there a characteristic enclosed within a gemstone, something that was trapped inside the stone while it was forming in the earth."

Marcel walked closer to Yaromir's work space. "And this one has no inclusions? Wouldn't that make it more valuable?"

The gemologist shook his head. "If a sapphire over three or four carats has no inclusions, for all purposes it is not real. I have been a gemologist for fifty years and have never seen a real sapphire of any size without inclusions." He gave a stiff nod. "Very few sapphires over five carats have the best clarity grade—what is called 'eye clean,' which means there are no inclusions visible without a jeweler's loupe."

Beau kept writing in his notebook. "So, the other gems are fine. Just that one is replaced with a fake?"

Yaromir nodded. "The largest and most valuable jewel. The original sapphire from Mother Russia is approximately twenty-five carats in size. It is nearly flawless in color and grade. Dark blue. Rare silk. That one stone alone is worth millions of American dollars."

"That one sapphire is worth millions?" Marcel repeated, stopping his pacing in the middle of the room.

Edmond let out a groan. The gemologist nodded.

"But all the diamonds and other sapphires in the crown are real, right?" Beau asked.

"Yes, but without the original large sapphire . . . even if the sapphire was replaced with another sapphire of similar size, the value of the diadem is still greatly diminished." Yaromir ran a slow finger along the crown.

"Diminished by how much?" Addy asked, unable to hold her tongue as she stood. This had happened in her hotel. On her watch. And she was already in Claude's crosshairs.

The older man softened his expression as he looked at Addy. "Millions of your American dollars."

"Millions, as in several? Even if replaced with the same size real sapphire?"

"Yes, Ms. Fountaine. The diadem loses many millions of value." Yaromir smiled softly at her. "Do you know the story surrounding the diadem?"

Addy stared at the tiara. "About it possibly being part of the missing Romanov crown jewels?"

Yaromir nodded as he took a seat on the barstool next to the table holding the tiara. "Yes. There are many who believe this diadem was part of the Diamond Fund. My father was one of the princely family's court jewelers before me, and his father before him. I was brought up having access to the best and most brilliant jewels known to man. My father, upon his retirement, took over the care of the jewels on display at the Kremlin. He stayed there until the day he died."

He lifted the tiara with such tenderness. "Even though my Mother Russia will not acknowledge this beauty as part of the Romanov crown jewels, mostly because of the Romanov family legend, I know it is genuine."

"If it's so valuable, why does the princess get to wear it?" Marcel turned to Katerina. "No offense, Princess."

She pulled out a pout, but Edmond glared at Marcel.

Yaromir tossed a harsh look at Katerina. "She should not have been wearing it here. It should have not left our country." He shook his head. "However, the new His Serene Highness, like his father and grandfather before him, does not believe the legend, nor my family's insistence and appraisals." The older man shrugged. "So while they are valuable in their own right, the princely family does not believe the diadem as a whole is invaluable. But it is."

Well, that made sense, but still . . .

"I guess you recovered my tiara before the thief could remove the other real jewels and replace them with imitations." Katerina looked at Beau. "I must thank you for that."

"Since the sapphire has been stolen, I'm sorry, but we'll have to keep the crown in police custody for now." Beau stood and nodded at Marcel, who moved to put the tiara back in the box they'd brought it in.

"Wait!" Yaromir reached for the tiara. "Let me secure it for you." He gently wrapped a piece of white cotton material around the tiara before easing it into the box.

"Do you have any idea when the princess will

get her tiara back?" Edmond's tone sounded as accusing as his stare looked.

Beau shook his head while Marcel took the box from Yaromir. "I'm sorry, but I don't. It just depends on how the investigation runs. We'll put out details, description, and information about the real sapphire to our sources." Beau looked at the gemologist. "Can you provide us with the description of the sapphire, please?"

Yaromir nodded, moved to the hard-sided leather case he had opened on the desk, and pulled out a folder. "Here is the legal description from the official appraisal I completed last year for the princely family." He handed Beau a piece of paper that looked like an award certificate. "This copy is for the police to have."

Beau tucked it into his notebook, then looked back at Katerina. "Princess, you said in your initial interview that you didn't know Jackson Larder, is that correct?"

"She said she didn't know him." Edmond put his arm around Katerina's shoulder.

"Mr. Jansen, I appreciate your thoughts and concern, but this is official police business, and I need to ask some questions and get direct answers from the person I ask. If you can't accept that, I'll have to ask that you leave." Beau looked more foreboding than Addy had seen him look.

It suited him in a macho, super cop kind of way.

"No, Detective, I did not know this Jackson Larder. I never met him." Katerina's accent had thickened with the arrival of Yaromir. Intentional? Perhaps not. Addy couldn't tell.

"The reason I ask is because we received his cell-phone records, and there are several calls logged from the number belonging to Rubin Hassler. These calls began about two weeks ago and ended on Wednesday, the day of the robbery and the day Rubin was killed."

Tears filled her eyes. "I do not know how they would know each other."

"Nor do we just yet, but we *will* find out."

Marcel met Edmond's harsh stare. "What about you, Mr. Jansen—did you know Jackson Larder?"

"I did not. Never met the man in my life." He tugged Katerina closer to him. "And I resent the implications of these questions." He shot a stare at Dimitri. "I'll be sure to let my father know how we were treated like common criminals."

"You're hardly being treated like a criminal, Edmond." Dimitri pushed off the table he'd been half sitting on the edge of and took a step toward the rest of the group. "The detectives are just asking a few questions. I would think you would want to know what happened not only to your deceased guard but the princess's missing sapphire as well."

Addy resisted the urge to clap. She'd never

thought she'd see the day that Dimitri took up for Beau, but here they were.

And she liked them all being on the same side.

"Of course we want answers, Dimitri. A royal employee was murdered here in your hotel. The princess's tiara was stolen from your supposedly secure safe. Yes, we most certainly want answers."

Addy's small victory crashed at her feet, and the back of her throat burned with acid. She looked at Katerina. "Again, we are very sorry and are working alongside the police to do whatever we can to find who murdered Mr. Hassler and to recover your tiara—Well, now the sapphire taken from it."

"Which would not have been available to be stolen had it never left our country." Yaromir's voice seemed to boom off the walls.

Katerina burst into tears and turned her face into Edmond's chest. He whispered softly as he kissed her very blonde temples and rubbed her back.

Yaromir let out a very loud and exasperated sigh.

Beau leaned closer to Addy. "The records show Hassler and Larder carried on lengthy conversations, thirty or so minutes, from two weeks ago through Wednesday mid-morning."

Marcel came along the other side of her. "Our cyber unit is pretty sure there had to be an inside

211

man. It's looking an awful like that person was Jackson Larder."

Addy hated to admit she hadn't known her employee all that well. She'd let Sully hire his own replacement when she'd had to promote Sully up to replace Geoff last year. She should have followed up. She should have paid better attention.

Dimitri was at her side in a moment. "You couldn't have known, Adelaide."

All her life, Addy had heard the phrase about cutting tension with a knife, but never fully understood it. Not until that exact moment, standing between Beau and Dimitri, who seemed to face off with a volume of unspoken words flying between them.

She wanted to vomit, but she needed to think. There had to be something she could do. Some way she could help. Something—"Luca!"

The guard turned at the mention of his name.

Katerina stopped her sobbing and turned from Edmond. "What about Luca?"

"Ask him if he knows Jackson. Or if he knew Rubin and Jackson were communicating. They were friends, yes?"

"I do not think Luca would know this security guard of yours." All of Katerina's tears ceased flowing as she looked at Addy.

"You didn't know Rubin knew Jackson, did you?" Addy asked.

Katerina frowned and shook her head. "No, I did not."

"Then maybe Luca knows Jackson, too, and you don't know that. Won't you just ask him?" Addy thought it was a simple enough request, but perhaps she'd misread the situation.

Edmond patted Katerina's knee. "Since this is official questioning, by the police, perhaps there should be a legal representative for Luca, my dear?"

Katerina nodded. "Yes. I think that would be best." She shook her head at Luca, who continued to stare at the group after hearing his name, then smiled at Addy. "To make sure there is no misunderstandings with the translations or anything."

Well . . . she had a point. Kinda.

Marcel gave a hard nod. "Perhaps you should arrange to have such a representative available here. Later today."

"So quickly?" Katerina's big blue eyes widened again.

Beau nodded. "The quicker we have all the facts, the quicker we can solve the case and possibly recover your missing sapphire."

"It's not missing, Detective." Edmond stood. "It was stolen from the hotel's safe that we had been assured was quite secure."

Addy's heartbeat kicked into overdrive and she opened her mouth to apologize again, but

Dimitri touched her arm and took a small step to be in front of her, just barely. "On behalf of the Darkwater Inn, I apologize to you, Princess Katerina. We will do everything possible to recover what was taken from you. We will adjust our insurance claim to ensure that as soon as our insurance company receives the final police report, they will have the estimate and appraisal in their hand. We are, of course, sickened by what has happened and hope that you know we will work alongside the police until the case is solved."

The corner of Addy's lip tingled in the beginnings of a smile, but she pressed her lips together. The testosterone in the room had become nearly stifling, but since most was released in order to stand up for her, Addy could breathe just fine.

# 19

## DIMITRI

"I don't take well to threats."

Dimitri froze outside his father's office, recognizing his father's tone all too well. Who on earth would be threatening Claude Pampalon in his own hotel?

"It's not a threat, I can promise you. We had a business deal."

"It's beyond my control that I no longer have it." The anger shook Claude's voice. "Trust me, I want to sell it to you more than you realize."

"Then you should reacquire it."

Dimitri could almost recognize the other man's voice. Just not quite.

"Don't you think I'm trying to do just that?"

"We have an auction lined up. We've invited various interested buyers. If we cancel, it will be damaging to our reputations."

An auction? Buyers? What had his father gotten into now?

"I'm working to recover it as best I can. I've even had a private investigator hired in an attempt to recover it before the police do."

Dimitri felt ill. He'd been an unknowing pawn in his father's nefarious scheme, and it made him so angry he could spit nails. But what was his father's plan? What was he doing?

"Yes, the police are better than I thought they would be. I was very surprised they recovered Katerina's tiara. I only wish they had acted faster in that aspect to have prevented the biggest stone from being replaced."

Dimitri sucked in air. The other voice was Edmond Jansen! "The theft was certainly at the most awful time."

"Are you sure about that, Claude?"

"Whatever do you mean?"

"It seems very coincidental that your hotel would be robbed when the princess's tiara was in there, along with the vase and flowers."

Claude's voice lowered to the point where Dimitri had to lean closer to the closed office door. "Are you implying that I had anything to do with the theft? If what the police have discovered is accurate, your country's private guard was involved in the robbery."

"Along with *your* hotel's guard. Our guard was murdered by yours during the course of the robbery."

"And our guard was murdered as well. At least the crown has been recovered."

"As I understand was your cash."

Dimitri moved away from the door as one of the office administrators made her way past the offices, heading to the lobby. As soon as she turned the corner, he moved back to listen again.

Claude cleared his throat. "Be that as it may, Edmond, I'm doing everything I can to recover it so I can sell it to you."

"Our auction goes live Saturday night. We'll need those poppies in hand before then."

"I said I'm doing the best that I can."

"If your best isn't getting it done, Claude, perhaps you should do something else. Whatever it takes. My father will not be pleased if we have to cancel the auction. He'll be furious."

"I said I'm handling it." Claude spoke from behind clenched teeth.

Dimitri could picture his father now: face red, veins bulging, jaw locked with the muscles popping. Controlled fury at its best.

"Are the police aware it was stolen?"

"No, of course not. I've gone on record that nothing of mine, aside from the hotel's cash on hand, was stolen."

"I heard tell that Ms. Fountaine claims differently. Could she have seen it?"

"No. She saw the pouch it was in but has no idea what was in it. There's no way anyone knows, or could even guess." Claude's tone had lifted a little.

Dimitri straightened in the hallway. His father sounded nervous. Maybe even a little scared. It was hard to tell because Claude was never nervous or scared, not that anyone could ever tell. Either way, it sent icy fingers down Dimitri's spine.

"I would hope not. For your sake, I hope you recover the vase and flowers soon."

"Don't you worry about it. I've spoken with the private investigator I hired to keep tabs on our independent person. My man understands the importance of reacquiring it with no one being the wiser that it was ever taken." Claude's voice was back to normal.

Yet Dimitri's gut was twisted into a tight blob. He'd been set up to play into his father's plan, whatever that was. How had he not seen it from the beginning? His father had hired someone to keep tabs on Rodney Ardoin after Dimitri had hired him? Adelaide had been right all along. His father had had something in the safe that was taken. Whatever he'd had stolen, he was desperate to get it back.

Dimitri moved to the other side of the hallway as one of the ladies in reservations smiled at him. He nodded at her as she passed him in the hallway. He waited until she'd turned out of his line of vision and moved back to his spot outside his father's office door.

Edmond's voice split the silence. "Let's see to it that it stays that way. I would hate for this deal to go south at this point because of one woman."

"Don't you worry about Ms. Fountaine. I have

that situation well under control. She won't be a problem for us."

"If you don't make sure, I will."

Dimitri's hands balled into fists of their own accord. "I said I have it handled."

"Then I'll look forward to hearing you've got the item in hand before Saturday night." Edmond Jansen's voice was louder, closer to the door.

Dimitri took a few steps back. It wouldn't do for him to get caught eavesdropping or just hanging out in the hallway. No, *that* didn't look suspicious at all.

*"Take the bull by the horns, son,"* Claude had always said. No better time than the present.

He sucked in air, tapped his knuckles twice on the wood door, pushed it open, and then stepped inside. "Fath—oh, I'm sorry. I didn't know you had someone in here. I'll come back later. Please, excuse me." He moved to turn.

"No, it's okay." His father stood up from behind his desk. "Mr. Jansen just came by to let me know how the police questioned him and the princess, as well as her staff." He frowned that disapproving scowl he wore so often. "I've offered our apologies and have pledged to assist them in a smoother experience from here on out."

Edmond cut his eyes to Claude, then nodded.

"Our conversation just ended, and he was just leaving." No mistaking the arrogance and authority in Claude's voice now. If Dimitri hadn't heard what he had, he wouldn't have believed Edmond Jansen had not only just threatened Claude Pampalon but bullied him as well.

And Claude hadn't been able to stop him.

Edmond paused for a moment, then gave Dimitri a hard look before brushing past him on the way out.

Claude let out a hard breath and sat back down in his leather executive's chair behind his overstated mahogany desk. "While your timing was perfect this time, Dimitri, I'm quite busy. What did you want?"

He needed to make sure his father didn't guess he'd overheard the conversation between him and Edmond. "I just came to fill you in on the case. The police gave us an update earlier, and I wanted to let you know."

"Mr. Jansen informed me the police recovered the crown from Jackson Larder's home, but had a jewel replaced. Our fifty thousand in cash was also recovered from Jackson's house, and a link has been determined between the princess's guard who was killed and our guard who was also murdered. The police had questioned him and the princess and plan to question her remaining guard. Is that about what you were going to tell me?"

"Pretty much. The police said they would be able to release the fifty thousand cash to us within a few days." Dimitri nodded, silently amazed at his father's ability to switch gears so quickly. Talent, or habit?

"Then if there's nothing else . . ." Claude looked up from his desk. "I have an appointment outside the hotel this afternoon and I must finish up some things here before I go."

"Of course." Dimitri turned and headed toward the door, but stopped. "Father . . ."

Claude sighed and stared at Dimitri. "Yes?"

"I'm not sure what is going on with you and Lissette, but—"

"There's nothing going on. She is trying to do everything she can to please me in hopes that I will continue to employ her after she turns twenty-four." Claude shook his head. "Yes, Dimitri, I can see by the look on your face that you've consulted with your little law friend and learned that I can, and most likely will, oust Ms. Bastien from this hotel and my life in mere months."

"But Father—"

Claude held up a hand. "Please do not insult me, Dimitri, by attempting to sell me on her attributes. As far as I can tell, she has none, just as her mother before her. There was a reason her mother meant nothing to me, why Lissette doesn't either. So please, do not try and justify her existence."

Dimitri couldn't even find the words.

"You'd do well to realize, my son, that crossing

me is not in your best interest. Or in the best interest of Ms. Fountaine."

"Father, she—"

"Don't apologize for her. At least her I can respect, because she believed something and stood up for that, even if she was wrong." Claude lifted his monogram-engraved pen from his desk. "I'll have to discuss *respect* with her, especially in front of other hotel staff, of course."

That sounded an awful lot like she wouldn't be fired.

"I believe she's done a good job here, so I'm willing to overlook this one lack of good judgment on her part. For now. We shall see how I feel after we speak." Claude dropped the pen back onto his desk. "If there's nothing else, Dimitri, I do need to finish up here so I won't be late to my meeting."

Not trusting himself to speak, Dimitri just left. Adelaide's position, for now, was secure. He just had to figure out a way to get Lissette settled, then work through whatever kind of jealousy she had going on about Adelaide.

## BEAU

"What do you make of the whole 'crown valued at millions' thing?" Marcel leaned back in his chair at the precinct and took a sip of coffee.

Beau shook his head. "I'm not into jewels and their worth, and I have no reason to disbelieve anything Orlov said, so I guess it's worth millions."

"What about it being part of the Romanov family jewels? Would be kind of neat if it was. I mean, that we've seen it and actually touched it and all."

Beau grinned at his partner. "I guess so." He glanced back to his notes. "Still, it seems odd."

"What does?"

"Well, we know Larder didn't have a lot of time."

Marcel shrugged. "He shoved the cash in a drawer. That doesn't take a lot of time. Or planning."

"But the missing sapphire. He not only got it out, but he had an imitation that would fit it on hand to replace it then wrap the tiara in a trash bag and duct tape it to the lid of his grill?"

"Hey, man, we've seen stranger things. He'd been talking to Hassler, planning it, so he probably had the right size piece of glass that he knew would fit."

Made sense. "Yeah." But it didn't feel right to him. Something was still off. Something he was missing.

"The money in the drawer . . . I don't think the security people knew the hotel kept such an amount of cash on hand. He opened the safe and probably figured it was a bonus and never told anybody else."

"Yeah, but that still doesn't tell us who killed him." Beau flipped through his notes. "He and Hassler plan everything weeks before, so everything goes off without a hitch: the hack, getting into the vault, all of that. Something happens to change the status quo. Either Larder plans the double cross or something happens in the vault—who knows, maybe they saw the cash and Larder didn't want to share with Hassler or something, but for whatever reason, Larder shoots and kills not only his coworker, but also his partner."

Marcel nodded and set down his mug. "Larder grabs the cash and the tiara and scrams. He heads home. He's already got the fake sapphire ready to switch out." He snapped his finger and pointed at Beau. "Maybe that's why he killed Hassler. Maybe they'd planned to sell it back to the princess all along, but Larder got greedy and decided to take the sapphire first, then sell it to the princess. He cuts Hassler out of the decision. He stashes the cash in a drawer and makes the switch, then secures the crown."

Beau nodded. "Let's say Larder planned to call Jansen and offer back the crown, but didn't plan to do it until the next day. He was supposed to go to work that morning. Maybe he wanted to see how the investigation was going before he did that. If there was too much heat, he could just sell off the stones of the crown, one jewel at a time."

"But someone killed him first. Who?"

"That's the million-dollar question."

"Or million*s*, as the case may be."

Beau flipped through his notes again. "I can't see there being another person involved in the setup. Larder clearly didn't see this coming any more than Hassler saw Larder killing him."

"Wouldn't it be a killer coincidence if whoever killed Larder had nothing to do with the crown at all?" Marcel took a sip of coffee.

*Ding!*

Beau turned to his computer. "Message from Nolan." He clicked to open his interoffice messaging system. "Prelim forensics report is in." He scanned through the information. "Still waiting on autopsy from Walt." He kept reading. "Fingerprints at the scene belonged primarily to Larder. A single thumbprint was found on the wooden footboard in the bedroom where the body was discovered." His heart and gut collided as he continued reading. "The print has been identified through an Interpol connection as belonging to one Luca Vogt, who is in the employment of members of the royal family of Liechtenstein."

Marcel nearly knocked over his coffee cup. "They'll either ask him now, or we'll haul him down here to ask him."

"I'll call the embassy for advisement and to

keep them in the loop as requested, then I'll bring the captain up to speed."

Marcel nodded. "I'll go ahead and request a German interpreter be ready. Just in case the princess doesn't want to ask him questions without a representative."

Beau dialed the number for the embassy, his pulse pounding.

They were about to get answers.

One way or another.

# 20

## ADDY

The sun set over the New Orleans' Basin City Projects, casting the last tendrils of shadows like eerie skeleton fingers reaching out to grab those who passed by the darkening alleys.

Addy shivered against the cooling breeze snaking over the area. Basin Street wasn't a place to be for a woman after dark, but the message she'd found on her desk had said Claude was adamant as to where they were to meet promptly at six. Surely this couldn't be the area where Mr. Pampalon was considering opening a small bed and breakfast. Addy double-checked the address with the GPS on her phone. No mistake, this was it.

Addy got out of her car, making sure to lock it, and looked around. She held her cell phone in a death grip as she made a slow circle in place, right next to her car, taking it all in.

A couple of teenage boys stood across the lot from her, the ends of their cigarettes blazing against the darkness. A radio thumped from a car passing on the street. A good block or three away a siren wailed. A woman down the street screamed, then laughed. Angry male voices carried on the wind.

Claude Pampalon had lost his mind. There was no way any type of legitimate business could succeed here. It might only be one block inland from the Quarter, but it ran parallel to Rampart Street, and as soon as that was crossed from either side of Canal Street, it was officially the bad part of town.

Basin Street, sometimes still referred to by older locals by its French name, *Rue Bassin*, had at one time been considered one of the finest residential streets in New Orleans. Around 1870, though, it became a red-light district, maintaining that status through World War I. It had housed the front of the Storyville red-light district, home to a line of high-end saloons and manors devoted to music.

Today the neighborhood was run down, full of low-income housing, with buildings in varying stages of dilapidation. This and surrounding neighborhoods were made up of more people of African and Czechoslovakian ancestry than nearly any neighborhood in America—over fifteen percent.

Addy held her cell phone as she made her way into the building the message had given an address for. Sure, there was parking aplenty, and these warehouses sat on good concrete foundations that had withstood hurricanes and swelling from the Gulf, but the investment would be wasted in this part of town.

Claude had been furious with her the last time they'd spoken, so maybe this was . . . No, she couldn't even think what was going through his mind to even consider turning this place into a bed and breakfast.

She opened the door to the warehouse. It moved without resistance, other than a creak from a hinge that cried out for oil. The dimmest of lights blazed in a room off to the side of the main space. Cold and damp, the place had the lingering odor of dead fish and mold. Not the best combination.

"Hello? Mr. Pampalon?" Addy made her way toward the room with the light.

No response. Not that she'd expected one. He was probably sitting in there enjoying what he knew had to be an ordeal for her.

A rat scurried across the floor. Addy's heartbeat instantly raced. Rats were filthy things, and Addy was very much afraid of them. The place was probably crawling with water bugs, too, being this close to the water. Definitely spiders with the darkness and mustiness. She shuddered, suddenly overwhelmed with the sensation that creepy crawlies were sliming all over her. Just the kind of setting her father would write about in one of his thriller novels. The murder scene.

This was ridiculous. Did Claude just need to prove he could put her in an uncomfortable position? That he had the power to make her go into dirty, stinky, rat-infested places on his command? Prove he could dictate to her like he did his own children?

She gripped her cell tighter and marched faster toward the room with the light. No job was worth this, no matter how much she loved it. Addy intended to give Claude Pampalon a piece of her mind. He might get his kicks ordering Dimitri and Lissette around, but Addy wasn't going to play this game.

Addy marched into the room. "Mr. Pamp—"

No sense continuing as she was all alone, save the furniture, sparse as that was. An old card table and one wooden chair. One of the arms had been broken off the chair. The light emanated from an electric hurricane lamp sitting on the table's corner. The fake flame danced against the glass of the lamp, sending flashes off the walls and revealing their peeling paint.

Where was he? When she found him, she was going to—

A sudden bolt of force just behind her right ear.

Hot, blinding pain. Her legs no longer supporting her.

She dropped to her knees, something digging into her skin. She toppled to the ground. Cold, wet concrete against her cheek.

The pain was too much. Darkness swallowed her.

# DIMITRI

"I'll be in the office if you need me," Dimitri told his sous chef, Yvette.

She nodded. "I'll find you if you're needed." Yvette went back to spooning gumbo into the white square bowls popular at the Darkwater Inn Restaurant.

He smiled to himself as he made his way to the little office just off the kitchen. It had been a long day, and he was thankful for Yvette's talent that allowed him to do what he needed to do.

Right now, he needed to figure out what his father had stolen that Edmond Jansen frantically wanted.

Adelaide had described it, if his memory was right, as maybe more than a foot or two long, tubular in shape, and maybe three or four inches thick. The possibilities of what it could be were endless. Dimitri thought back to the conversation between his father and Edmond. If Edmond and his father were having an auction to sell it, the item had to be worth quite a bit of money.

What was it Edmond had said? Dimitri struggled to remember. Edmond had just threatened Adelaide. Claude had assured him that he had everything under control. Edmond had told Claude that he hoped he recovered the vase and flowers. Vase and flowers.

Edmond had said that earlier in their conversation too. He'd told Claude it seemed too coincidental that the hotel was robbed when the princess's tiara was in the safe along with the vase and flowers.

There wasn't room in the safe's drawer for a vase and flowers. The description of the black pouch from Adelaide certainly couldn't contain a vase and flowers. That had to be code for something.

He opened the laptop sitting on the desk, then opened the browser. He ran a search on *vase and flowers* for which a multitude of florist listings was returned. Page after page. He tried again, this time using *a vase and flowers* in the search bar with quotations. This time, in addition to a few floral listings, several still-life painting sites loaded.

A painting could fit Adelaide's description. A canvas cut from its frame could be folded and/or rolled and put inside a pouch to be put in a safe to be kept secure until such time when it could be sold. But to go up for auction it had to be a very expensive painting.

None of the ones listed on the search results looked to be worth enough to warrant so much planning and trouble.

He sat back in the chair and closed the laptop, thinking. After a moment he pulled out his cell phone and called Adelaide. She loved art and recognized all the pieces in the hotel's collection. His call went straight to voice mail. "Hi, Adelaide. Please call me when you get this. Thanks. It's Dimitri."

Surely his father wouldn't take one of the hotel's paintings and sell it. No, that just didn't make sense. Besides, as far as he knew, none of the paintings from the hotel were worth a large amount of money. All were insured, and to sell one would open them up to insurance fraud. Claude knew this and wouldn't put himself at risk. Dimitri might not know about paintings, but he knew who did.

He searched through his contacts list, found whom he was searching for, and made the call.

Zoey Naure answered on the second ring. "Hello, there, Dimitri. I was just thinking about you."

"Were you?" He smiled even though she couldn't see him.

"I was, truthfully." She laughed, her husky voice sounding like smooth whiskey. "Because I'm pulling up to your hotel right now."

The smile slipped away. "You are?" He remembered how not too long ago Zoey had frequented the Darkwater Inn's bar a little too often with a variety of men. A variety of men who paid for her company.

"I'm actually delivering a print to one of your guests." She laughed again. "Don't panic, I'm not going back to my old ways. I'm just dropping it off, and then I'll be on my merry way."

Dimitri whispered a silent prayer for God's perfect timing. "Actually, I need a favor."

"Name it. You know I owe you big time."

Last year, he'd learned that Zoey was a single mother in need of a steady, respectable job. He'd reached out to various friends and was able to get her a job in one of the warehouse district's art galleries. She'd been grateful, but his friend had been even more grateful, telling Dimitri that Zoey had a natural eye for art and was a great asset to her gallery.

"You don't owe me, but if you could spare a few minutes, I'd really appreciate it."

"Of course. Like I said, I just have to drop this off at the client's room. I'm walking to the elevator now. Love your valet parking, by the way."

He grinned. "Come on to the restaurant when you're done."

"I'll see you in less than fifteen, my friend."

Dimitri wove through the labyrinth of pathways in the kitchen and restaurant itself to the hostess's station, stopped many times by regular guests and diners who wanted to say hello. Normally he enjoyed the conversations and feedback on his creations, but tonight . . . Tonight everything felt off to him. Nothing felt right.

Arriving at the front of the restaurant, Dimitri

pulled out his phone. No missed calls. He tried calling Adelaide again. His call went immediately to voice mail again. He left another message, a niggle of worry bubbling up inside him. She never turned off her phone, and it was unlikely she'd be on a call so long. He lifted the in-house receiver and dialed her office's extension. It rang four times.

"Hello, stranger."

Dimitri hung up the phone and turned.

Zoey's hair was red and straight, and she had those big, round, dark eyes, but it was her almost transparent skin that made her truly stunning. She smiled wide as she wrapped her arms around him and hugged him tight. When she released him, she laid a hand on the side of his face. "You look really good, Dimitri."

"As do you." That wasn't just lip service— she looked amazing. She'd always been a head turner, but instead of the clingy dresses she'd once worn, she now wore a clean-cut, tailored pantsuit. Her eyes that had once boasted rings of makeup were now softened with just the slightest use of mascara. "It's really good to see you, Zoey."

"You too." She smiled. "What can I help you with?"

Apparently she was still all about the value of her time. Then again, he remembered she had a young child she was probably anxious to get home to after work. "Come on and I'll show you." He led her back to the tiny kitchen office.

"Well, this is a downgrade from your other office." She shut the door behind them.

Dimitri glanced at the confined space. "Yeah, but I like this one better."

"It shows." She shrugged. "And it suits you."

He opened the laptop and pulled up his search history. "I overheard someone talking about a vase and flowers so I was searching which painting they might be referring to, but there are so many. The one I'm looking for would be very valuable and—" He stopped as Zoey shook her head. "What?"

"I think the painting you're referring to is sometimes called *Vase and Flowers*, but its real title is *Poppy Flowers*. Could that be what it is?"

Wait . . . He'd overheard one of them talk about poppy flowers. What had they said? They were arguing about the auction. Yes, that was it—Edmond had told Claude they would need poppies in hand. "Yes, that's it. What can you tell me about it?"

Zoey perched on the edge of the desk for lack of anywhere else to sit and pulled out her smart phone. "Well, it is very valuable. About fifty million or so. It's a Van Gogh."

Dimitri's hopes were deflated. There was no way his father owned a real Van Gogh to sell. They had to be referring to a different painting.

Zoey read from her phone. " 'The painting, which is of a vase of yellow and red poppies, is contrasted against a dark background. It is said it's a reflection of Van Gogh's deep admiration for Adolphe Monticelli, an older painter whose work influenced him when first he saw it in Paris in 1886.' "

While interesting, it wasn't what his father and Edmond had been arguing about.

Zoey continued. " 'Interestingly enough, the painting was stolen twice from the Mohammed Mahmoud Khalil Museum in Cairo, Egypt. The first time was in 1997, and it was recovered ten years later in Kuwait. It was stolen again in 2010, during which, according to sources, the painting was cut from its frame and was just walked out of the museum. At the time, police blamed poor security since none of the alarms at the Khalil Museum were working and only seven out of forty-three security cameras were, and though the museum had only ten visitors that day, the thieves remain at large.' " She looked at Dimitri. "And the painting is still missing."

Dimitri's stomach tightened as his pulse raced. His father *had* had the stolen Van Gogh.

Now it had been stolen a third time. From the Darkwater Inn.

# 21

ADDY

Darkness enveloped her. Addy knew she was awake—coherent—but she couldn't open her eyes. Her lashes rebelled against a blindfold pressing tightly to her face. She strained to hear. Off in a distant part of the building in which she lay, she could just make out muted voices in heated conversation. She couldn't even tell if they were male or female.

A sour odor wafted under her nostrils, causing her stomach to heave. She attempted to hoist herself up from her lying position but fell against the restraints holding her legs together and her hands confined.

Fear surged as her recollection dawned—she'd been in Claude Pampalon's old warehouse and had been knocked on the back of the head.

Reverberations of footsteps bounced off the walls surrounding her. Addy's palms sweated. Whoever had hit her and tied her up was coming closer. Her heartbeat echoed in her head.

*Shuffle, step. Shuffle, step.*

Rank body odor assaulted her sense of smell as he came closer.

*Shuffle, step. Shuffle, step.*

His breathing sounded strained, coming in bursts and pants. She could smell his brewery breath in the close room.

*Shuffle, step. Shuffle, step. Step, stop.*

Panic overtook her. While she couldn't see for the blindfold, she could feel his presence. Feel his stare. Feel the fear rising in her chest. Her body rebelled. She wanted to scream, to yell, but she wouldn't. Couldn't. She bit down on her tongue. The metallic taste of blood tinged her taste buds.

Addy snorted air through her nostrils. The air was moist—stale. She took another deep breath and her nose tingled. Stirred-up dust wafted upward and settled in her nostrils. With another intake of air, Addy sneezed.

A man's throaty breathing filled her ears.

She cleared her throat and assembled as much bravado as she could. "Who are you? What do you want from me?"

He cleared his own throat. "That's not important."

"You have to want something." Images of her father's face flitted in her mind. Back when he'd had the stalker who'd threatened him, Vincent had gone into "Super Dad over-protection" mode. She'd gotten irritated that he'd been so serious. Now she understood.

"For now, you just stay put and know that you're being watched. Don't try any funny business."

Addy wheezed in the total darkness that surrounded her. "I need some water, please."

A moment passed. Two. Had the man left? She hadn't heard him walk off, but she couldn't even hear him breathing now. "Hello? Are you still there? I need some water, please."

A heavy sigh cut through the silence. "Stay there." He chuckled, obviously amused at his own joke.

*Shuffle, step. Shuffle, step. Shuffle, step.*

His movements faded to where Addy could hardly hear his broken gait. Clearly the man wasn't Claude, but it could be someone he'd hired. That didn't make a lot of sense, since Claude would just fire her if he wanted her gone.

Her father's stalker? Or another one of his rabid fans? Over the last several years, they'd relaxed their once vigilant guard and precautions. She had been at her father's last night. If someone had been watching the house, they would've seen her come and go. Her father always said his worst nightmare would be someone taking her to get to him.

But how would he have gotten her to this warehouse? No, the stalker theory didn't hold up. Vicky had given her the message that Claude had called and wanted her to meet him at this address at six o'clock to discuss him possibly opening a bed and breakfast.

It didn't make sense.

*Shuffle, step. Shuffle, step.* "Here."

Before she could speak, a strong grip on her right shoulder brought her into an upright position. "Open your mouth."

She jerked backward and rammed back into a wall. "I thought you were thirsty."

"I'm not going to drink anything unless I can see what I'm drinking." He could give her anything, something that might kill her. "Then I guess you're going to be thirsty."

*Shuffle, step.*

"Wait!" Well, to be fair, if he wanted her dead, she'd already be dead. But maybe if she could see him . . . There had to be a reason she was blindfolded. Either she would recognize him, or he didn't want her to be able to later. The last part boded well for her eventual release. "Please. I really am thirsty."

"It's bottled water. Listen and you should be able to hear me opening it." His voice had softened drastically.

Sure enough, she could. A twist and a little snap.

"Open your mouth and I'll give you some." The stench of his body odor nearly made her gag, but she resisted.

Every instinct in her told her not to, but the dryness in her throat screamed for her to open her mouth. Cautiously, she parted her lips.

A splash of cold wetness hit her mouth.

She gulped, leaning closer to the source. Her lips touched the plastic bottle. She sucked as he poured more. Then he pulled it away.

"That's enough for now." The gruffness was back in his voice.

*Shuffle, step.*

No room for argument.

*Shuffle, step. Shuffle, step. Shuffle, step. Step. Step.*

Panic rose in her throat as she sat alone in the darkness.

# Beau

"Let's do this." Beau nodded at the translator who stood beside him outside the interrogation room at the back of the precinct.

They had picked up Luca Vogt and brought him back to the precinct. The German translator had been waiting, but they'd had to wait for the representative the embassy sent to arrive. She had and had been afforded private time with Luca.

Their fifteen minutes alone was over.

Beau opened the door. He sat across from the big Liechtenstein man and the small woman the embassy had sent. Marcel dropped into the chair beside Beau while the translator took the chair on Beau's other side. Beau handed the copy of the Miranda rights to the translator, who recited them in German.

Luca nodded when she was done. "*Ja.*"

The translator set the card on the table. "He understands his rights."

"Do you know why we brought you to the police station?" Beau asked, then waited for the translator to repeat the question in German.

Luca shook his head. "*Nein.*"

"Do you know Jackson Larder?"

Again Luca shook his head. "*Nein.*"

Really? Beau held the big man's stare. "Your fingerprints were found where we found Jackson Larder's murdered body."

Luca's eyes widened before the translator finished speaking. The small woman the embassy had sent leaned over and whispered something to him in their native tongue. Luca shook his head and replied.

"How are your fingerprints at the scene where Jackson Larder was murdered?" Marcel asked.

The woman put her hand on Luca's forearm, but he ignored her, speaking so fast the translator had to rush to keep up.

" 'I did not know him, no, but he killed Rubin. He shot Rubin. He deserved to die.' "

Not quite a confession. "Did you kill Jackson Larder?"

The woman tightened her hold on Luca's arm, earning a glance from him. She spoke to him, shaking her head while he spoke back rapidly.

Beau looked at the translator, who began translating. " 'If you admit to murdering him, you are confessing to a crime. The country cannot help you if you do this.' "

Luca shrugged off her hand. "*Ja.*" He nodded. "Yes." Luca met Beau's stare. "*Ja, ich habe ihn getötet.*"

The translator sat straight in her chair. " 'Yes, I killed him.' "

There was the confession. Beau took out his notebook and opened it. "Why did you kill him?"

Luca sighed before he spoke, triggering the translator. " 'I already told you. He killed Rubin, so he deserved to die.' "

Revenge. Pretty cut and dry. On the surface. "Did you talk to Jackson Larder before you came to the United States?" Larder's phone records had not reflected he'd talked to anyone other than Hassler, but Vogt could have used Hassler's phone.

"*Nein.*"

"Did you know about the plan to rob the hotel and steal the princess's tiara?"

"*Nein.*"

"Did you speak to Jackson Larder prior to going to his house with the intent to kill him?"

"*Nein.*"

"How did you get to his house?" Marcel asked.

"I took a . . . trolley."

"How did you know which of the streetcars to get on and the schedule and where to get off?" Marcel pushed.

"The map and schedule were in the hotel room."

The room went silent save the gentle ticking of the clock on the wall.

Beau stared at his handwritten notes. "How did you know he killed Rubin?"

Suddenly, the big man clammed up and sat like a stone.

Marcel looked at the translator. "Did he not understand the question?"

She spoke to him again in his native tongue. He nodded but didn't speak.

The small woman spoke, and Beau looked at the translator.

"If you understand the question, why are you not answering? You have already confessed to a premeditated murder, so telling them how you knew he killed your friend will not get you in any more trouble."

He shook his head.

Marcel stood and began his series of pacing, which often loosened up witnesses. Intimidation or just familiarity, Beau didn't know, but it often worked. "I hear you. Somebody shoots my friend Beau here, and I find out about it? I'm going to even the score."

Luca nodded as he watched Marcel pace.

"I mean," Marcel continued, "you don't just shoot my friend, right?"

Luca nodded as both the translator and woman waited.

"Somebody tells me who shot my friend, and I'm ready to make sure they pay. Am I right?" Again Luca nodded.

Marcel stopped pacing and placed his palms on the table across from Luca and leaned almost into the big man's personal space. "I understand you, Luca. I get it. Who told you Jackson killed Rubin?"

The man sat silent, his gaze to the corner, avoiding Marcel's eye.

The small woman looked at Beau. "I am sorry. He is not going to answer this question."

Beau looked at his notes. He hated to think this was possible, but considering Luca's personality and how he acted, it was the only thing that made sense to Beau. It was a long shot, but they had nothing else.

He lowered his voice to barely a whisper. "How did Princess Katerina know Jackson Larder killed Rubin?"

# 22

## ADDY

Addy shifted against the wall, her legs growing numb against the cold floor. When the sun had set, so had the warmth. Here in the warehouse with no electricity, the wind pushed the chill in between the boards of wood. She shivered. Relaxing her neck muscles, she tried to relieve the tension in her body. With any luck, she'd be back home soon. If only she knew why she'd been abducted.

Her captor hadn't returned after taking away the water. While his presence was frightening, at least she hadn't been alone.

Goodness, that made her sound really pitiful.

A scratching sound to her right stiffened every muscle in her body in an instant. What was that?

Trying to twist around despite the confines, she fought against the restraints holding her arms behind her back.

Rustling sounded to her left. Was that something moving across the floor? A snake? A mouse? She shuddered as fearful, horrible images formed in her mind. She didn't do reptiles, nor rodents. Panic rose like a tidal wave as she heard the noise again.

Arching her back, she tested the tightness of the ropes. Maybe one was loose enough that she'd be able to work her hands or feet loose. Rocking herself on the hard, cold floor, she pushed and pulled. No such luck. The ropes were tighter now than they were before.

Relaxing her body, she emitted an exhausted sigh. Desperation circled her like a buzzard over roadkill.

She needed to focus. Where was her cell phone? If it was still on, Beau could track her GPS and find her. If someone reported her missing and if her cell phone was still on and here at the warehouse. For all she knew, her captor could have destroyed the phone.

Her car. That would be a little harder to get rid of. She moved around. Her keys were still in her pocket! She had OnStar, so if Beau needed to find her car, he could.

But someone needed to know she was missing to know to call Beau.

Friday night. She didn't have anything special scheduled. As usual, she'd planned to work, then go up to her suite, have a light supper, then take a long, hot bath. Maybe finish the latest murder mystery she'd been reading, or maybe just sit on the balcony and look over the city.

Wow, she'd never realized how isolated she'd become. She was around people all day and had a standing supper date with her dad every Thursday night, and she and Tracey tried to get together at least once every two weeks, but she hadn't had a date since . . . Okay, it'd been far too long since she couldn't remember. Not a *real* date.

She'd come to terms with the sexual assault that had happened to her in college, and knowing that Kevin Muller aka Brayden Colton was dead and would never be able to hurt another woman again made acceptance easier. But she hadn't really done much in changing her lifestyle. That needed to change. She needed to change. She needed to get back to doing things that had brought her peace and happiness.

Like keeping a journal. She'd always kept a personal journal, ever since she was a teenager. She'd stopped when she felt like she couldn't risk actually giving words to the emotions she was feeling. But then she'd picked up a blank notebook when she'd been in Europe and started writing through what she was feeling. It'd been exhilarating to have a pen back in her hand.

And sketching. She'd never been good at it, not even close, but she'd loved drawing flowers and such. Her journals had always been decorated with little doodles along the sides. She hadn't done that in a long time.

Years ago, she'd written poetry. Not just written it, but recited her original poems as live performances. She'd loved expressing herself that way. Once Brayden had . . .

Well, she'd stopped performing because she didn't want to bring attention to herself.

She shouldn't have. She shouldn't have stopped any of these things. It was letting Brayden win. Well, no more. It was past time for her to step into her own skin again.

She wanted to live life fully again.

She paused in her thinking, her mind jumping back to earlier this week when she'd pulled her old Bible from her desk drawer. For the first time in a very long time, she'd seen it, touched it, opened it without any of the anger and resentment that had filled her anytime she thought of God. Of faith. Perhaps there was something else she needed to reintroduce to her life. Perhaps it was time . . .

*Hey, God. It's me again. If You're still listening, I could really use Your help.*

No bolt of lightning came down. No rolling thunder. Just her in some old warehouse of Claude Pampalon's. But maybe He heard.

Addy let out a slow breath. She refused to give in to fear. She had a life to live. She willed her breathing to regulate. She needed to be smart . . . to think. She needed a plan. Did anybody know she was missing? Beau? Dimitri? Hopefully she'd been on their minds today. After all, she'd finally told both men that she was ready to date. And she was. Ready to date . . . ready to start getting back to enjoying life . . .

ready to become who she was always meant to be.

If she survived this.


## DIMITRI

"Hey, Dimitri." Elise hollered out to him as he stormed into his father's home.

He paused. "What are you doing here?" It took him a moment to realize that he'd been so furious with his father that he hadn't registered their housekeeper's Mustang was parked in the circular drive.

"Aunt Tilda wanted to bring over the king cake she baked for Mr.Claude. Something told me I should come with her."

He knew she was referring to the spirits and voodoo, but he didn't have time to delve into the nonsense at the moment. "It's nice seeing you, Elise, but I need to see my father. I'll talk to you later."

She replied, but he didn't hear her because he was already heading toward the kitchen.

Tilda was alone, shutting the refrigerator. "Mr. Dimitri. I was just—"

"I know, bringing Father a king cake. Do you know where he is?"

"He was in the study a moment ago."

Without another word, Dimitri headed to his father's study. He didn't knock, just barged in.

"What are you doing, Dimitri?" Claude sat in his oversized and overstuffed leather recliner, his feet up, the daily newspaper in his hand, and a crystal tumbler with a drink on the table at his side. "Have you lost your senses, barging in here like some thug?"

"We need to talk, Father." Dimitri stood behind the high-back chair that faced his father's recliner.

Glaring, Claude folded the paper and set it in his lap, folding his hands neatly over it. "By all means, let us talk."

Dimitri gripped the brocade fabric of the back of the chair. "I know about the Van Gogh."

His father's façade slipped, but only for a moment before his expression went back to his normal sternness. "I have no idea what you're talking about." Yet there was a little hitch in his voice.

"Yes, Father, you do. I'm talking about the painting titled *Poppy Flowers*, the Van Gogh that was stolen twice in Egypt: once in the late nineties, recovered ten years later in Kuwait, then stolen again in 2010."

His father didn't respond, just scowled at him.

But Dimitri wouldn't be intimidated by his father this time. Not today. He tightened his grip on the chair and stared down his father. "You know, the one that was stolen from the safe when Jackson stole the tiara and the cash. I'm assuming he took the painting as well. The one you were going to sell to Edmond Jansen, who is now furious that you don't have it and he might have to cancel his precious auction."

Claude's eyes widened and his brows lifted.

"Yes, I know all about it. I also know that you hired someone to follow the private investigator I hired in hopes that you could recover the painting before the police find it." Dimitri found his body surging with an energy he'd never felt before, and he couldn't stop. "I bet it made you a thousand kinds of nervous when they recovered the princess's tiara and the cash. They probably would have recovered the painting, too, had they known to look for it."

Claude sat as silent as a statue.

"Did you ever think that perhaps Edmond was behind the theft? That he arranged it, using their guard Rubin Hassler as the contact person with Jackson? Or did you arrange the theft yourself? Steal the crown so you could have it, but also provide a very convenient excuse for not having the painting anymore. Did you want to have your own private auction? Cut Edmond out of the deal?"

"You have no idea what you're talking about. I knew nothing of the theft or a plan thereof until we were robbed."

"So maybe it was Edmond who orchestrated the whole thing."

"I doubt that. His father wouldn't allow it."

Dimitri fisted his hands. "Maybe he finally had enough of his father's control. I can certainly understand that sentiment."

"Son, you don't understand. You—"

Dimitri shook his head. "No, don't 'Son' me. All this time, Adelaide was right. You had the painting in that black pouch. She saw it. Knew it was there. Knew it'd been stolen. But you couldn't claim it. Couldn't tell anyone, could you? Because it's stolen." He swiped the top of the chair. "Where did you get it, Father? There's still an open reward for it."

Claude sat up, setting the folded newspaper on the coffee table. "I acquired it from a friend of a friend. And yes, I thought about turning it in for the reward."

"Why didn't you?" He wanted so desperately to see something—anything good and noble—in his father, but Claude continued to disappoint.

"You can't possibly understand the nuances of the business dealings I have to conduct. I have built our fortune from nothing. Nothing, Dimitri." Claude shot to his feet. "I owe you no explanations. I have given you everything you've ever needed. Wanted. I provided you with a stable home, the best education, the best things money could buy. I exposed you to a lifestyle most people only dream about."

"That has nothing to do with a stolen painting."

"But it does, Dimitri. Everything is because of something else. All of the things I've provided for you haven't come cheap. I started with nothing and built my empire into what it is today because I wasn't afraid to cross a line or two."

"It can't be just about the money. You don't need more money, Father."

"One can never have enough money, Dimitri, but it isn't just about the money. It's about paying back a favor to someone who helped me at one time. It's about conducting a business transaction not because it is in your best interest but because you owe a debt of favor to someone. And I know Edmond wasn't involved in the theft because it's his father I was doing the favor for."

Claude moved to the wet bar and poured himself a shot of whiskey from the decanter. He downed it in one gulp, then set the tumbler back on the cherrywood. "There are things over the years that I've had to do to maintain our lifestyle." He turned and faced Dimitri. "I do them for you. To keep my estate plentiful for you . . . for your future children."

Dimitri shook his head. "No. That's not why you do anything, Father. You do things for your own wants and needs, not mine. It's never been about me."

"I—"

Dimitri held up his hands. "No, I can't listen to this anymore."

"Then why are you still here?"

"I want to know why you had a meeting with Adelaide tonight. Were you scared she was on to you? What did you say to her?"

"I don't know what you're talking about."

"Father, don't try to deny it. I went to your office to ask you about the painting, and I saw your appointment calendar. You had noted a meeting today with Adelaide. At six."

Claude's face went slack, and he slowly shook his head. "Dimitri, I can assure you that I did not have a meeting planned with Ms. Fountaine. I didn't have one scheduled at six, or any other time today, nor have I spoken to her this afternoon."

Dimitri's chest tightened. "Don't lie to me."

"I'm not lying to you, son. There was no appointment with Ms. Fountaine on my calendar when I left."

His father had just admitted to owning and almost selling a stolen Van Gogh. Why would he lie about an appointment?

So where was Adelaide?

Dimitri pulled his phone from his pocket and tried her again. His call went straight to voice mail. He ended the call and pointed at his father. "You'd better not be lying to me." He didn't wait for a response before turning and rushing toward the front door.

"Dimitri! Dimitri!" He'd never heard that

concerned tone from his father, but now wasn't the time. Something was wrong with Adelaide. He knew it. He could feel it.

"How can I help?" Elise met him in the entryway.

"It's Adelaide Fountaine. She isn't answering her phone—my calls are going straight to voice mail. I'm going to go back to the Darkwater Inn and check her apartment."

Elise nodded. "I know her friend, Tracey. I'll call her."

"Thanks." Dimitri paused. "If you hear anything, learn anything, whatever, please call me."

"I will."

He rushed out the door and into his car.

*Please, Lord, keep Adelaide safe. Wherever she is and whatever is happening, please keep her in Your protective hand.*

# 23

## ADDY

Stuck in a room with only darkness as a companion, Addy lost track of time. Was it still Friday night? Surely, but she couldn't be sure. Maybe it had segued into Saturday already.

Two Mardi Gras parades were scheduled today. One was Claude's, at noon today. Princess Katerina would ride on the float he'd spared no expense in having created. Claude's krewe was the Krewe of Aion, who was the Greek god of eternity. Claude had designed the back of the float to be a huge zodiac wheel with a naked Aion standing in the center as if holding it up. Katerina would sit on the throne beside the depiction of Aion. It would be quite the sight to see.

Too bad Addy would miss it.

She was so thirsty again. She wanted to ask for water, but she hadn't heard anyone for a while. Had she fallen asleep? Surely not. If only she—

Her captor spoke, off in the distance. Wait. She couldn't hear him clearly, so he obviously wasn't talking to her. If not her, then who was he talking to?

Her heart thumped. Should she try to call for

help? She opened her mouth, then stopped. He hadn't gagged her, so he must be pretty certain no one would hear her if she yelled. He was probably just on the phone. Yelling probably wouldn't be her smartest move.

Maybe whoever he was on the phone with would hear her. Not likely, though. Addy tilted her head and used her shoulder to rub against the tie of the blindfold. Why she hadn't considered doing it before . . .

It moved an inch!

She moved her shoulder frantically and bobbed her head. She pinned the blindfold fabric with her shoulder and jerked her head quickly to the side. Part of the blindfold lowered, just enough to drop below her right eye.

She blinked against the light from the lamp on the table. It was so much brighter than she remembered.

"Don't worry. She's fine. She has no idea who I am or why she's here." His voice was closer than before.

*Shuffle, shuffle, step.*

"Come peek in at her and you'll see she's okay."

Addy froze. There were two of them, and they were going to look in on her. She could turn her head and duck it and maybe they wouldn't notice the blindfold had slipped.

*Tap. Tap. Tap. Tap.*

That was the sound of a woman's heels. A woman was involved in her abduction. Addy couldn't believe it. Didn't want to. Who?

The footsteps stopped outside the door. The door creaked. Addy ducked her head and held her breath.

A minute passed.

*Shuffle, step. Tap. Tap.*

Addy opened her eyes and used the wall to slide up. She wobbled to a stand and looked out the open door.

A big man with shoulders the width of an LSU blocker stood with his back to her, talking to a woman, blocking her from Addy's line of vision. He stood with most of his weight on one side. Must have an injury, which would explain the dragging when he walked.

As he talked, he moved, affording Addy a clear image of the woman involved in her abduction.

Addy sucked in air and felt her heart free fall. Lissette Bastien!


# BEAU

Beau strode across the lobby of the Darkwater Inn toward the elevators. While Luca hadn't said another word during the rest of their interrogation, Beau hadn't missed the man's expression when he'd been asked how Princess Katerina knew Larder had killed Hassler. Katerina had been the

260

one to tell Luca, no question, and Beau intended to find out how the princess knew that. While Marcel finished processing the paperwork on the Liechtenstein guard, Beau was determined to get answers from the princess, and probably her fiancé too.

"Beauregard!"

Stopping just outside the elevator bay, Beau turned to Dimitri. He'd always detested Dimitri's habit of calling people by their full name. It was annoying.

"Thanks for waiting. She's not up there." Dimitri shook his head. "I haven't been able to get in touch with her in hours. I'm guessing you haven't either."

"What are you talking about?"

Dimitri wrinkled his forehead. "Adelaide, of course. That's why you're here, yes? Because calls are going straight to voice mail?"

Beau's gut tightened into a ball. "When was the last time you talked to her?" He immediately began trying to remember the last time he'd spoken to her. Earlier that day, when they were all in the gemologist's suite?

"I haven't spoken to her since we left Yaromir Orlov's suite."

"That was about, what—" Beau did the mental calculations back past the interrogation of Luca Vogt. "—four or so?"

Dimitri nodded.

"How many times have you tried to call her?"

"Five or six at least. Every time, they go straight to voice mail."

Indicating it was turned off. Beau pulled out his cell. He had to try himself. His call, too, went straight to voice mail.

"I've banged on the door to her apartment, but there's no answer."

Beau stared at him. "Do you have keys to it?"

"No. I mean, security has master keys to every door in this hotel, but . . . I checked the parking deck. Her car isn't here."

Where was she? It wasn't like her to just go off the grid. Someone usually always knew where she was. If not work, then . . .

"Hang on." Beau called Vincent, who answered on the third ring. "This better be important, son. I'm knee deep in autopsies for researching."

Beau struggled to keep his tone even. "Sorry for interrupting. I was just wondering if Addy was there."

"Here? No. Why?"

"She's just not at the hotel, so I thought you might have called her."

"No, I didn't. I talked to her early this morning, but I haven't this evening. Is something wrong?"

"No." The denial burnt Beau's tongue. While he didn't know anything was wrong, every instinct in his detective psyche screamed that there was. "I just wanted to ask her something.

She's probably out jogging or something. I can catch her later."

"Are you sure? I can try to call her for you."

"No, that's okay. If you see her tonight, just tell her to call me, okay?"

"Beau, are you sure nothing's wrong?"

He forced the laugh. "Well, there's a lot wrong with my caseload and piling up of laundry if you'd like to help me with that."

Vincent chuckled. "I'll take my autopsies, thank you very much. I'll let Addy know you were looking for her, if I hear from her."

"Thanks. 'Night." He disconnected the call and shook his head at Dimitri, who had been staring at him. "He hasn't heard from her."

"Jogging?"

Beau nodded. Addy sometimes went running, mainly when she wanted to clear her head because something was weighing on her. This case would definitely do that, not to mention that they had a date coming up. He glanced at Dimitri. She might have a date with him too. Maybe she was just in Jackson Square getting fresh air, a little exercise, and her thoughts in line. Maybe—

His cell phone vibrated. He checked the display before he answered the call. "Hi, Tracey."

"Hey. Do you know where Addy is?"

Was that the question of the night or what? "No. Why?"

"I just got a call from Elise Hubert. Her aunt is the Pampalons' housekeeper."

"I know who she is." Beau narrowed his eyes as he stared at Dimitri. "What did she want?"

"She said that Dimitri was worried because his father had an appointment on his calendar set with her at six, but Claude said he didn't have one."

Why hadn't Dimitri told him that himself, if he was so worried about Addy? "I'll call you back." Beau ended the call and glared at Dimitri. "What's this about Addy having an appointment with your father?"

Dimitri's face reddened. "There's an appointment written on his desk calendar saying he was meeting Adelaide, but Father swears he has no idea how that got on his calendar. He's at home and has been there for some time."

"Why didn't you tell me this from the beginning?" Beau marched toward the hallway of executive offices. "You should have told me that immediately."

"I wasn't trying to keep it from you." Dimitri matched Beau's stride.

"But you didn't tell me. In my line of work, that's called a suspicious action."

Dimitri opened his father's office, flipped on the light, and went to the desk.

"Your father doesn't keep his office locked?" Beau followed him.

"Rarely. He doesn't keep anything in here." Dimitri turned the desk calendar schedule around so Beau could see it. "Except his schedule.

He checks it several times a day because his assistants add appointments as they are scheduled."

Beau read the notation Dimitri pointed to: *Adelaide 6pm*. It was written in nondescript block letters.

"That's it? Nothing else?" Beau set the book back on the desk.

Dimitri shook his head. "That's all there is."

Beau flipped a couple of pages and read the other entries.

"What?" Dimitri moved closer.

"Well, all the other entries are in the same format: time, location, and person or detail. This one has the name first and the time second. There's no location."

"That is odd. Father is particular about consistency. He has instructed his assistants and secretary on the format to use on his schedule entries, I'm very sure."

That feeling in the pit of Beau's stomach spread, filling all the space in his gut. "Does Addy have a calendar like this?"

Dimitri shook his head as he straightened the calendar back to its place on the desk. "She uses an app on her phone exclusively. I know this because I've heard her assistant complain

265

that she has to give Adelaide messages to make changes or updates."

"Can you call her assistant? See if she remembers anything about this supposed meeting?"

"Yes. Come on, let's go get her number." Dimitri led the way to his former office, now Lissette's. "We keep personnel files in both Adelaide's office and here." He pulled open the file cabinet and began flipping through folders.

Beau looked around, his gaze taking it all in and logging everything. The framed picture on the desk of Lissette and an older woman, hugging and all smiles. The piece of pottery on top of the credenza behind the desk beside more photos of Lissette and the woman Beau could only surmise was her mother, a picture of Lissette and Dimitri at last year's Mardi Gras ball, and a little weird figurine. It was made of black stone or something and was the shape of an old man. Two feathers stuck out the top of his head, one a two-tone blue and the other a deep wine. The body had small shells glued on it and little . . . What were those—pins?

"Vicky, this is Dimitri Pampalon."

Beau glanced over his shoulder to see Dimitri leaning against the file cabinet, his cell pressed against his ear. "I apologize for calling this late, but I need to know if you recall any appointment Adelaide might have had this evening."

Beau went back to surveying the desk. Pens stuck in a cup, some with lids, some without. Perfume bottle missing a lid. Desk calendar. Beau turned that around and studied the month at a glance listing.

"Thank you, Vicky. I'll look into that." Beau straightened and faced Dimitri.

"No, there's nothing else. Thank you." Dimitri slipped the phone into his pocket and shut the filing cabinet. "She said she didn't make an appointment but saw a message about an appointment this evening sitting on her desk when she set some papers on Adelaide's desk around four."

Beau tapped the desk calendar. "Look at this."

Dimitri moved behind the desk and studied it. "What? Lissette doesn't have an appointment with Father or Adelaide listed."

"Look at the format. Name, then time. No location or other information. Most all of her appointments are like that."

Dimitri was silent, but Beau didn't miss the slight micro-expression nuances.

"Is there something I should know about Addy and Lissette?" Beau couldn't help but feel his frustration growing along with the knot in his gut.

Dimitri sighed. "Lately, Lissette has been showing signs of jealousy regarding Adelaide. Little things."

"Like what little things?"

"Just little snide remarks here and there. Comparison comments." Dimitri shrugged. "Simple things like that."

Jealousy was a funny emotion: lots of things could trigger it, and it was never the same for different people. One thing Beau did know from experience, though, was that it was never simple. Nor it did ever bode well for the focus of someone's jealousy.

"What was Lissette jealous of Addy over?"

The tips of Dimitri's ears reddened. "Lissette overheard a conversation I had with our father. It seems that his legal obligations of forced heirship to include Lissette in his estate will expire on her birthday later this year. He was informing me of this, and when I argued with him, he also pointed out that it was within his power to fire Adelaide."

"I'm not following. He'd fire Adelaide for what?"

"To hurt me." The red crept up Dimitri's neck and across his face. "Father used Adelaide to keep me in line. If I don't do as he wishes, he'll fire Adelaide."

"Wow." What a class A jerk.

Dimitri nodded, as if he'd heard Beau's thoughts. "This time, Lissette heard the threat and jumped to the conclusion that I would agree to her being ousted to save Adelaide's job." He shook his head. "That was not the case, of course, because Father will oust Lissette simply because he doesn't want her here, period. Lissette didn't want to understand that."

Beau didn't know whether to feel sorry for Dimitri for the way his father treated him or to think less of him for not standing up to his father. It didn't really matter at the moment. Neither emotion would help Addy. "Basically, she felt like you would throw her under the bus to save Addy's job?"

Dimitri hung his head. "Yes."

Beau let out a sigh. "So, let's say she's jealous of Addy and believes you've chosen Addy over her. She's angry. She obviously makes a bogus appointment for Addy with your dad. Why?"

Dimitri shrugged. "Maybe she wanted to talk to her and was afraid Adelaide wouldn't meet with her? She knows Adelaide wouldn't miss an appointment with my father."

"Doesn't sound like Addy. She'll try to work things out with just about anybody." Another reason Addy had his heart. "Have you called Lissette?"

"I tried calling her earlier, but she rejected the call. Let me try again." He made the call, placing it on speaker. It rang three times, then went to her voice mailbox. Dimitri pocketed his phone. "I didn't really expect her to take my call since she's pretty upset with me. We had an argument."

"About Addy?" Beau's uneasy feeling was getting stronger.

Dimitri nodded. "She told Father that Adelaide had been telling everyone he was a liar about having something in the safe when it was stolen. Father wasn't pleased."

"That's irrelevant now since we recovered the money and the crown and didn't find anything else."

Dimitri's eyes widened. "Did you know what you were supposed to be looking for?"

"Just a black pouch, that's all Addy said. Why?"

"Oh, it's very relevant, and you should know what you should be looking for."

# 24

## ADDY

Lissette left the warehouse, her heels tapping the cadence of her departure.

Addy let herself slip down to the floor, leaning back against the wall. Her mind wouldn't accept what her eyes had seen. How could Lissette be involved in this? What had she ever done to Lissette? This was crazy.

She played everything over in her mind. The conversations she'd had with Lissette for the last day . . . week . . . month. Nothing stood out as to why Lissette would do this to her. Sure, she hadn't been as enthusiastic as Dimitri about her coming on and jumping up the ladder to become CEO of the Darkwater Inn, but surely that was understandable.

*Shuffle, shuffle, shuffle, step.*

Addy did her best to slip the blindfold back in place. She wasn't scared anymore, but the more she thought about Lissette's involvement . . .

*Shuffle, step.* The door creaked open.

Addy lifted her head, pretending she hadn't known he was on his way. "Hello?"

"I brought you some more water."

"Thank you."

They went through the routine again. The water was cold and refreshing but did little to cool the anger burning in her chest.

The lid twisted back on the bottle.

*God, if this is the way You're helping me . . .*

"Look, I know you don't want to tell me what's going on, but can you at least just talk to me?" Maybe if she got him talking, he'd give away more than he'd intended. She had to try. Besides, the silence was killing her.

"Talk?"

He came across as a bit simple to Addy. Maybe she could use that to her advantage.

"Yes." Addy knew women who could play the damsel in distress card at the drop of a dime. She never had, but perhaps now was as good a time as any to learn. "I'm scared and in the dark. I don't even know what time it is."

His breathing caught.

Addy held her breath. Dare she continue? Would it do any good?

"It's ten twenty-one."

"Thank you." An open door was an open door was an open door, as her Daddy always said. She'd step through. "So, are you going to the parades tomorrow?"

The single chair's legs scraped against the floor. The wood creaked as the big man sat down. "I usually don't."

"I do. I love the parades." She needed to keep

him talking. Build a rapport. "My boss has his own krewe, and this year he brought in a real princess to ride on his float."

"Get out!"

Despite herself, Addy smiled. "No, he really did. Then again, my boss is Claude Pampalon who owns the Darkwater Inn hotel. Do you know him?"

"You work at the hotel?" The question was loaded.

Addy realized he had no idea who she was. If he didn't know who she was, did he realize who Lissette really was? "Yes. Yes, I do. I'm the general manager there, actually. Have you ever been there?"

"You're the general manager?"

If she'd had any doubts about his simple-mindedness before, she didn't now. Maybe this was her opportunity. "Yes. I've been there for about six years. I love it. Mr. Pampalon is the owner and can be a little demanding as a boss, if I'm being honest." She kept going, hoping he . . . well, she didn't know what, but she kept on talking.

"His son, Dimitri, used to be next in charge, but he never liked being in that position so he's the chef now. Mr. Pampalon's daughter, Lissette, is training to take over for Mr. Pampalon. She's only been there less than a year."

"Wait, what?"

273

Ah. He didn't know. She would so use information to her advantage. But she needed to keep it simple enough that he could follow her. "Yeah, it's confusing, I know. None of us knew Mr. Pampalon had a daughter, but DNA proves Lissette is really his. Apparently her mother died not too long ago, so she got in touch with Dimitri, who helped her confront Mr. Pampalon. Now, Dimitri and I are training her in all aspects of the hotel business so she can take over when Mr. Pampalon retires."

"Lissette is going to take over?"

"That's the plan at least. She's trying really hard to learn everything." Maybe if she talked nice enough about Lissette, he'd tell Lissette and they'd let her go. Wasn't likely, but then again, what were the odds that Lissette would have Addy abducted? And it had to be her plan. No way this simple man was capable of concocting such an idea. "She seems to be catching on rather well, too, so I'm guessing she'll be able to run the hotel in no time. Talk about a real rags-to-riches story. It's like a fairy tale."

If only Addy could figure out what Lissette hoped to accomplish with this. Nothing about it made sense.

"Fairy tale?"

"Well, yeah. I mean, Lissette said she and her mom could barely afford groceries sometimes. Her mom got sick, from what I was told, and so it was really hard on Lissette. No one should have to grow up with that. But now . . . Well, now she's Claude Pampalon's daughter. She's being groomed to take over the hotel. Has a really big and pretty office. Dimitri helped her get into a big apartment in the arts district, so she's got a real nice place to live. She's drawing a pretty healthy paycheck from the hotel."

She hoped she wasn't laying it on too thick, but she needed to do something. "Oh, and last year she went to a Mardi Gras ball and met New Orleans's most eligible bachelor, Malcolm Dessomes. I think they're dating." They'd gone out a couple of times, but Malcolm traveled a lot and was extremely busy. He might be a millionaire, but he was in no way a playboy who didn't work for his money. "This is the stuff of a fairy tale. Not like my life."

He grunted. "What's so wrong with your life?"

Oh, where did she start? Dare she even tell him things about her?

Personal things about her life? Could she? Should she?

Why not? She really didn't have much to lose. Maybe it would make him feel sorry for her and let her go. A long shot, maybe, but she was willing to try anything. "My mother was an alcoholic. Lousy mother. Left me and my father to fend for ourselves. She embarrassed me all the time. I never knew what I'd come home from school to find. She tried to set our house on fire a couple of times. Once when I was inside."

"That's rough."

She nodded and rested her head against the wall. She didn't really like revisiting painful memories, but if it helped build a bond between her and this man . . .

"Yeah. She eventually died from cirrhosis of the liver, but not before she put all of us through the testing procedures. I think my dad has a lot of guilt for not being there all the time, but he had to work to pay the bills and put food on the table. I don't blame him at all."

"Yeah. My dad wasn't around at all when I was a kid, so you're lucky there."

"My dad is really awesome. That's the good part of my life. He's always loved me and supported me. Maybe more than usual because of my mom." Vincent had always been her rock. Never had she doubted her father's love and devotion for her.

"Sounds like your dad made up for the roughness of your mom."

"He did. Then I went to college." Addy let out a long breath, surprising herself as she continued sharing, opening up about a subject that a year ago she couldn't even tell the people she loved the most. Now she was telling a stranger very intimate details of her past, and it was okay.

"I was attacked while in my sophomore year.

I was stupid and went off campus with a guy I didn't know, and it turned out very badly. I tried to do the right thing and report it, but . . . Well, I dropped out of college and came back home, but didn't tell anybody the real reason why." The pain of what had happened so many years ago still could scrape across her heart, but she realized it was the first time she'd actually thought of the ordeal as part of her past. Telling it didn't bring it front and center this time.

"That is rough."

"Yeah. Keeping it to myself didn't help. Oh, I tried. I saw a therapist and eventually went back to college and got my degree, but I was always scared without even knowing it. Without even knowing why. Every little sound in the night put me in a panic."

Could she go for the reach? Why not? "That's why I'm so scared now. I mean, I'm here against my will, tied up, and blindfolded. I don't know you. I don't know what's going to happen to me."

She bit her lip, praying she hadn't pushed too far.

"I'm not going to hurt you like that. Gosh, no. Don't you worry about that." The concern in his voice told her many things.

She could use that. "I thought I could trust the other guy too. I couldn't. So you scare me."

"I promise you that I'm not like that."

"Yet I sit here in an abandoned warehouse, tied

up, and in a blindfold. At least he just attacked me, but then let me go."

His breathing filled the room. She'd carried it too far. He was going to retaliate. Her pulse pounded.

"I can't prove to you I'm not gonna hurt you, but how about I untie your hands? At least you might feel better then. You'd have to promise not to remove your blindfold or try anything, though."

Her heart sped up. "Yes. Okay." Progress!

"Just for a little while, okay? Just so you can drink on your own. I have a candy bar you can eat, too, if you're hungry."

"Yes, thank you. That would be very nice." First the hands, then her feet. And once those were gone? She was going to run.

Run like her life depended on it.

## Dimitri

Beau stared at him as if he'd sprouted another head. "Let me get this straight. You're telling me that your father somehow got his hands on a missing Van Gogh painting that's estimated to be worth fifty million dollars and planned to sell it to Edmond Jansen for Jansen to hold a black market auction to sell it, only to have it stolen from his safe inside a vault?"

Dimitri nodded.

Beau chuckled and shook his head. "Guess the universe told your dad in no uncertain terms: no."

In spite of everything, Dimitri smiled. There were many things he didn't appreciate about Detective Beauregard Savoie, but his sense of humor wasn't on that list. He could understand why he and Adelaide were such good friends.

Friends . . . That's all he hoped they were. A lump formed in the back of his throat. "I guess that would be accurate." And explained why his father had acted the way he did.

Beau pulled out his phone. "Let me call my partner and update him."

Dimitri nodded and pulled out his own phone. No missed calls. He tried Lissette's cell again. Three rings, then to voice mail. He tried her home number again, just on the off chance she'd gone home and her phone was somewhere else. No answer.

What was she up to? That she wasn't answering made him extremely nervous. Surely she didn't expect him not to find out what she'd done.

"We're sending a unit back to Larder's to go through everything, this time specifically searching for the painting. Marcel pulled up a picture of the stolen painting online and will get it to the unit."

Dimitri nodded. "What about Adelaide?"

"If her phone is off, I can't ping her GPS to locate her."

How could this be? Were they just supposed to sit around and wait? Dimitri didn't think he could take it.

"However, her car is equipped with an online service that can give us the location."

Relief flooded Dimitri's chest. "How long will it take you to get a warrant to do that?" Hopefully not long.

Beau smiled. "Getting a warrant could take several hours, but I don't need a warrant." He waved his phone, then made a call. "Vincent? Hey, it's Beau again. Sorry to bother you."

Dimitri ignored the jealousy that Beau was so easily and longterm embedded in Adelaide's life. Right now, all that mattered was finding her.

"I don't want you to worry, but we think Addy might be in a bit of a jam. No, no, we don't know for sure. She's just not where she should be and her phone is turned off."

If only he knew what Lissette was thinking. That she could be involved in Adelaide missing was almost unbelievable. Almost, but the facts didn't lie.

"No, I don't think that's necessary yet. We know she left in her car. Addy had told me years ago that you had her password for her OnStar. Could you get that information for me so I can call them and have them locate her car for me?"

Dimitri opened the desk's drawers. He didn't know what he was looking for, but maybe there was something here that might give him an idea of what Lissette was up to.

"Thanks, Vincent. I'll call you as soon as I know something. Yes. Yes. I will."

Dimitri slammed the top drawer shut. There was nothing besides cardstock and rubber bands in there.

"Yes, this is Detective Beau Savoie with the New Orleans Police Department. I need to get a vehicle's location, please. I have the account number and the password."

Dimitri shut the second drawer. Only hotel paperwork in there. Beau rattled off the account number and password, then waited. Nothing in the drawers. What was Lissette's end game? What had she done? Getting Adelaide out under the premise of meeting Claude . . . why? Did she want to talk to Adelaide? There'd be a much easier way to have a conversation than this. There had to be more.

The possibilities of whatever that *more* was were endless, and many of them sent cold chills down Dimitri's spine. He wasn't one to just sit around. He had to be able to do something. At least Beau was doing something.

Dimitri refused to let his own envy make him do something foolish. Sadly, he had a feeling that Lissette had let her jealousy make some bad choices.

"On Basin Street? Got it. Thank you." Beau

slipped his phone into his pocket. "OnStar was able to ping the location and found her car. I know that part of town. It's no place I want Addy to be."

Dimitri understood all too well. He knew the Basin City Projects area was a low-income neighborhood. Like eighty-five percent lower. Definitely not a place Adelaide should be. "What's the address?"

Beau rattled it off. "I don't know what's there, but Addy shouldn't be."

Dimitri felt the blood rush from his face. "I do. I know that address."

"What?"

Dimitri slowly nodded. "That's real close to one of my father's old properties. He bought some of the old warehouses after Hurricane Katrina, intending to resell them when the property values went up. They never did. Instead they took an even stronger nose dive. He couldn't dump them all."

"So what's there now?"

Dimitri stood, every muscle in his body tensed to capacity. "The warehouses are abandoned. Nothing's been there since Katrina hit in 2005. Probably wasn't much there before then, to be honest."

Beau whipped out his phone as he rushed from the office. "Marcel, I need you to meet me at an abandoned warehouse." He rattled off the address on Basin Street as he left the hallway and crossed the lobby. "Send backup and have emergency services on standby. It's Addy." He turned and locked stares with Dimitri as he continued. "We have reason to believe she's possibly been abducted and is being held at that address."

Dimitri clenched his fists and watched Beau automatically reach back and touch the handgun at his side. "Yep. Meet you there." He put the phone in his pocket and started across the lobby toward the front door.

"Hey, I'm coming with you." Dimitri fell into step alongside the policeman.

"No, you aren't. This is now a police matter."

"You don't know that to be certain. We don't know. She could be sitting there with Lissette just talking." He didn't believe that, of course, but it was possible.

Unlikely.

Beau turned to stare at him. They held eye contact for a moment.

"Please. I need to be there to see that she's okay." Dimitri had never pleaded before, but this was Adelaide. "If you leave me here, I'll just get in my car and follow. I'm technically one of the property owners. I can authorize you to enter."

"Fine. Come on."

Dimitri followed, sliding into the passenger's seat as soon as Beau unlocked it. He fastened his seatbelt as the detective slammed the car into drive and gunned off.

His heart raced as fast as Beau drove.

*Please, Lord, let her be okay. Let us be making more out of this than there is. I pray that You keep her safe. Amen.*

His cell phone vibrated, and he leaned to dig it out of his back pocket.

Beau took a hard left, nearly slamming Dimitri into the window. "Sorry." But he didn't sound too sorry.

The phone vibrated again. He glanced at the display, and his chest constricted. He slid to answer the call, but lightly punched the detective's arm and spoke loudly. "Hi, Lissette. Where are you? I've been trying to call you."

Beau motioned to put the call on speaker, so he did.

Lissette's voice filled the car's cabin. "I see. Look, I had some things to do. I know you're mad, but so am I. That you didn't stand up for me really hurt my feelings. I thought we were on the same page."

"We are. We are." Beau made a motion to keep talking. Dimitri nodded his understanding. "I'm sorry you felt like I wasn't taking your side. That's not the case. I've already put in another call to the lawyer's office, demanding that they figure out something we can do."

"I don't know, Dimitri. I looked up the forced-heirship laws. If I turn twenty-four and Claude's still around, well, then I get nothing."

"I told you before, even if something like that were to happen, I wouldn't let it. I'd give half of whatever I got to you."

"But there's nothing we can draw up that would legally bind you to that."

Dimitri didn't like the sound of her voice, nor the way she was answering. "So what do you suggest we do?"

"Nothing. I think Claude will mess up, do something bad or something. If he does and goes to jail, say, then his estate would fall under the forced-heirship laws and everything would be divided between you, as his named heir, and me as his forced heir."

"Lissette, what are you up to?"

"Don't worry. Just wait, brother. Just you wait." The phone went dead in his hand.

# 25

## ADDY

"Thank you." Addy rubbed her wrists where the rope had been. It hadn't been too tight, but any kind of restraint . . .

"Just remember not to touch your blindfold."

"I won't."

"Here's some water for you."

She held her hands out and gripped the water bottle he put against her palms, then opened it herself and took a drink. Small victories, but she was grateful. Who knew? Maybe God was working for her and she didn't know it yet. That's what she could hope for.

At least she'd made progress with her captor. He didn't seem so bad or scary now. Well, he *was* taking orders from Lissette. "So, tell me about yourself."

"What?"

"I told you about my life. What about yours?"

He was silent, but his breathing sounded a little heavier in the otherwise silent building. It was more than a little eerie, but Addy chose to not think about that.

She focused on getting him to talk. Maybe he'd say something she could use to help herself. How, she didn't know, but it was worth trying. "Hey, you don't have to tell me, but what's it going to hurt? We're just two people in an old warehouse passing time." She took another sip of water. When she bent her head, she could see a sliver over the blindfold from where she'd worked it loose earlier.

He had a scraggly beard, but the scar running along the length of his right cheekbone drew the attention. Even though by the look of it the injury had happened years ago, its anger still vibrated as he spoke.

He stared at the floor, his hands resting on his knees. "My dad ran off when I was little. I don't remember him much at all."

"I'm sorry. I know how that must have hurt." Addy did a quick check of herself and realized she really did feel sorry for the little boy whose father had abandoned him. She couldn't imagine her life without her father.

Even though he didn't realize Addy could see him, he shrugged. "My mom worked a lot to make sure we had food. She wasn't home a lot."

Addy took another sip of water.

"I didn't do so great in school. I never liked it much. I was never any good at it. I couldn't play sports because I didn't have a ride. We didn't have money for the fees anyway. And I had to babysit my little brother."

Sadly, his story was a common one.

"I dropped out of school and went to work, helping my mom with the bills. I have two brothers, one older and one younger. My older brother started hanging out with the wrong people and doing things we all knew were wrong. He didn't use drugs or anything, but he made our lives miserable. One of his friends even hurt me once." His finger went to the scar on his face. "My brother was sorry, but it didn't stop. One day . . . I'm not real sure what the truth is on what really happened, but my brother was shot by the police and died."

"I'm so sorry." It sounded so lame to keep saying that, but she was sorry, and that's all she could think to say.

"There was a lot of political mess about my brother's shooting. Some say my brother wasn't armed, others testified that he was. The cop took a lot of heat, and when the investigation ruled that the cop didn't do anything wrong . . . Well, I'm sure you know all that happens in situations like that here."

Addy nodded. Unfortunately, she did know. The climate between many neighborhoods and the police made her worry so much about Beau. Right now, she wondered if she'd ever see him again. Or Dimitri. Her chest tightened at the thought.

Her captor kept talking. "My mom was desperate to save us, worrying that me or my little brother would follow in our older brother's footsteps. She met with some women in Jackson Square who told Mom they could put some protection spells on us."

"And that worked?" Addy asked, truly interested. She knew about all the voodoo and hoodoo beliefs, of course. Growing up in New Orleans, everyone knew, but she'd always wondered about how people felt who had such things willingly done to them.

He shrugged again. "Guess so, because me and my brother were never shot or anything. He moved to Texas about five years ago. Got married and had a kid. We don't see each other much. His life is a lot different than mine." He paused, and Addy kept her head down so he wouldn't notice she could see a little, but she sure wished she could gauge his expression. "Do you believe in voodoo?"

Wasn't that a loaded question. "Well, I know many people who do. My best friend, for example, is very respectful of it." In spite of the situation, Addy let out a chuckle. "Of course, she kind of has to be. It's her business. She runs one of the St. Louis nighttime cemetery tours."

"Really? I grew up with some people who kept me safe with voodoo after my mom died. I owe them my life."

Well, if he believed in all that, maybe he'd be impressed with Tracey's supposed lineage. "My friend is actually a descendant of Marie Laveau."

No mistaking his quick intake there. Everyone knew who Marie Laveau, renowned Voodoo Queen, was, even people who didn't live in New Orleans.

Why not really impress him? Tracey's pedigree was respected in the circles. "My friend is a direct descendant of Marie's look-alike daughter, the second Marie."

"That's the dark one." No mistaking the awe in his voice.

All native New Orleanians knew the story of Marie Laveau and Louis Christophe Dominick Duminy de Glapion, her left-handed husband. Rumor had it de Glapion was a man of noble French descent in the 1830s and was in a *placage* relationship with Laveau. Together, it was said, they had at least seven children, but only two survived: both daughters named Marie, one the look-alike of Marie Laveau who embraced the darker side of voodoo in Bayou St. John. Although not confirmed anywhere, it was said that the second Marie murdered her own older sister, Marie Philomene Glapion, the only other living descendant of Marie and Louis Christophe. This was Tracey's heritage.

"Yeah. Tracey's got the direct-line thing going, so I am really aware of how serious voodoo is to the people who believe in the practice."

"Your best friend's name is Tracey?"

She nodded. "Yeah, Tracey Glapion. Do you know her?" That would be too sweet, and extremely helpful to her current situation.

"I know of her. She's a powerful woman." That awe in his voice again.

It would be amazing if Trace was one of the people he credited with saving his life. "Is she one of the people who you said saved your life after your mom died?"

"No." He swallowed loudly. "I didn't really know her back then."

"Oh." Well, there went that possibility.

"I've stayed close with two, even after all these years."

"That's good. Tracey and I have been friends since high school. She's the one I can always count on to be there for me." All she could do now was keep him talking and try to pick up on any clues he gave her. Anything that would help her.

"Well, these two weren't my best friends. It was a mother and her daughter. They kinda took me in and shared their lives with me. Made me feel like part of their family. The mother passed away not too long ago."

"I'm sorry." Addy hated that it sounded so lame to just keep saying that, but there really wasn't any other proper response.

"Me and the daughter, well, we talk almost every day. I do owe her a lot, but she doesn't

291

let me forget it. Every time she wants me to do something for her, if I don't want to, she brings up how much she and her mom helped me."

Addy forced her breathing to stay regular and her voice to remain even as her mind raced as she began connecting the dots. "Oh, that's not good. If someone helps you, that's a wonderful thing for them to do. But you shouldn't be indebted to them for their decision to be a good person and help out their fellow man."

"Right! I mean, that's what I think, but she doesn't see it that way. She's always holding it over my head. Telling me that she could always just remove the protection over me and my brother."

Addy felt more nauseated now than when she'd felt something crawling on her. While he was allowing himself to be manipulated, the threat over his little brother . . . Well, it was despicable. "I'm by no means an expert in voodoo, but if you want my help, I can ask Tracey."

He hesitated. "You're just saying that so I'll let you go."

"No, I'm not." As she thought about it, Addy realized that strangely enough, it was true. She *did* want to help him. "Look, I don't know you, but I've kept my word to you just like you've kept yours to me. I haven't so much as touched my blindfold since you untied my hands."

"Why would you want to help me? I hit you

292

on the head and tied you up and am keeping you here."

She softened her voice. "Because we both know none of this was your idea. This wasn't your plan. It's all hers, isn't it? The girl who helped you when you didn't think you had anybody else. The girl whose mom stepped in and filled that role for you when your own mom died. The girl who used voodoo to protect you. The girl who is manipulating you to do what she wants by threatening your brother. It's all her, isn't it?"

"Yes." His voice was softer too. "I'm sorry."

Addy dipped down her head so she could see over the top of the blindfold with her right eye.

He sat with his head hung.

The anger returned to Addy with a vengeance. "Don't be sorry. Do something."

"What?" He lifted his head. "There's nothing I can do. I don't know how voodoo works or how to control the power like she does."

Addy jerked her head upright as well. "Don't let her do this to you. Don't let her use you like this." Her heart raced.

"I can't. It's not just me. She'll hurt my brother, and he's happy. I mean, really happy. Has a good job. A wife. A little boy."

"What can she do to him? You said he lived in Texas, right? Has a job and a family. I bet he doesn't even believe in voodoo anymore. I don't know a lot, but I do know if you don't believe in it, you're ahead of the game."

"He lives over in San Antonio."

"That's a good bit away. He's out of her reach."

"You don't know that. Voodoo knows no distance. She would do something, I know it. Something just to prove to me she could."

Addy snorted. "Even if that's true, we can get Tracey to help. You said yourself that she was powerful." Oh, Trace was going to get a real power rush over this one. "Tracey's ancestor is the voodoo queen herself."

"How do you know she'd be willing to help me? You could just be saying all this to make me let you go."

Oh, she'd had enough of this. Addy jerked off the blindfold and stared at him. "Really? No. Tracey will help you because it's the right thing to do, but also she'd do it for me." She hoped she was right—on her gut instinct of what was going on with him and on who the woman manipulating him was.

His eyes widened, and he staggered to his feet but he didn't bear down on her.

She reached down and started untying the ropes around her ankles. "And I'll help you because while I'm mad you hit me and tied me up, I know that deep down you only did it because you wanted to keep your little brother and his family

294

safe. You wanted to protect the people you care about."

He made no move to stop her, just stood there staring as if his feet had been cemented in place. The scar on his cheek stood out angrily against the paleness of his skin tone. His bushy beard was uneven and very unkept.

"Helping you is the right thing to do, and I'll do it. But right now, you need to help me up so that we can stop that woman from whatever plan she's got cooked up." She held out her hand, hoping he didn't notice her slight tremble.

He took one step toward her and took her hand, then gently helped her stand.

Relief almost made her legs give out from under her. Or maybe it was that they'd been in the same position and confined for too long. Either way, she swayed. He wrapped an arm around her and caught her. The stench of his body odor was overwhelming, but she didn't care.

"Whoa, there. Steady."

She smiled at him. "Thank you. I don't think we've met properly. I'm Adelaide Fountaine, and it's a pleasure to meet you. Do you know where my cell phone is?"

# 26

"Stay here." Beau glared at Dimitri over the roof of the cruiser. Their open doors illuminated the darkness with the car's cabin lights. They were in the parking lot on Basin Street and had parked right beside Addy's car. Beau put his hand on the hood. It was cold.

Dimitri snorted. "I'm not staying out here."

"Look, I let you come. I appreciate your argument, but if Addy's in there being held against her will, then it's a police matter." Beau tried her car door. It was locked.

Whatever reply Dimitri had was lost as Marcel whipped his car beside them, his headlights off.

"Trying to replace me?" He nodded toward Dimitri as he stepped onto the parking lot. His own car's cabin added to the area illumination.

"Uh, no. Mr. Pampalon here is the owner of those two abandoned warehouses and has granted me permission to enter the premises."

"Nice." Marcel nodded. "Okay, what's the story?"

Beau quickly brought his partner up to speed as he walked alongside Addy's car, taking note that there was nothing to indicate any foul play. At least nothing he could detect in the darkness.

"Which one do you want to check out first?" Marcel pulled two police vests from the trunk of his car and passed one to Beau.

"Don't suppose it matters." Beau pulled the Kevlar vest over his head and tightened the Velcro. He pointed at Dimitri. "Stay put. I mean it. If you start following, I'll handcuff you to my steering wheel."

Dimitri lifted his chin and straightened his shoulders. "You wouldn't dare."

Beau glared. "Try me." He nodded at Marcel. "Let's go."

Both of them pulled their guns as they made their way toward the entrance to the warehouses. No lights blazed in the upper-story windows. Beau glanced over his shoulder to make sure Dimitri stood by the cars.

"You okay here, Beau?" Marcel lowered his voice as they crossed the pothole-littered parking lot full of trash, loose gravel, and rocks.

Beau nodded. He hadn't taken the time to consider what he'd do if he found her in the warehouse . . . No, he wouldn't finish that thought. She had to be okay. Had to be.

"Okay." Marcel glanced back over their shoulder. "Can't believe you brought him."

"Didn't really have a choice."

"I'm guessing that was a fun car ride."

Beau glanced over his shoulder to check on

him again. Darkness had swallowed most of the space, yet he could make out Dimitri's outline by the car's dashboard lights. "Yeah. Defined *awkward*."

Marcel chuckled. "I bet." He sobered as they got closer to the entrance, his gaze darting as he took in the details. "Right or left?"

"Doesn't matter."

"Hey." Marcel put a hand on his shoulder to stop him. "No matter what we find inside, it's okay. All right?"

No, if it was bad . . . If Addy was hurt, or worse, he didn't know that it'd ever be okay again. But that Marcel had his back was enough. It was all he could expect at the moment. He nodded, then pointed to the warehouse on the right. Through the dirty window, a flicker moved, like a flame dancing in the night breeze. He nodded.

"Right it is."

Marcel moved to the door on the right. Beau fell in line behind him, watching his back, staring up at the windows to make sure no movement revealed someone might soon be shooting at them, then scanning the row of darkness in front of them. He did a quick self-check, as he always did just before going into an unknown, to make sure he was good to go.

Vest, check. Gun, check. Extra magazine loaded, check. "Let's go," he whispered.

Marcel stole up the stairs silently yet quickly.

His gun was in his hand as he reached for the door and swung it open.

Beau was at his six as they entered the warehouse.

A light blazed down the hall. Footfalls fell on their ears.

He and Marcel both took their stances and lifted their guns. A silhouette moved into the hallway.

"New Orleans Police. Freeze!"

"Wait. Don't shoot!" A slender figure pushed up alongside the larger silhouette.

"Addy?" Beau's heart caught in the back of his throat.

"Beau! It's me. I'm okay. Don't shoot." She moved toward him, but the silhouette moved with her.

"Addy, what's going on?" He nodded at Marcel, who kept his gun trained on the shadowy figure, and holstered his own gun. He took a few steps toward her.

"I'm okay. So is he."

Beau rushed toward her, and in seconds she was in his arms. She'd never felt so good. He held her tight and sent up silent prayers of gratitude.

Addy took a step back and looked up into his face, her hands on either side of his cheeks. "I've never been so happy to see you." She leaned forward and gave him a peck on his lips, then drew him tight to her in a bear hug.

He wanted nothing more than to stay just like this for the rest of his life. Unfortunately, though, Marcel cleared his throat and clapped his shoulder. "Happy you're okay, Addy. Want to tell us what's going on?"

She eased out of his embrace. "Yes. First, this is Willie Neyland." She motioned for the man to join them. "Now, before you two say anything, I need y'all to hear me out, okay?"

Beau held up a finger. "Hang on a second." He reluctantly moved his arm from around her. As much he didn't want to include Dimitri, he knew how worried the man had to be. They'd both been to the breaking point. It wouldn't be fair to keep Dimitri on pins and needles.

Opening the door to the warehouse, Beau let out a whistle. His car door opened and closed, and in moments Dimitri was at the stairs. "Did you find her? Is she okay?"

Beau just held the door open and let him inside.

Dimitri caught sight of her at the same time she recognized him. "Dimitri!"

He ran to her and swept her in his arms. "Oh, *mon chaton*, I was so worried about you."

Beau turned so he didn't have to see Addy in Pampalon's arms. He sent a quick text to Vincent that Addy was okay and they would call him soon.

"I'm okay. I'm fine." Addy hugged Dimitri back, then eased out of his embrace. She smiled and winked at Beau. "So, I guess you need to know what happened here now."

He nodded.

"Let's turn on some lights." Dimitri headed across the large, empty space and pulled a lever. Instantly, light flooded the room. Everyone blinked to get their eyes adjusted.

Dimitri shrugged as he returned to the group. "Father keeps the electricity on so he can write off the monthly bill."

"How do you fit in here, Willie Neyland?" Marcel hadn't let the bigger man out of his sight since he'd followed Addy down the hall.

The man let out a hard breath. "I'm the one who hit her and tied her up."

Both Beau and Marcel reached for their guns.

Addy stepped in front of Willie. "No, wait. He was blackmailed into this."

The man had hit Addy. Blackmail or no, the man was going into handcuffs. Beau pulled his set from the back of his belt.

"No, Beau. He's as much of a victim as I am."

He shook his head. "Doesn't matter, Addy. This is my job." He handcuffed Neyland, then turned back to her. "He hit you. Let me see."

She shrugged off his touch. "It's a bump on the head. No big deal."

"Did you lose consciousness?" He glared at the man. "Did she lose consciousness?"

"No," she said at the exact same time the man nodded. "A little, yeah."

Beau took a slow breath in through his nostrils, then exhaled.

"I'll call the EMTs." Marcel had his phone out.

"I'm fine. I don't need any ambulance or anything." Addy shook her head, but winced as she did. Her head was obviously hurting—she just didn't realize how badly yet.

"It's protocol. We have to call it in. Marcel will let them know it's a nonemergency, though." But Beau would feel much better once they got here and checked her out.

"Oh." She chewed her bottom lip.

"Tell us what happened." Marcel spoke so softly that even Beau had a hard time hearing him.

She looked like she was ready to drop. Beau took her gently by the shoulders and led her out to the door. He swung it open, and led her down the stairs to sit on the bottom one. Dimitri sat beside her, while Marcel ushered the handcuffed Willie Neyland to stand on the concrete.

"Thanks." She smiled at Beau, and he knew she understood that he'd do whatever it took for her to be as comfortable as possible considering the circumstances. She let out a sigh.

"Okay. What happened." Marcel pointed at both Beau and Dimitri. "No interruptions. Let her tell her story."

Beau pulled out his notebook and pen.

"So, I found a message on my desk this afternoon that Claude wanted me to meet him here at six. I put it in my calendar and didn't think about it again until my alert went off that it was time to leave."

"Does Claude often request meetings outside the hotel?" Marcel asked.

She shrugged. "Sometimes. If it has to do with what the meeting is about. Like here. The message I got said he wanted to discuss his possibly opening a bed and breakfast at this property location."

She noted the skeptical gazes of the men surrounding her and held up her hands. "Yeah, I know. As soon as I got here, I realized this would never work. I know. I know. I should have called him right then and told him I was getting in my car and going back to the hotel. But honestly? I was so irritated at him that I marched in here, ready to give him a piece of my mind." She shook her head. "I realize now that wasn't the smartest of things to do."

Marcel grinned. "We've all been there. So, you came in . . ."

She nodded. "But there was no one here. I saw the lamp on in the back, so I headed that way. I went in there, but Claude wasn't there. Next thing I knew, I—" Addy cut off and stared at Willie.

"I hit her on the back of the head. She went

down, and I tied her hands behind her back, tied her feet at the ankles, and put a blindfold over her eyes." He kept his head bent, gaze on the concrete parking lot.

Beau gripped his pen so hard it was a wonder it didn't snap.

"I guess I did lose consciousness for a few minutes because when I tried to open my eyes, I was already blindfolded and tied up."

Beau really wanted to punch Willie Neyland right in the face. No matter that the man was bigger than he was, Beau wanted to smack him for daring to lay a finger on Addy.

"But Willie didn't leave me alone. He gave me water, as soon as I asked."

"How noble." Beau couldn't stop his sarcasm from slipping out.

A police cruiser pulled in, shining headlights on the group. Two officers got out. "Detectives."

Quickly, Marcel gave them enough details for them to pull a crime scene kit from their trunk and head into the building. He turned back to Addy. "Sorry. Please, continue. Willie gave you a drink of water."

"Right." She shivered. "At one point I realized that I was alone in the room, and I worked and got a piece of my blindfold off so I could see."

Willie's head snapped up.

"I'm sorry I didn't tell you that. I could see you when you were talking to her down the hall, through the little part of the blindfold I managed to move."

"So everything you said in there was a lie. To get me to untie you!" Willie took a step forward.

Beau pulled out his gun and focused it on him. "No, Beau, it's okay."

"No, Addy, it isn't okay."

Marcel grabbed Neyland by the handcuffs and jerked him back. The big man didn't put up a fight, just stared at Addy like she'd just run over his puppy.

"I didn't lie to you, Willie. Every single thing I said was true. I just didn't tell you that I'd seen you talking to her."

"Wait a minute. Back up. Talking to who?"

Addy sighed and looked back at Beau. "When I was able to work my blindfold down, I saw Willie talking to a woman. Well, I *heard* him talking to someone. I figured out it was a woman before I saw her because I could hear her footsteps. I knew they were women's heels." She let out a little half laugh. "It's funny how distinct certain sounds are that you never realize until you can't see. Then those sounds are so loud in your head that it's all you can hear."

"So you heard a woman's heels, then heard Willie talking to her," Marcel prompted.

"Yes. So I looked down the hall and saw him talking to someone. I could make out him saying that I didn't know anything. I couldn't see who he was talking to at first because he was blocking my line of sight." She paused. "Then he stepped aside and I saw her. I recognized her, and I have to admit, I almost threw up."

Addy shifted to look at Dimitri. "It was Lissette."

# 27

## DIMITRI

Adelaide looked at him with such sympathy. "I know you don't want to hear that and are probably having a really tough time believing it, but I promise you, Dimitri, it was Lissette."

As if he wouldn't believe her?

Dimitri pulled her into a sideways hug as they sat on the stairs outside the warehouse. "Shh, *mon chaton*, I believe you." For the umpteenth time since he'd laid eyes on her, he sent up another prayer of thanks that she was safe.

An ambulance pulled into the lot beside them, paramedics opening the back doors. Quickly, Marcel filled them in on the situation, and they got Adelaide sitting on the cot while one paramedic checked her head and the other checked her vitals. Dimitri, Beau, Marcel, and the handcuffed Willie Neyland stood in a semicircle outside the back of the ambulance, watching and waiting.

"Can I still talk to them?" Adelaide asked the EMS technician taking her blood pressure.

"Sure," the woman replied.

"Okay." Adelaide looked back at Beau.

"Lissette left. She never spoke to me or any-thing, but I knew it was her. Then Willie came back to check on me."

Dimitri stared at the man. He was so big. Hitting Adelaide on the head. His beefy hands on her as he tied her up. Dimitri wanted to rip his head off.

"We started talking, and he untied my hands. He gave me another bottle of water."

"So generous," Beau said.

His partner shot him a disapproving look, but Dimitri didn't think he and the good detective had ever been as much on the same page as they were right at that moment. Dimitri wanted to applaud, but figured Detective Taton just might handcuff him, too, if he did.

"I told him things about my family, and he told me things about his. We talked about some of the rough things we'd been through. Willie, everything I told you was true. About my mother. What happened to me in college. And my friendships."

He met her stare, not saying anything, but his expression softened. Beau and Dimitri shared a look for just a split second. She'd shared about Kevin Muller? She really had come so far emotionally in the last year.

"He told me about his father not having been around and his mother looking out for her three sons. How his older brother was shot by a cop, which brought a lot of tension to the neighborhood." She looked at Beau, including Marcel in her gaze. "Y'all know how that can be. It's hard on everyone involved."

Both detectives nodded, their faces grave.

"He told me how he dropped out of school to help with finances, and he'd been looking out for his little brother. A woman and her daughter stepped in to help. They told his momma that they could use voodoo to help keep her two remaining sons safe."

Dimitri knew where this was going, and he wanted to scream. At the very least he wanted to pull Adelaide into his arms and hold her. Instead, he remained still and listened to her continue.

"His momma died, but the woman and her daughter took in Willie. His little brother moved to Texas where he got married. But Willie stayed here. The woman died, leaving just Willie and her daughter."

The EMS technician finished taking Adelaide's vitals and sat back, obviously interested in the tale as well.

"This daughter manipulated Willie to do what she wanted. Told him that if he didn't, she would not only remove the protection around him and his brother, but threatened to put curses or the like on his little brother."

Dimitri could relate all too well. Just a year ago, he'd had curses and spells put on his house and him, and, as he figured, probably by the same person.

"That person, that daughter, that woman is Lissette. She threatened to hurt Willie's little brother if he didn't subdue me, tie me up, and keep me here."

While Dimitri understood the man's dilemma, this was Adelaide being abducted and man-handled. He wanted to hit something very, very hard.

"What do you think she hoped to accomplish by keeping you here, Addy?" Marcel asked. "I mean, what was her endgame?"

Adelaide shrugged. "I don't know exactly." She glanced at Dimitri.

At first it didn't make sense. But then he considered Lissette's words to him on the phone. And the coldness of her voice . . .

She'd intended to kill Adelaide. Or have someone else do it. Dimitri couldn't imagine a world without Adelaide.

"She said she was going to have someone take you out of Louisiana as soon as she could make plans," Willie volunteered.

"Who?" Beau asked.

Willie shook his head. "I don't know. She knows I can't drive, so I couldn't. She said she was making plans and it would all be over in a few days. That's all I was supposed to do—keep her for a few days."

Dimitri wanted to rip someone apart at the moment.

The paramedic examining Adelaide's head put a cold compress against her wound and moved from behind her. "You're good, but we need to get you to the hospital and have your head checked out."

"Oh, it's okay. This is all I need." Adelaide pressed the compress against the back of her head and grimaced. "I'm good, thank you. Thank you both." She smiled at both the ladies, but pain was evident in her face.

"We need to rule out a concussion, and the doctors will check you out." The EMS technician stood and jumped from the back of the ambulance. She smiled wide at Marcel. "We'll meet you at Tulane Med."

Dimitri stepped forward. "May I ride with you?"

"Sure." Adelaide looked at the paramedic. "Is that okay, I mean?" The EMS technician looked at Marcel and Beau.

Marcel turned to Dimitri. "Until we conclude taking her statement, we need her not to be alone with anyone else. I'm sorry, but you'll need to just meet her at the hospital."

Not what Dimitri wanted to hear, but he guessed he understood. "Come on, I'll give you a ride to the hospital." Beau slipped his notebook back into his pocket. "We'll use the sirens and everything, so we'll get there about the same time."

"You think so? Should I take that a challenge?" The EMS driver grinned. She glanced at Adelaide's widening eyes and laughed. "I'm just kidding. We'll cut them off." She winked and shut the doors.

"I was just kidding about the lights and sirens. Don't rush. Precious cargo there." Beau gave the paramedic a volume of information without saying a word.

A slow smile crossed her face. "See you there, then, Detective." She moved to the driver's door of the ambulance. "Better take the back route. One of the krewe's parades is going on, and there are streets closed."

"Yep. I had a bully of a time routing around to get here." Marcel turned to his partner. "I'll make sure the unit knows what we need before I meet you at the hospital. I'll be there soon."

"Come on." Beau jerked his head at Dimitri.

They were buckled up and on the road before Beau asked, "Do you have any ideas on what Lissette planned? I'm trying to figure out what she thought she could get out of it, but I'm coming up empty. She made a plan, even though it seems very flawed, so I'm guessing she had an end result in mind. Do you have any thoughts?"

Might as well get his suspicions out, and probably better to do it out of Adelaide's earshot.

"This might be crazy, and I have nothing to back this up, but I think she planned to kill Adelaide and set up my father for it."

"What do you mean?"

Dimitri held up his hands to ward off the detective's argument. "Just hear me out. She left the message for Adelaide about a meeting with my father. Not her, not me . . . my father. She did it in such a way that Adelaide's assistant, Vicky, would see the appointment was with him. The time was specific as well. As was the location, although Vicky couldn't remember that. I'm betting that the actual message itself would show up afterward that had the address. Vicky would be able to recognize it was the message she saw."

Beau nodded as he pulled up to a stop sign and spared a glance at him. "You've got my attention." He slowly made the turn.

"She made sure to also log the appointment on Father's calendar, which I saw and did exactly as Lissette intended: thought my father in fact had a meeting with Adelaide. We would assume that Adelaide met my father at the Basin Street warehouse at six."

Beau nodded as he steered. "Still, you said he was at home when you went to confront him. With other people as witnesses."

"Detective, would you believe the alibi of a man's son and housekeeper if something had happened to Adelaide? When all evidence would show that he met her at the place where her bod—where she would have been found?"

"No."

"Me either." Dimitri stared out the window into the downtown lights still blazing. Carnival season in full blast, justifying New Orleans's earned nickname as the "most unique" in the United States. "But the most compelling to me was what she told me on the phone. That if Father went to jail, then his estate would be divided between me, as his named heir, and her, as his forced heir. You heard her—I asked her what she planned to do and she told me she had taken care of everything. I think that meant she had everything planned out, at least in her mind."

Beau nodded. "She'd laid the groundwork well, that's for sure. Enough to cast suspicion on Claude from the beginning."

"If something had happened to Adelaide, her vehicle found in the parking lot, with the meeting documented . . . and no sign of Adelaide . . ."

"And we would pull GPS records on her car and verify the time. We would also do the same with her phone and see what data our forensic techs could pull off of it."

Dimitri gripped the side of the console as Beau turned down another side street. "I'd bet that Lissette took Adelaide's phone with the intent to put it somewhere connected to my father. His car, a coat pocket, somewhere that would dispute

Father's claims that he never had a meeting with her."

"And that would catch him in another lie, making him look all the more guilty." Beau let out a low whistle. "That's cold of her. To set up y'all's father."

"I think she's gotten desperate. Learning that Father planned to cut her out of his estate as soon as she turned twenty-four put her back against a wall." On one hand he could understand her desperation. But alternately, he'd told her he would take care of it. Of her. Maybe that was just too hard for her to believe, considering the lack of trust she had in men overall.

"There's the ticking clock that she's up against. She turns twenty-four this year, you said, right?"

"Yes. In the fall."

Beau turned down another back alley and pulled to a stop at the main road. He turned to glance at Dimitri, the graveness of his face illuminated by the dashboard lights. "Do you really think Lissette is capable of murder?"

Dimitri paused. Just considering it made his heart ache, but he had to. He took a slow breath. "My initial response is there's no way she could do such a thing, but considering everything . . . She truly believes in the voodoo. She probably planned to get rid of Adelaide by that method." He shook his head. "But when that didn't work? She would have to have a backup, because I

315

don't think she could physically do it herself. She would probably manipulate that Willie fellow or someone else. I think she was desperate enough."

"Tell me, what do you think is her main beef with Addy? Surely it can't be just that she thought you chose Addy's job over hers."

Staring out the front windshield, Dimitri sat in silence for a minute. Then two. This was about to get awkward, but there was no other way around it. "I think Lissette realized the depth of my feelings for Adelaide. I believe she learned of our planned date this weekend, and it was a catalyst for her desperation."

"How so?" Beau didn't ask about the date, so Dimitri could only assume that he either already knew, suspected, or had his own date with Adelaide. None of which made this conversation any less uncomfortable.

"If things progressed with Adelaide as I hoped they would, then Adelaide would stand to be more than just the general manager at the Darkwater Inn."

"Oh." Beau pulled the car into the emergency-room lot at Tulane Medical Center. He parked and twisted to look at Dimitri. "I know this is an odd and difficult situation for us to both be in, both of us feeling the way we do about Addy. I get that." He unfastened his seatbelt and let out a breath. "And I really wish neither of us were in this situation, but here we are."

Dimitri clicked his seatbelt release as well but didn't move.

"I guess what I'm trying to say is that I don't like our situation, but it is what it is. You're a good guy, Pampalon, even if your father isn't. If there's anything we need to tell each other, for the sake of the case, let's just do that. We're both men and capable of handling hearing things we might not like."

Dimitri nodded. "I agree. And I appreciate that you came out to get me as soon as you knew Adelaide was safe. You could have left me in the dark longer."

Beau nodded. "So you think that Lissette considered if things got serious between you and Addy, she would be ousted, so that made her put her plan in action?"

"Sadly, yes." Dimitri hated to think Lissette was so callous, but that's what her actions defined. "She didn't trust that I would make sure she was not excluded." That was what broke his heart. He'd done everything he could to prove to his sister that he was on her side. From accepting her even before the DNA results were in to going with her to confront their father to demanding Father include her in the hotel business, Dimitri had done nothing to indicate he wouldn't stand with her.

Yet she didn't trust that he would.

"I suppose this was her way of killing two birds

with one stone, pardon the pun. Getting rid of a woman she saw as her competition, in a warped and unrealistic way, and punishing the father who abandoned her, making sure he suffered in a way that would be torturous for him personally." Dimitri felt ill.

"Let's finish up with Addy, then go see if your theory is right." Beau opened the car door and got out.

This was one time Dimitri hoped he was wrong. But he was pretty sure he wasn't.

# 28

## ADDY

"Beau, you can't blame Willie. Lissette threatened to hurt his brother and family if he didn't do what she said." Addy sat on the little cot sandwiched into a small space in the emergency room, waiting on the doctor to read her CT results. Having been brought in by ambulance apparently put her as priority.

That or the escort of two police detectives might have had something to do with it.

"I understand what you're saying, Addy, but I don't get to pick and choose who gets charged. That's a decision for the DA."

"But if you don't arrest Willie, they won't charge him." Her heart went out to the young man that Lissette had so shamelessly manipulated.

Beau gave her the look he'd been giving her since they were kids when she wanted something so obviously unattainable. "You know that's not an option. I can't just look the other way."

She knew, and his strong sense of ethics was one of the things she most admired about him. But Willie . . . "I know he broke the law, but he really felt like he didn't have a choice, and I know what that can feel like."

She'd had things done to her that were definitely not her choice, and the resulting feelings later made her feel completely out of control. "He did let me go, and he gave me back my cell phone."

She pulled it out of the pocket she'd slipped it into before Beau and Marcel had shown up at the warehouse. "Well, the glass is cracked, and the battery's dead, but still." Addy knew she was reaching, but Willie didn't deserve to be punished for being gullible. "Lissette is the one who orchestrated everything."

"You know that?" Beau pulled his notebook out of his pocket.

Addy let out a little groan. "I don't know it to be fact, of course, but Willie told me."

She saw the look that passed between Beau and Marcel. "Well, Willie's not lied to me that I know of, but Lissette has proven to be a liar." She glanced over Beau's shoulder. "Is Dimitri just hanging out in the waiting room?" She hated to leave him out there.

Beau nodded. "He's on the phone with the hotel right now. Then he was going to call his dad."

Oh. She'd rather not be around for that call. Although, on second thought, maybe Claude would be relieved since he'd made it clear he didn't want Lissette around at all. Maybe he'd known something the rest of them hadn't.

320

"Can you think of anything else?" Beau tapped his pen against the notebook.

She shook her head, then regretted it. All of a sudden, the bump on the back of her head really hurt. Maybe because people had been poking and prodding it or maybe because she was just now letting herself register the pain. Either way, it sure hurt like the dickens.

"Okay. I'm going to head back to the precinct with what to book Neyland on, double-check that the patrol unit got everything we needed, then I'm calling it a day." Marcel looked from her to Beau several times. "Unless there's something else?"

"No. Thanks, Marcel." Addy gave him a smile. She was starting to come around to liking him.

"I'll talk to you in a bit. Go ahead and tell Dimitri he can come back now." Beau pulled up the chair beside the little cot and dropped beside her. "I was really terrified when we realized you were missing."

She took his hand. "I know. I was scared too." Scared she wouldn't see her father or Beau or Dimitri again. The emotions still filled her chest. "Thank you, Beau. For everything." Tears burned her eyes.

Man, she must be really tired.

He kissed her hand, then ran a thumb over her knuckles. "You aren't supposed to scare me like that."

"I didn't mean to." Her voice cracked as emotions threatened to hold her voice hostage.

"Just don't do it again." Beau's voice sounded as thick as hers felt.

"Ads, are you okay?" Tracey parted the white-and-green curtain and stepped into the small space. She reached over and wrapped her arms around Addy.

Beau stood up and moved aside. Tracey gave him a glare. "You can't tell me Addy's missing, then just hang up on me. We'll work on your manners later." She sat on the edge of the narrow cot and hugged Addy again. "Dimitri said you got hit on the head. Are you okay?"

"Where is Dimitri?" Addy asked. Marcel was supposed to have told him that he could come back here.

Tracey gave a flick of her wrist. "Marcel said only one person could come back because of space restrictions, and I told Dimitri he'd have to wait since he'd already seen you. He didn't argue much, but I told him I wouldn't take long."

Beau inched closer to Addy. "I guess I'll let you two catch up." He leaned over and gave Addy a hug. "I'll be in touch soon."

"Hey, Beau." She grabbed his hand and held it tight. "Will you do what you can for Willie? Please?"

"No matter his reasons, he assaulted you, Addy."

"Please, Beau."

He let out a sigh. "I'll keep my opinions out of the report. That's the best I can do."

"Thank you."

Beau had barely slipped out of the curtained area before Tracey smoothed the blanket over Addy's legs. "So, you and Beau?"

"Have a date on Saturday." Tomorrow or—she glanced up at the clock on the wall—today.

"Really?"

Addy nodded, then regretted it again. "And I have a date with Dimitri on Sunday."

Tracey chuckled. "Um, Ads, when I told you to date both of them, I didn't mean every other day."

"Is that bad?" Funny how that possibility didn't bother her at the moment. Being tied up and not knowing what was going to happen next had made Addy realize she didn't want to waste any more time. She wanted to figure out where her heart was and what she wanted for her future.

"No, it's just . . . sudden. Well, for you. But hey, it's past time."

"I agree. I tell you, girl, they both showed up today to rescue me. Together."

"What?"

"Yeah, surprised me too. It was kind of nice. Awkward, though."

Tracey laughed. "I can imagine. Well, not really."

Addy laughed with her, and it felt good. Really good. "Trace, thank you."

"For what?"

"For being my friend all these years. Listening to my problems for forever and never judging me. Giving me advice, even when I didn't take it. Putting up with me when I'm all whiny and pouty."

Tracey chuckled and hugged her. "Girl, that's what friends are for. You do the same for me."

"Maybe, but I just wanted you to know that I might not say it enough, but I love you and I'm thankful for you."

Tracey hugged her again. "Oh, the same." She sat back on the bed and dabbed at her eyes. "Look at you, making me mess up my makeup. Do you know how long it took me to put this eyeliner on?"

Addy grinned.

"So, Beau came in to the rescue like a knight in shining armor?"

"He did. I have to tell you, I was never so happy to see him as in that moment. He came in with Marcel, guns blazing."

"Swoon!" Tracey fanned herself with her hand. "Girl that's the stuff of romance novels."

"Tell me about it. Once he saw I was okay and he didn't need to shoot Willie, all I wanted to do was let him hold me. His arms felt really good around me."

"I bet, and I want to hear all about that, but who is Willie?"

## BEAU

"Hey, what all did you find in Larder's trunk?" Beau leaned back in his chair at the precinct and stared across the desks at Marcel. He'd gone through the inventory list from Jackson Larder's house and there was nothing listed that could remotely hide the Van Gogh painting. Of course he was past exhausted. Yesterday had been a long day, and Beau and Marcel had dropped Addy's car off at her father's before going into work this clear Saturday morning.

At least Addy had still been asleep. She needed the rest. With any luck, her dad would be able to keep her home today.

"I don't think we've gotten that listing from evidence yet."

"Get it. We need to double-check any list of a painting. He wouldn't have known immediately what he had, but he'd know it was valuable because it was in the safe. I'm betting a couple of internet searches or carefully asked questions to certain people would let him know what it was and how much it was worth."

Marcel nodded and started typing on the computer on his desk. "Thanks for coming in early."

"Hey, I want the collar just as badly as you do. I'll be glad when somebody locates Lissette."

"You and me both, my brother." They had a BOLO out on her, but no one had seen her. Not at her apartment. Not at the hotel. Not even at Claude Pampalon's house. The regular voodoo haunts like Jackson Square and places in the Quarter hadn't turned up a single sighting. Unless someone was covering for her and hiding her. He wouldn't put it past the voodoo people.

As a courtesy to Addy, Beau had contacted Willie's brother and made sure they were okay. Both Addy and Willie had been relieved to hear the news.

"If we can find the painting, we can link it to Claude Pampalon and make an arrest."

"It'd be ironic, don't you think?"

Marcel leaned back in his chair. "What do you mean?"

"Well, Lissette went through an awful lot of trouble to get Claude arrested so she could be sure to get her piece of the Pampalon estate. She didn't need to do a thing since Claude already had things in motion that would have him arrested. She could've just sat back and waited a week or so. Ironic."

"Okay, here we go." Marcel sat up and studied his computer. "It's there. Listed as a painting of flowers." He shot to his feet. "Holy Toledo, we have a Van Gogh in our evidence locker."

"Take it to Nolan, and have him contact someone who can verify it's really the Van Gogh. If it is, we'll need to contact the owner. The museum in Cairo, Egypt, where it was stolen. I don't know who all else."

Marcel nodded and rushed out of the room.

For the umpteenth time Beau checked the time. Barely eight—way too early to call Addy. He hoped she was getting to sleep in. Her father had shown up right after Tracey had arrived, none too happy. The hospital had discharged her last night, and Vincent had demanded she go home with him so he could watch over her. There was no arguing with Vincent Fountaine. Not when it came to his daughter.

Beau could understand. He wanted to stand guard over her, too, but knew that aside from being in his protection, Addy was safest with Vincent. That was the only comfort that had allowed him to sleep last night.

Not that he'd gotten much sleep anyway. Horrible dreams had haunted him. Dreams of Addy in a casket. Addy tied up and gagged. Every time, he'd awoken in a cold sweat, heart racing.

He let out a breath. Until Lissette was located, that case was on hold, but right now, they had a Van Gogh. Most likely a Van Gogh. They could certainly haul Claude Pampalon in for questioning. At least it would keep his mind busy so he didn't dwell on Lissette being out there somewhere.

Marcel walked back in. "Nolan's already got someone on his way to verify the authenticity of the painting. I don't think I've ever seen the guy so excited." He held up his cell phone. "I took a couple of photos, just in case we needed them. So, what do you want to do while we wait? Please tell me that we get to arrest somebody."

"How about we go talk to Claude Pampalon? I can't promise an arrest, but maybe he'll slip up and say something he shouldn't." The man couldn't be so lucky *all* the time.

"What're we waiting for?" Marcel grabbed the keys and led the way.

They were on the road to the Pampalon's house in the Garden District when Marcel spoke next. "So, are you still keeping your date with Addy tonight?"

"I'm planning on it. Unless she doesn't feel up to it." Marcel nodded. "I'm starting to like her more, you know."

Beau grinned. "I think that feeling is mutual. I knew you two would like each other if you just gave each other a chance."

Marcel shrugged as he sped toward Pampalon's address. "Maybe subconsciously I didn't want to like her because she's the only woman you've ever been really interested in since we've been partners. Don't get me wrong, I love my ladies, but you've never been one to play the field."

"Haven't ever thought there was much point. Addy's had my heart for years."

"Just be careful, bro, that she doesn't break it. I don't want to pick up the pieces. Then I won't like her again."

Beau laughed as Marcel parked in the front drive. "Let's do this."

An older woman answered the door. Beau flashed his badge.

"I already told the officers who came by last night and earlier this morning that Mr. Pampalon hasn't seen or heard from Lissette."

"We're not here about that. We need to speak to Mr. Pampalon."

She hesitated, then let them in. "Have a seat in here. I'll get Mr. Claude."

They stood in what could only be described as a formal den or sitting room, Beau didn't rightly know what the upper crust called rooms like this. Rooms with expensive furniture that was usually uncomfortable as all get-out, ugly pictures on the walls only there because of the photographer's or artist's name, and trinkets that did nothing but sit on shelves requiring dusting because they were some collector's edition or something. And books? Those were only like first editions or rare books. A totally useless room that was as environmentally stuffy as its content was stifling.

"Detectives, how may I help you?" Claude

Pampalon looked like he'd gotten a good night's sleep. No bags under his eyes, grey hair still damp from the shower, and already decked out in the rich man's uniform of khaki pants and a designer golf shirt.

"We need to ask you a few questions about the robbery at the hotel."

"Oh, not about Lissette?" He cocked his head to the side, then waved them toward the set of four chairs in the center of the room, sitting atop one of those expensive imported area rugs. "Sit, please."

Beau sat on the edge of one of the chairs. It was as uncomfortable as he'd assumed. "No, we have a BOLO out on Lissette, so it's only a matter of time before she's apprehended and brought in for questioning."

Claude sat in one of the other chairs, glancing up at Marcel.

"Sorry, I need to stand. Stretch my legs and all."

"So," Claude ignored Marcel and looked at Beau. "What can I do for you, then, Detective?"

Beau pulled out his notebook and pen. "Let's discuss having *Poppy Flowers* in your possession, shall we?"

# 29

## DIMITRI

"Thank you for coming, Mr. Dimitri." Tilda opened the door as soon as he drove up and got out of the car. "I didn't know what else to do. They said it has nothing to do with Lissette." She stepped aside so he could enter. "They're in the sitting room."

Dimitri smiled at Tilda, but he couldn't really assure her. He knew why the detectives were here, and he'd been the one to tell on his father. Claude would blow a stack when he found out, especially because Dimitri would have to testify against him, if it came to that. Claude's threats of disowning him would probably come true this time. Only problem with that was he'd still be behind bars. Unless Beau and Marcel couldn't find the Van Gogh.

He took a deep breath outside the sitting-room doors. *Lord, I need Your guidance. Your word says to honor my father and mother, but You are also a God of justice. You are the God of truth. It's one of Your commandments not to steal. Please, Lord, give me wisdom and strength. Amen.*

Dimitri exhaled and opened the door. His father and Beau sat in chairs across from each other. Marcel stood behind his partner, facing Claude.

"What are you doing here?" Claude's face went pale. He knew Dimitri had all the information necessary to put him away. Even if it was Claude's word against Dimitri's.

Dimitri sat down, nodding at Beau and Marcel. "Tilda called. She thought I might be needed here."

"You aren't. You should leave." Claude's expression was hard.

"It's fine if he stays." Beau tapped his pen on his notebook. "I asked you about the Van Gogh painting *Poppy Flowers*, and you said you didn't know what I was talking about." Beau glanced at Dimitri, then back to Claude. "It's been a minute, so maybe you've had a chance to reconsider that answer."

His father glared at him, but Dimitri didn't flinch. His father had been responsible for many horrible things over the years, and finally his deeds had caught up to him. Dimitri wouldn't lie to save his father's hide. Not when his father had made the choice time and again not to be the best person he could.

"Here, let me remind you what it looks like. It's an oil painting on a canvas. Smaller than most of Van Gogh's work, it's only about two feet by two feet at most. It's a painting of yellow and red poppies in a vase, with a dark background."

Beau looked up from his notes to stare at Claude. "Ringing any bells with you yet?"

"I see a lot of paintings by renowned artists. The hotel has many of them in the vault. Perhaps this is one of them?" Claude tried to appear nonchalant, but Dimitri recognized the nervousness in his demeanor.

"Funny you should mention the vault, Mr. Pampalon." Beau flipped pages back in his notebook. "It seems that Addy Fountaine was right in that you had an item in the safe in the vault at the time of the robbery. An item that was a couple of feet long, tubular, in a black pouch." He glanced over his shoulder at his partner. "A size that would match a rolled-up two-foot-by-two foot canvas, wouldn't you say, Detective Taton?"

"I do. Almost a perfect match, I'd say."

"I've already told you that Ms. Fountaine was mistaken. I filed no claim of anything of mine missing from the safe, except for the hotel's cash." Claude looked at Dimitri, his eyes pleading his son not to dispute his statement.

It was beyond that. The police already knew.

"No, she wasn't mistaken, Mr. Pampalon, and you're lying. I know this because we have a copy of the video surveillance from your hotel on Monday morning of you carrying in that exact item to your vault. You leave minutes later without it. Twenty-four-hour video from that time until the robbery shows you never went back and removed the item. It was in there, and you didn't report it because it's the stolen Van Gogh painting." Beau shut his notebook.

"Here's a photo of it to jog your memory." Marcel stuck out his cell phone to Claude's face. "It's in police custody, being authenticated at this exact moment."

Claude's eyes went wide, and he stood. "This discussion is now over, gentlemen. If you'd like to speak to me again, please do so through my attorney."

"That's okay." Beau pulled his handcuffs from the back of his belt. "You can call him from the precinct yourself. You're under arrest for the possession of stolen goods, attempting to sell stolen goods, and that's just to start. Please put your hands behind your back."

"Dimitri, tell them. This was Edmond Jansen's doing. It's his painting. He's having an online black-market auction. It was supposed to be tonight, but the painting was stolen. Tell them it's not mine. I didn't set up the auction."

Beau put the handcuffs on Claude, then paused, looking at Dimitri. "Son . . . tell them they've got it all wrong. It was Edmond and his father, not me."

A million memories washed over Dimitri in a flash. As a child, when he ran to greet his father with arms outstretched, but Claude pushed him away. Giving his father his report card, so proud of the honor roll he'd struggled to make, and Claude asking why he hadn't made all As. His mother begging Claude to give Dimitri attention, and Claude denying his son any affection. Every rude comment to employees. Every harsh word spoken. It all flooded Dimitri into emotional overload.

"Son . . ."

Dimitri stood, pulling up to his full height. "No, I won't lie for you, Father. You acquired that stolen painting and brokered a sale of it to Edmond Jansen. Yes, he planned an auction to sell it to the highest bidder, but he had to buy it from you first."

"You can't prove anything," Claude basically snarled, spittle waggling from the sides of his mouth.

"Maybe not, but I heard you and Edmond Jansen arguing. I heard the entire conversation where you admitted to having the painting before it was stolen from our safe."

"It's my word against yours, and who would believe you over me?" Claude's sneer was all too familiar.

"I would." Beau jerked Claude toward the door by his arm. "And I'm betting the district attorney will as well. And we haven't even talked to Edmond Jansen yet, but that's next on my to-do list, and I'd bet he'll sell you out since he never actually took possession of that stolen painting. Now, let me read you your rights. You might want to pay attention to this first one. You have the right to remain silent . . ."


## ADDY

She opened her eyes. Sunlight splashed across the room. Wait, her window wasn't on that side of the wall.

Where was she?

Addy bolted upright in the bed, blinking several times. The panic subsided as she recognized she was safe in her bedroom at her father's house. She let out a slow breath.

Maybe her ordeal in the warehouse yesterday had affected her more than she'd originally thought. At least the headache she'd nursed all the way home from the hospital last night had subsided.

She stretched, appraising that while her wrists and ankles were a little sore and her head still had a goose egg, she seemed no worse for wear physically.

Addy moved to the window and stared out. The blazing sun felt good against her face. It'd be nice weather for the parade.

Parade!

What time was it? She turned and picked up her cell phone that she'd had charging on her bedside

336

table. Nine fourteen? Oh, mercy . . . she was later than she'd ever been before. She needed to get a move on.

Thirty minutes later, she was showered, dressed, with makeup on and hair fixed, and in her father's kitchen waiting on the fresh pot of coffee she'd made to finish brewing. Vincent walked in from the front door just as she poured her first cup and dropped her bread in the toaster.

"Good morning, Addybear." He kissed her temple as he reached for his own coffee mug. "How'd you sleep?"

"Too soundly, apparently. I think my alarm might be messed up along with the cracked screen." She set her cell on the counter and grabbed the butter and knife.

Her father gave her a quizzical look as he poured creamer into his cup. "You should probably take your cell to be checked. No telling what all is messed up."

That might make sense why the alarm didn't go off. She nodded. "I'll add that to my list today. I'm already so late. Why didn't you wake me up?" The toaster popped. She quickly buttered her toast and stood over the kitchen island to eat. "I've got so much to do today. Claude's krewe's parade is at noon."

"Surely you aren't going in today?"

"Why wouldn't I?" She sipped coffee in between quick bites.

"Seriously, Addy?"

She set down her mug and met her father's stare. "Yes, seriously. I'm fine. The doctors told you last night that I was okay. I'm quite capable of doing my job."

"I talked with Beau this morning. He arrested Claude this morning."

Wait, what? "For what?"

"That item you knew he had in the safe?"

She nodded and chewed, then washed the toast down with coffee. "Apparently it was a stolen Van Gogh. Beau and Marcel recovered it from the security guard's house. Beau said they made the arrest this morning."

"I knew it! I knew he had something in there." She nodded and took another drink of coffee. "Yeah, it was about the size of a rolled-up canvas. A stolen Van Gogh?"

"That's what Beau said."

"Wow." She finished off the toast and stuck the plate in the dishwasher before grabbing her cup. Claude would probably be out on bond soon, but still . . . "Then that's all the more reason for me to be at work."

Vincent let out a heavy sigh. "Lissette Bastien is still out there somewhere."

That's what had him worried? "Daddy, Lissette isn't going to try anything. She played her hand, put her master plan in motion, and I'm okay. Now she's wanted by the police. Trust me, the last place she'd show up would be at the Darkwater Inn."

"Maybe you should take today and rest."

She took the last sip of coffee, stuck the cup in the dishwasher, then crossed the kitchen and pulled him into a hug. "Daddy, I can assure you I'm fine. I love you for worrying, but really, I'm okay."

He hugged her tight for just a second longer than usual. "The doctor also told you to take it easy."

Addy pulled back a little so she could look into his eyes. "I'll take it easy."

He gave her The Dad Look, as she and Beau had dubbed it when they were teenagers.

"I promise. I'll sit behind my desk a lot. I'll let Dimitri feed me lunch."

Her father gave her another quick hug and kissed her crown. "I couldn't stop you if I tried." He held out her keys. "Beau delivered your car this morning."

She smiled and took them. "That was really sweet of him. I thought I was going to have to beg you for a ride."

"He's a thoughtful one, that Beau."

Addy put her hand on her hip. "Daddy, I need to tell you something."

"What now, honey?"

"I have a date tonight." She let that sink in for a minute. "With Beau."

Her dad grinned. "Well, it's about time."

The heat shot up the back of her neck. "What?"

"Addybear, that boy's been heartsick over you for years. It's about time you put him out of his misery and went out with him." He nodded. "I approve, by the way. Not that you were asking for my approval or that you need it, but you have it anyway."

While happy to hear her father approved, Addy knew she had to go ahead and tell her dad the whole thing. "And I have a date tomorrow with Dimitri."

That pulled the smile right off his face. "Addy!" No denying the disappointment in his voice and in his expression. "You can't string two men along."

"I'm not." Yet she felt awful at the insinuation. "Both men know I have feelings for both of them. I've told both of them that I'm going out with them to see how I feel. I'm not stringing either along." She let out a sigh. "Daddy, I'm trying to be as honest as I can, to them but also myself. I care about them both, and at this point I don't know which one more in a romantic way. Dating them is the only way I'm going to figure that out."

"Just so long you stay honest. A man's emotions and intentions are nothing to play around with."

She nodded. "I know, and I promise you I'm not playing with them. I'm truly trying to figure out my own feelings, and as soon as I know which way my heart leads, well, I'll just have to make that choice." Just the thought of that nearly made her break out in hives.

The vibration from her cell phone drew their attention, followed by a sick-sounding beep.

"Well, guess I will need to get my cell looked at." She picked it up. The display was blank. Definitely would need it repaired. "Hello."

"Ms. Fountaine, this is Vicky. I'm sorry to bother you, but neither Mr. Pampalon nor Ms. Bastien is here."

"That's not a problem, Vicky. I'm about to head to the hotel anyway. What's the problem?"

"It's the princess, Ms. Fountaine. She's asking about her crown for the parade today. I don't know what to tell her."

"Tell her I'll be there soon. I'll take care of it."

"Yes, Ms. Fountaine. Thank you."

"I'll see you in a few." Addy ended the call and gave her father a final hug. "I love you, Daddy." She paused, then gave him an extra hug. "Thank you for everything." Emotions thickened her throat, so she rushed out the door and to her car.

Once on the road she tried to analyze herself. So emotional lately. Maybe she should grab a new journal and see what happened. She certainly felt like expressing herself here lately.

Addy didn't know if that was necessarily a good thing or not.

Guess she'd find out soon enough.

# 30

## DIMITRI

"Are you very hungry?" Dimitri had been watching Adelaide for the past hour as she helped Princess Katerina get ready for the parade. She'd been escorted to the float by Sully and a hired driver about ten minutes ago.

He'd finally gotten Adelaide to sit down on a barstool in the hotel's kitchen for a few minutes, and he now pushed a bowl of grapes in front of her. She'd been going nonstop since she arrived at the hotel, and Dimitri worried she was overdoing it and would tire herself out.

"I am, actually." She popped a grape into her mouth. "I wonder where Edmond Jansen is. Katerina's very upset she hasn't been able to locate him."

Dimitri began chopping onions and celery to whip her up an early lunch. "I'm sure he's heard about my father's arrest and is running scared somewhere."

"Maybe, but I'm not so sure. If he was running, I think he'd tell Katerina." She ate another couple of grapes.

"Perhaps you're right. My father was just arrested a few hours ago." As far as he knew,

342

Claude hadn't been released yet. Then again, he hadn't called and checked, nor had he called his father's law firm to inform them. Let Claude do his own work. Dimitri had already had to cancel his contract with Rodney Ardoin and tell him it was likely he was being followed by someone Claude had hired.

The reach of his father's dastardly deeds was long.

Dimitri slipped the chopped onions and celery into a skillet coated with olive oil.

"How are you doing with that?"

"Well, it's not easy, that's for sure." He sautéed with a wooden spoon as he shrugged. "I don't really know how to feel. I mean, he's my father, so I should feel bad, right? But I don't, and that makes me feel guilty."

"Oh, Dimitri. You can't feel guilty over that. Your father has done some horrendous things over the years. Not to mention that this time three men died. Not that their deaths are his fault, but he didn't really care. He worried more about finding the Van Gogh and not getting caught with it. You can't feel guilty for not being upset that he's been arrested."

He could always count on her to make him feel better. It was a natural gift she had, and he appreciated it. There was just something about Adelaide that made him want to be a better man. "I know."

In a big mixing bowl, he whisked together an egg, mayonnaise, dry mustard, garlic powder, onion powder, and ground red pepper and then added the tender celery and onions. "I just wonder how many more stolen items he's brokered over the years." He shook his head. "It's staggering to think about it."

"I'm sure the police and the district attorney have all that being investigated." She finished off the last grape, then grabbed the water bottle he'd set before her.

"Tilda's beside herself. She was literally wringing her hands when they took Father out. I told her that everything would be okay, but she's distraught. I'll have to go by this afternoon and check on her." To the mixing bowl, he added bread crumbs, fresh crab meat, and diced red and green sweet peppers. He stirred everything together,

"Dimitri, you're a good man, which is why I care so deeply about you, but you cannot, and should not, have to go behind your father and correct all the wrongs he's committed. It will wear you out."

His heart swelled as he began forming the mixture into little crab cakes. "I know, but Tilda's like family. Hey, she practically raised me."

"I know, and I appreciate that. I'm just telling you to monitor yourself. It's not your job to clean up Claude's messes. If you try to do it too much, it can take over your life. That's exhausting. I know because I tried to do that behind my mom." She shook her head and ran her fingers along the water bottle. "She was such a drunk that she was mean to so many people. Damaged stuff. Was just awful and never even so much as apologized. It drove me insane."

"I'm sorry, *mon chaton*." He dropped the crab cakes into the skillet with more olive oil. "I never realized." He hadn't known her or her family when she was a child—he was only three years older than Adelaide. Sure, once they were older, and Claude learned who Vincent Fountaine really was, he'd known all about the whole family. He couldn't imagine what the young Adelaide had had to endure with such an alcoholic as a mother.

She took a drink of water and shrugged. "It is what it is, but I'm just giving you a friendly warning: you can't undo what they do, what they say, who they hurt. Even apologizing for them doesn't matter because it never matters how regretful you are, it's they who need to be apologizing and making amends."

Dimitri laughed a humorless laugh. "Like Claude Pampalon will ever apologize for anything. Ever." He flipped the already nicely browned cakes over.

"Then it's not for you to do. I'm serious. I spent years apologizing for my mother's rudeness,

345

in words and deeds, and it was never enough. Once I even used my allowance to buy old Mrs. Fontenot a new tulip plant after my mom ran hers over in one of her drunk-driving excursions. At first, she was really nice, until she realized that my mother wasn't even with me. She threw the potted tulip off her porch and slammed the door in my face. She had to be at least seventy or so, and she hurled that off her porch like it was nothing."

Dimitri had never wanted to slap an elderly woman that he'd never met more than he did right at that moment. "Talk about rude." He waited a minute more for the cakes to finish cooking, then pulled them out and let them sit on a paper towel for a moment.

"Yes, but I later realized it wasn't the actual tulips that were the issue. It was that my mother hadn't even cared. No matter how many apologies I made or tulips I bought, it would never be enough because it wasn't my amends to make. It was a lesson that I can only be responsible for myself and no one else."

"True. But that Mrs. Fontenot was still rude." He put the crab cakes on a plate, added a fork, then set it in front of Adelaide.

She laughed. "She was, but now every time I see a tulip, I smile. Funny that they turned out to be my favorite flower. Or maybe that's not so funny after all." She took a bite. "Oh, merciful heavens, Dimitri, these are wonderful. Crispy, but melt-in-your-mouth fabulousness."

He grinned and leaned on the counter across from her. Her pleasure in eating his creations brought unexplainable happiness to him. He loved cooking for her. They were good together. They balanced each other and complimented the other's personality.

"Ms. Fountaine!" Vicky burst into the kitchen. "Excuse me, but you told me to let you know if anyone saw Mr. Jansen."

"Yes?" Adelaide stuck another bite in her mouth even as she hopped to her feet.

"The doorman reported him when he entered the hotel, and the elevator attendant took him to the princess's suite."

Adelaide pulled out her phone. "I'm calling Beau."

"Thank you, Vicky." Dimitri nodded at Adelaide's assistant. "Please keep us informed if the elevator attendant brings him back down."

"Yes, sir."

Adelaide had connected. "Beau, Edmond Jansen just returned to the hotel. What do you want us to do?"

Dimitri liked how she used the plural pronoun referring to them. Made them sound like a couple, which he definitely liked.

"Okay. We will." She set the phone on the counter. "He said not to do anything. He and

Marcel were already in the car, so they'll be here really quick." She scooped a last bite into her mouth, then lifted the plate.

Dimitri took it from her.

"I'm quite capable of washing my own plate, thank you."

"I know that, but you don't have to." He moved to stand very close to her. Close enough that he could smell the Chanel perfume she wore. The heady one that, whenever he caught a whiff anywhere, immediately made him think of Adelaide. She'd made the scent hers. He ran his thumb down her inner forearm, from elbow to wrist, then took the plate from her and set it on the counter by the sink. "I like doing things for you."

She looked up at him, and his lungs froze. Everything in his world was right here, right in front of him. Did she feel the pull too? The undeniable draw like two magnets.

Gaze never leaving hers, Dimitri bent his head to hers. Slowly.

Softly, he brushed his lips against her, his skin barely touching hers.

His heart raced as if he'd run a marathon.

He wrapped his arms around her, moving to touch her lips again.

*Zzzzzaaaa*—

They both jumped at her cell's warbled vibration, then chuckled. She lifted her cell.

"Hello." Her cheeks flamed bright red. "Beau. You're here?" She smiled and nodded at Dimitri, but headed out of the kitchen.

Detective Beauregard Savoie had the worst timing ever. Or the best, depending upon who was asking.

Dimitri followed her as she crossed the marble floor and met Beau and Marcel in the lobby. He nodded to both men.

"Edmond is in the princess's suite." She led the way to the elevators. "Katerina isn't here. She's on the krewe's float as planned." She held up the master key card. "I'll be able to open the suite even if he doesn't answer."

Beau looked like he was eager to question the man. "We just need to bring him in for questioning. See if he'll turn against Claude and be willing to testify." He looked at Dimitri. "The inspection of the painting was concluded, and it is the missing Van Gogh. Your father is being charged with a myriad of things. We'll probably need you to be willing to testify to what you overheard if Jansen won't own up to anything."

Dimitri nodded. Claude might be his father, but he'd already come to terms about doing what was right. "Any chance his lawyers will get him out today?"

Beau shook his head. "Not likely. The DA is ready to contest his request for bail once we

349

finish charging him. His legal team is none too happy, but he has the means to flee, so the DA thinks the judge might deny bail, or set it really high." He hesitated. "I don't know how anything works legally, but maybe you should ask a lawyer about freezing your father out of access to the hotel accounts and such. Just in case he does get bail and gets out. You might not want him to be able to run."

Oh, Claude Pampalon wouldn't consider it running, he'd tell people he was taking a leave of absence, but he'd make sure it was in a place like Montenegro—the former Yugoslav country in Europe that didn't have an extradition treaty with the United States, unlike its neighbors Serbia and Croatia.

"Thanks. I'll call my attorney and see what I can do."

Beau nodded as the elevator opened. All four of them stepped inside.

The tension, while obvious to all of them, wasn't as suffocating as it had been before yesterday. Dimitri felt he and Beau had . . . well, they hadn't really connected, but they had formed a sort of truce. It made moments like this bearable.

"Willie Neyland will probably be released on his own recognizance today, though."

Adelaide's head snapped up. "Oh?"

"Yeah. The attorney Dimitri sent over has really

pushed to get his hearing before a judge today."

She turned to Dimitri. "You hired him an attorney?"

He nodded.

"Thank you." Her bright smile was truly all the thanks he needed.

The elevator attendant held the door open, and all three men allowed Adelaide to step into the hallway first.

"Addy, why don't you give Dimitri the key and you stay here?" Beau asked.

Dimitri appreciated Beau's desire to keep her from harm's way.

Not that Edmond Jansen was dangerous.

"I'm fine." She moved to lead the way to the penthouse suite.

Dimitri recalled Edmond's voice and threats in his conversation with Claude. He reached out and put a hand on her arm. "Beau's right." He gently took the key card from her and handed it to Beau.

He and Beau shared a look before the two detectives headed to the penthouse suite.

"I'm not some helpless female, you know." Adelaide glared at him but didn't move to follow the police.

"I didn't say you were. I'm here too. It's police business now, not the hotel's. Just like you don't want anyone interfering in hotel business, they don't want anyone interfering in theirs."

Marcel knocked on the suite's door.

She raised one of her perfectly arched brows at Dimitri.

"What?"

"I just never thought I'd see the day that you defended Beau to me."

He shook his head. "It's not defending him as much as just stating facts."

She grinned. "If you say so."

Marcel reached to knock again, but the door swung open. From their position in the hall, Dimitri could see Edmond standing in the doorway.

"Mr. Edmond Jansen, we'd like you to come to the precinct with us to answer some questions," Marcel said.

"About what? I'm late to the Mardi Gras parade my fiancée is in." Edmond might sound like he hadn't a care in the world, but Dimitri recognized the uncertainty in his voice.

"It wasn't really an invitation, Mr. Jansen. We're taking you to the precinct to answer some questions regarding a stolen Van Gogh titled *Poppy Flowers* that Mr. Claude Pampalon secured for you to auction off."

"That painting was being sold to us by Mr. Pampalon. He assured me and my father that he had acquired it legally." No mistaking the alarm in his voice now.

"Yes, you can tell us all about it at the precinct."

Marcel moved from in front of the door and waved him into the hallway.

Edmond caught sight of Adelaide and Dimitri in the hallway. "Your father was going to sell us a stolen painting? I had no idea."

"Don't respond, please." Beau held up his hand to Dimitri. "Y'all should wait for the next elevator."

Dimitri shook his head as the elevator door shut behind them, Edmond still proclaiming his innocence.

But, of course.

# 31

ADDY

"I guess we need to make an announcement to the hotel staff. About Lissette. And Father. Everyone will hear about it soon enough, if they haven't already." Dimitri paced the floor in front of the big window in Addy's office.

"I'm sorry. I know this has to be hard on you. I hope—" A knock sounded on her door.

"Come in." She moved from behind her desk as Mr. Orlov stepped into the office.

"Ms. Fountaine, I apologize for the interruption."

"Is anything wrong, Mr. Orlov?" Adelaide switched effortlessly to hotel general manager.

"Yes, yes, there is. I need to speak to you, and it is of the utmost importance." He included Dimitri in his look. "You as well, Mr. Pampalon."

What now?

"May I get you something? Water?" Addy gestured him to the sitting area in front of the window. She sat on the loveseat in her office facing the old gemologist.

"No, thank you. I am okay." Dimitri sat down beside her.

She smiled at Mr. Orlov. "How may we help you?"

"It is about the diadem."

There weren't words to express how sorry she was that it had been stolen and the big sapphire removed. "Again, Mr. Orlov, I'm truly sorry. Our insurance company has the claim we filed and will remit a claim check soon. Although it can never replace the original sapphire, as you say, that's all we can do."

"That is just it, Ms. Fountaine. I do not believe the sapphire was recently removed."

"What?" That made no sense. Addy glanced at Dimitri, then inched to the edge of the loveseat. "I'm sorry, I don't understand. I thought you said the sapphire was a fake?"

"It is." He nodded.

"Then what are you saying?" Dimitri asked, clearly as confused as she was. At least it wasn't just her due to the knock on her head yesterday.

"I have been reviewing my photos and records from my inspection and appraisal last year as well as photos taken with members of the royal family wearing the diadem since."

"You mean aside from Katerina? I thought she was the only one who wore that one." Dimitri leaned forward as well.

"No. Some other princesses in the princely family wear it on occasion. Weddings and the like."

Addy nodded, although she had no idea where Yaromir was taking the conversation.

"I concluded my inspection of the diadem last April, as that is when I do all inspection on the royal family jewels. Princess Marie wore it at a wedding in June. Look at the photos." He pulled pictures from his jacket pocket and set them on the table in front of them.

"What are we looking at?" Dimitri asked.

Yaromir tapped the picture of just the diadem. It was stunning, no doubt about that. The sapphire and diamonds, elongated and pear shaped, shined in the silver setting. "You see the sapphire here in the center, the one that has been replaced?"

Kinda hard to miss a jewel that large. Addy nodded. "Look at the metal around the sapphire."

Addy did, but saw nothing. Just the shiny silver.

Yaromir touched the other photo. "This is Princess Marie wearing it at the wedding in June. See the sapphire in the center?"

Again, hard to miss the big jewel, but Addy nodded.

"Look carefully at the metal around the sapphire in this picture." Addy lifted it and studied. She squinted, having no idea what on earth she was supposed to be looking for. Maybe the bump on her head had really—Wait a minute. She glanced at Yaromir, then back to the photograph. "Are those little scratches up on the left side, by those little diamonds?"

Yaromir grinned and nodded. "You see."

Dimitri shook his head. "What does that mean?"

Addy had a strong feeling she knew exactly what it meant.

Mr. Orlov sat back in his seat and ran a finger along the side of his nose. "I, of course, noticed the scratches when I inspected the diadem here. They were clearly caused by the sapphire being removed and replaced with the imitation. I assumed that the replacement and scratching had occurred here, after it was taken from the safe." He sat up and tapped the second picture again. "This photograph tells a different story."

"So, what are you saying?" Dimitri asked.

"I am saying that based on these photographs, I believe the original Russian sapphire was stolen before. Sometime after April third but before June fifteenth."

Addy stared at the photographs, then met Mr. Orlov's eye. "Stolen months before, back in Liechtenstein?"

Mr. Orlov's head bobbed. "Yes, that is what I believe."

"Which would mean that Jackson Larder didn't steal the sapphire at all. He stole the tiara itself from the safe, but he didn't remove any of the jewels. Is that what you're saying?" Dimitri asked.

"Yes."

"But . . ." Addy shook her head. "I don't understand how that could have happened."

"I have checked my records, and the diadem was only worn three times in April, May, and June. In early April, Princess Katerina wore it to Easter church service. Princess Katerina again wore the diadem to an event in conjunction with the Treisenberg spring festival. It was not worn again until Princess Marie wore it at the wedding where she is photographed in it there. Where it already had the scratches."

"I'm sorry, but we don't know the policy of how the diadem is kept. You might need to be a little more specific." Dimitri might have spoken without inflection in his voice, but Addy could feel the tenseness of his posture. He was on the edge of his seat with excitement.

So was she. If that sapphire had been stolen back in Liechtenstein, the Darkwater Inn wasn't responsible.

"All of the royal family's jewels are kept in a highly protected manner, much like you have a safe and vault here. The royal family has a safe place as well. The prince and princesses can access these areas and remove the jewels for when they are wearing them, under the permission of the hereditary royal family. These are the only people who have access."

"So, someone couldn't have gotten the tiara, pulled out the real sapphire and replaced it, then put the tiara back without anyone noticing?" Dimitri asked.

Mr. Orlov shook his head. "Absolutely not. There are, as you say, surveillance cameras and other security measures. I have reviewed them as well. No one touched the diadem except when one of the princesses wore them to approved events."

Addy's mind raced. "You're telling us that the sapphire had to have been taken when it was in Princess's Katerina's custody?"

"Yes." Yaromir scooped the pictures up and looked at them. "That is my conclusion after a thorough investigation."

This was . . . Addy didn't even know what this was. "So how can we help you?" Dimitri asked.

"If the sapphire was not stolen here in the United States, your policeman can give me the diadem to take back to Liechtenstein, is this correct? He said he only had to keep it for the investigation, but if it is intact as it was when Princess Katerina arrived here, then we can have it returned."

Well, it did make sense.

"So I need you to tell the police this and have them return the diadem to me to take home."

Put that way, it seemed very logical. Addy nodded. "I can't guarantee anything, of course, because I have no authority over the police, but I can call Detective Savoie and have him come here, and you can show him the pictures and tell him what you've told us and see what he says."

"Thank you, Ms. Adelaide Fountaine. You are a lovely woman."

She smiled and pulled out her phone. "Let me call him right quick." She stood and stepped a few feet away and called the number she'd known by heart for years.

"Hello, Addy. We just finished up with Jansen. The DA is working out a deal with him right now as we speak. Looks like Claude Pampalon's not going to get away this time."

She was happy, of course, but also sorry for Dimitri. Not because Claude was a good father, but because he wasn't.

"I think I need you to come back to the hotel," she told Beau.

"Yeah? Why's that?"

She quickly told him what the gemologist had told them. "He's pretty adamant, Beau. I studied those pictures hard, and I think he's right."

"Good gravy, this is getting complicated, but uncomplicated too."

"Yep. So, will you find a magnifying glass on your way? Just to see the picture better."

"Of course. I'll be there quickly. I want to make sure I get off work on time today. I have a hot date tonight."

Her cheeks heated, and she couldn't stop the smile. "Do you, now?"

"I do. With the most kind and wonderful and beautiful woman in the whole French Quarter."

"Wow, lucky man. Guess you'd better hurry then so you aren't late for your very important date."

"Consider me on my way."

She ended the call, took a moment to wipe the grin off her face, then returned to the little sitting area in her office. "Detective Savoie said he'll be on his way shortly. Can I get you some water or something while we wait?"

Yaromir Orlov shook his head. "No, thank you, Ms. Fountaine, but you can tell me when Princess Katerina will return. It seems I need to ask her a few questions."

## BEAU

"So the sapphire wasn't stolen here." Beau shook his head. But those facts . . . "What that implies is just crazy."

"I just can't believe the princess would allow this to happen." Addy looked at Yaromir Orlov from the loveseat in her office, where Beau and Dimitri flanked her either side. "There has to be some other explanation."

"I cannot think of one. The evidence shows what it shows. Princess Katerina is the only person who had access to the diadem during the timeframe."

Marcel stopped pacing. "What about royal housekeepers or whatever? Wouldn't they have access to the crown?"

Orlov frowned. "No. No housekeepers or other employees have access to the royal jewels. They are kept secured until being worn."

It made sense in theory, but realistically?

Beau just couldn't wrap his head around it. "I can't see Katerina having the foresight to find a stone the same size and shape of the sapphire to make the switch." It didn't fit with her as a person, and in his line of work he'd learned that people, for the most part, didn't really go against their ingrained natural bent.

Sitting in the chair across from them, Orlov's brow puckered even deeper into his aged skin. "I did not imply that Her Highness Princess Katerina physically did this herself. I am stating that it happened when she had the diadem in her possession."

"That she had it done? That's what you're saying?" Dimitri asked. He sat on the other side of Addy on the loveseat facing Orlov.

"Yes. As much as I do not want to believe it, that is what the evidence shows. She had the diadem with the sapphire, then it was replaced before it went back to safe keeping."

Beau tapped his pen against his notebook. "That took planning. I mean, I'm no expert, but I would think matching the size, shape, and general color of the sapphire wouldn't be something that could be done in hours, or even a day."

Orlov shook his head. "*Het*. No. It would take time to find such a stone. The glass in there is close enough to the color to fool most in photographs. I never questioned it, and I am closer to the jewels than just about anyone else."

This was definitely a game changer.

"So, you see, you can return the diadem to me and I will secure it back to Liechtenstein. I can assure you nothing else will happen to it."

This could get dicey. Usually, when an investigation was concluded, items logged in as evidence were returned to the owner. One would normally think, in this case, that would be the princess. However, considering that she herself had told them that the crown didn't belong to her, but to the country . . .

He needed to call the embassy as well as run it by Captain Istre. "We'll try to get the crown returned as soon as possible, Mr. Orlov."

The older man nodded as he stood. "I will be returning home this evening."

Dimitri also stood. "We'll have someone ready to drive you to the airport as soon as you're ready, of course."

Orlov gave a slight bow. "I have already spoken to the representative of His Serene Highness, the ruling hereditary prince of Liechtenstein, and informed them of my findings. I am to return to our country as soon as I can with the diadem." He hesitated. "And with Princess Katerina as well. As you can imagine, the royal family is very . . . anxious to speak with her."

Oh, Beau could well imagine. He could only hope that his captain would defer the whole thing to Liechtenstein since, technically, the tiara wasn't an instrument of a crime here. It was just a recovered piece of stolen property that should now be returned to the rightful owner.

*Zzzzzaaaa—*

Addy snatched her cell from the table. "Sorry, apparently my sounds aren't working." She stood and walked toward her desk with the phone against her ear. "Hello."

"We'll call you as soon as we get permission to release the tiara to you, sir." Beau stood and shook Mr. Orlov's hand. "I'll see if we can get that processed as soon as possible."

"Thank you." The old man left Addy's office, walking much faster than expected of a man his age and with his gait.

"He left too soon." Addy set her phone on the corner of her desk and stared at Beau, Marcel, and Dimitri.

"Why's that?" Beau asked.

"Because the parade is over, and Sully is on his way back to the hotel with Princess Katerina."

# 32

## DIMITRI

"Here's some water." Dimitri handed a cold bottle to the princess, who had just returned to her suite. Adelaide sat beside Katerina on the little sofa, smiling gently. Just her presence would make this hard situation a little easier.

"Thank you."

For a moment, Dimitri felt sorry for the princess. She had to feel alone and isolated without Edmond or Luca or Rubin, and there were four of them facing her: Dimitri, Adelaide, Beau, and Marcel paced the narrow space behind the couch. She had to feel the uneasiness that had settled over the sitting area of the suite. Even Adelaide's presence couldn't replace that.

The smile Katerina offered was weak. "I am very tired, so if there is nothing else, I would like to rest now."

Beau sat on the sofa, opposite the end where Dimitri sat. "I'm sorry, princess, we have a few questions for you."

"Okay." Katerina took the lid off the bottle of water.

"It seems that Rubin Hassler and Jackson Larder planned the theft of your tiara." Beau's ever-present pen tapped against the notebook he held in his lap. "Weeks in advance."

"That is disappointing." She blinked rapidly and took a drink.

"No, it's premeditation," Marcel corrected.

"But if they planned this together, why did your Jackson Larder kill Rubin?"

Dimitri felt a pang. Their own murdered guard, Leon, seemed to be forgotten in the midst of everything else.

"That's the rub." Beau shifted on his seat. "Apparently Mr. Larder decided to double-cross Mr. Hassler and killed him."

She didn't reply, just took another sip of water.

"Here's the thing: we brought your fiancé in for questioning regarding another issue, and he was quick to talk about anything in order to avoid being charged himself." Marcel went back to pacing. "We knew he wasn't involved in the robbery because something he wanted was also stolen at the same time. So we made a call a few minutes ago to ask what he knew about the tiara after it was stolen."

Dimitri nodded. Edmond had been furious that the Van Gogh had been stolen and messed up his auction because he knew his father would be furious. Seemed ironic that Dimitri and Edmond had both had to face issues recently in efforts to live up to the standards their fathers had set forth.

Beau picked up the questioning. "Edmond told

us that Mr. Larder had contacted you, through him, to sell you back the crown. Edmond wanted to assist, but claims you were adamant that you would have Luca go and make the sale and retrieve your crown. But that didn't happen that way, did it?"

This was news to Dimitri. By the look on Adelaide's face, it was news to her too.

But not Katerina. Tears filled her eyes, and she shook her head. "No. You must understand, I did not tell Luca to harm your Jackson Larder. He was just angry because Rubin had been murdered. Rubin was his friend."

"And you knew that, right?" Marcel stopped pacing and faced her. "You sent Luca to Jackson's house because you knew he would take care of your problem."

"I do not understand." She set the bottle on the end table.

"Come on, Princess, we already know what happened." Marcel sat on the arm of the empty chair diagonal to the loveseat.

Dimitri had an idea, based on everything they now knew, but he hadn't heard the private conversation the two detectives had had prior to Katerina's arrival. Beau had told Adelaide that the police captain had talked with the embassy and had directions, but hadn't had opportunity to offer more explanation. Or maybe they weren't able to say more yet.

"What do you know?"

Beau set down his notebook. "We know that you orchestrated Rubin Hassler contacting someone at the hotel to arrange the theft of your tiara. We know that Rubin worked with Jackson Larder, then Jackson double crossed Rubin, killing him. Jackson then came to Edmond to make the offer to you to sell you back your tiara, but you never wanted that to happen, so instead you told Luca that Jackson had killed Rubin, knowing that he would retaliate."

Katerina gave a nervous smile. "Interesting theory, Detective, but there is no proof of any of this."

Marcel shook his head. "Oh, but there is. We have copies of phone records that prove Rubin and Jackson planned together. We have Edmond's statement that Jackson contacted him about buying back the tiara, but that you told Luca to handle it. We have Luca's prints at the murder scene at Jackson's house."

"None of that has anything to do with me." Only she didn't look so confident anymore.

"Perhaps not." Beau leaned forward. "But we have Luca."

Her face paled a little. "Even if what you say is true, Luca would never betray me."

"Really?" Marcel crossed his arms over his chest.

"Who exactly do you think Luca is more loyal

to? You or his country?" Beau leaned back again. "It seems the royal family is sending their own person here to sit in on the questioning of Luca. They are interested in the truth."

Her face paled even more. "Why would I have been involved in my diadem being stolen at all?"

"Because, as Mr. Orlov proved to us today, you had already stolen the sapphire from the setting."

Her face went totally ashen, and Dimitri was afraid she would faint. He handed her the water bottle from the side table. She gave him a most pleading look, but he couldn't do anything.

Like his father, she had acted on her own bad decisions and now had to face the consequences of those choices. He could only listen and watch the destruction unfold.

## ADDY

Princess Katerina looked as if she was going to be sick.

Addy could understand—she felt sick just hearing it all. She wanted so badly to empathize with the princess, but Leon had been an innocent bystander in the scheme and was now dead. Addy needed desperately to understand. She owed getting an answer for Leon, to honor his memory at least. She glanced at Beau, the unspoken request in her eyes.

He understood and gave a little nod.

She turned back to the princess. "I just don't understand the motive here. Why would you take the sapphire from your own tiara?"

Katerina's eyes glistened with tears. "I needed a very large amount of money and could not explain to my family why I needed it. Selling the jewels was the only option I believed I had at the time."

Addy leaned forward, closer to the edge of her seat. "I think we all want to understand but are having a hard time grasping why a princess would need such a large amount of money quickly."

Katerina slowly shook her head. "You do not understand the diplomatic relations of my country."

"You're right, we don't, but we want to understand."

Beau, Dimitri, and Marcel were all silent, which seemed to allow Katerina a moment to organize her thoughts. The princess hauled in a deep breath, then nodded. "To understand, you need to know some of the history of my country. After World War II, what was then Czechoslovakia confiscated property belonging to my family. Not just a little bit, but almost ten times the size of our current holdings. It was mostly farming land and forests in Moravia, but also included some of our family palaces and the accompanying land parcels."

She paused, taking a long drink of water before

continuing. "My family has declared that we were neither German nor Nazi collaborators during the war, but Czechoslovakia continuously refuses to reopen their past. My family knows Czechoslovakia stole not only some of Moravia's finest castles but also one and a half thousand square kilometers of our land."

Addy might not understand minute details of diplomatic relations, but stealing the royal family's property, castles and land alike, had to cause a rift. "I can see how that would be a problem between your family and Czechoslovakia." Still, that didn't explain why the princess would steal her own crown's jewels.

Katerina clasped her hands together in her lap. "Because of this situation, my country did not recognize, in the legal sense, the Czech Republic or Slovakia from the end of the war until near the end of 2009, when Prince Hans-Adam II made political decisions that allowed my country to resume diplomatic relations with the Czech Republic and Slovakia. While most of the ramifications with this dispute affected few personally, there are a few exceptions."

The princess reached for her water bottle, tightening her grip until the plastic popped against the pressure. She released it and took a sip, then set it back on the table. "Some years ago, I met a family who had been separated because of the dispute. Half of the family was living in the Czech Republic and the other half was in my country. They desired to be reunited, but lacked the money to pay for either side to relocate and join the other." She paused to take another sip of water.

"A friend of a friend came to me and told me about the tragedy that had befallen this family. The woman who lived in the Czech Republic had become quite ill. Physicians said she would not live long. It was her dying wish to see the grandchildren and her daughter she had left back in my country."

Addy's heart ached. While her own mother had been a drunk and the least maternal person she'd ever encountered, she knew how close Beau and his mother had been before she'd been killed by a drunk driver. Family dynamics could be the best . . . and the worst.

In spite of everything, Addy found herself softening toward the princess as Katerina continued. "Since my own mother had died when I was young, it broke my heart to think this woman would die without seeing her daughter again, or have the opportunity to meet her grandchildren. I knew I needed to help this family."

The princess took another drink of water and pressed the back of her hand against her mouth. "I inquired through various people the possibility of my royal family giving financial assistance to this young woman and her children to travel to the Czech Republic for their family to be reunited. Despite the resuming of diplomatic relations, there were still hard lines between my country and the Czech Republic. My inquiries of possible assistance were met with disapproval. There would be no happy reunion, at least not on Czech Republic soil. Had the family been able to reunite in my country, the royal family would likely have assisted financially, but the woman was too sick to travel."

Addy had a feeling she knew exactly where this was going, and her mouth went dry.

Apparently, so did the princess's. She took the nearly empty water bottle and drained it. "I was—how do you say it—ill equipped to argue for the right to help and unable to direct funds to provide assistance, but I knew I needed to help this family. I sought advice from friends and trusted advisors, and no one provided me with any workable solution. I needed to figure something to do to help."

"What did you do?" Beau's voice was barely audible.

"I figured out how much money it would take to get the daughter and her three children out of my country. It was not just the travel provisions, it was being able to support them once they arrived in the Czech Republic. I knew they would need to have very substantial funds in order to get settled and live, and to take care of the ailing woman, medical charges and living expenses, for a good period of time. I did not want this young woman to worry about how to provide for her children as she took care of her mother during this end-of-life time. This would be much more money than I have access to or could acquire."

Addy nodded, her chest tightening.

"My family had just had the appraisals concluded on the royal jewels, and I had easy access to the tiara." Katerina shook her head. "I am not proud of what I did. I know it was wrong, but I had no choice. Or I thought I did not." Her big blue eyes pooled with tears.

Addy reached over and squeezed Katerina's hands.

"The person who was willing to give me the money I needed wanted the sapphire. I tried to talk him into one of the other stones, one of the smaller ones that would not be as noticeable, but he was adamant. I did not have the choice to find another person I could trust to keep the agreement, so I took the tiara and let him replace the sapphire with an imitation. He paid me the amount we had agreed upon, and I gave the money to the woman, and she and her children were able to go to the Czech Republic and be reunited with her mother. They are comfortable and happy and have the financial stability to live out the rest of their lives together and in peace, so I do not regret assisting them."

She locked stares with Addy. "But I knew that the annual inspection of the diadem would come in April, and there was no way I could deceive Mr. Orlov. He would know, and I would be exposed and disowned and so many other things."

She had the room's attention. Everyone remained quiet, although Beau's pen scraped against the notebook.

"I thought the easiest solution would be if the diadem was stolen, but there was no way for that to happen in my country. I began to try and think of ways to get it out of Liechtenstein before April. When Edmond mentioned he would be planning a trip here in February for the carnival, I saw this as my opportunity."

Still no one spoke as Katerina continued. "I begged Edmond to let me join him, and he relented. I made plans immediately and, as you figured out, had Rubin hire someone here to steal the diadem from the hotel so the blame would not be on us." She looked at Addy. "I am sorry."

Addy wanted to nod and smile, reassuring Katerina, but she just couldn't. Leon had died. Rubin and Jackson had died, and although they were by no means the innocent in this situation, like Leon, they still didn't deserve to die.

And yet that woman hadn't deserved to be

separated from her mother because of political issues either.

Life was complicated. And messy. And definitely challenging at times.

Katerina sighed. "No one was supposed to get hurt. I did not expect Jackson to turn on Rubin and kill him. The plan was for him to steal the crown, remove the jewels, and sell them all separately. He got greedy and wanted it all."

"Or maybe he didn't want to go through all the hassle of selling everything piecemeal." Marcel stood and started pacing again, as was his way of thinking, Addy had figured out.

"I'm guessing he didn't know you were behind the idea. He didn't know you'd already removed and replaced the big sapphire, did he?" Beau asked.

"Of course not."

"So he would, naturally, assume you would pay to get the crown back. Less work and more money, and no time delay." Marcel sat back on the arm of the chair as if he didn't really know what to do.

The princess's eyes filled with tears, but no one reached out to comfort her, so she continued. "When Edmond told me Jackson had called him, I panicked. I told Edmond that I would have Luca handle it because I did not want him involved." She nodded at Beau. "I did tell Luca that Jackson had killed Rubin. I am not proud of this, but I thought it was the only way to keep you from finding out."

"And it was perfect for you that Luca doesn't speak or understand English." Beau's voice was barely a whisper.

"Yes. When he did not find the diadem, I did not worry. I thought if it was ever recovered later, everyone would assume that Jackson had taken the sapphire. Nothing could link it back to me." She lifted a shoulder. "Well, not that I knew of. I thought everything had been resolved and no one would ever be the wiser for what I did."

"Except Mr. Orlov noticed the scratches in the pictures and figured things out."

"I am not proud of what I have done. I did the only thing I could think of to help someone, then everything else I had to do to keep that secret. I never thought it would turn out like this. Not with so many dead." She let out a slow breath. "What happens now?"

"According to my captain, an official representative from Liechtenstein is already on their way. When they get here, they will take you and Mr. Orlov and the tiara back to your country." Beau closed his notebook and slipped it into his pocket.

"What about Luca?" Katerina asked.

"He committed a murder of an American on American soil. Your country supports our right to hold him accountable. He is officially charged. An embassy legal representative is working with our district attorney to work out a plea arrangement so there won't be a trial."

Addy could empathize with the princess only so far. There were three people dead and one in custody, all because of the choices Katerina had made.

In that moment, Addy realized it was much like Willie's situation. He had made choices because he had felt he had no alternative and needed to help someone else. While no one had died, crimes against others had still been committed.

Addy looked at Beau, understanding completely now why he'd had to arrest Willie. It was never a matter of what he wanted to do but what he was obligated to do.

What was right.

# 33

## BEAU

"We just got a hit on the BOLO on Lissette Bastien." Marcel raced to his and Beau's desks and set down his mug, sloshing coffee over the lip.

"Where?" Beau automatically stood and reached to open the drawer securing his gun.

Marcel mimicked his movements. "Congo Square."

*Going back to her voodoo roots.*

Beau holstered his gun and tossed the car keys to Marcel. "Let's go."

Once in the car and on the way, Marcel filled in more details. "Patrol spotted her car parked in the area. As per our instructions, uniformed officers were removed from the area. Two undercover cops verified her with a visual ID in the square itself."

Congo Square was an open space located in the southern corner of Louis Armstrong Park, just across from Rampart Street, north of the French Quarter, and had a rich history worthy of its belonging to New Orleans. Back in 1724 *Code Noir* was implemented, which gave enslaved Africans Sundays off. Even so, there were no laws giving them the right to congregate in public. Despite being constantly threatened, they often gathered in remote and public places. On Bayou St. John at a clearing called *la place congo*, these groups congregated.

In 1817 the mayor of New Orleans restricted any gathering of the enslaved to that one location of Congo Square—or, informally, Place Congo, the "back of town." Today, local voodoo practitioners still considered Congo Square a spiritual base, many still gathering at the Square for voodoo rituals and rites.

It was only natural that Lissette would run back to the place where she felt she could blend in. Back to her voodoo upbringing.

Marcel stopped the car behind the unmarked police cruiser, outside the arched entrance to Armstrong Park. One of the undercover cops leaned against the trunk, smoking a cigarette.

In character.

Beau and Marcel headed toward him, taking notice of the people around them, watching.

"Hey, you." Beau approached.

The undercover threw down his smoke and straightened. "I wasn't doin' nothin'."

"It's okay." Beau stepped closer. "Where is she?" he whispered.

Holding up his arms, the undercover whispered under his breath,

"Back where all the voodoo stuff is being

380

traded." He lifted his voice. "I don't want no trouble." He took two steps, then jogged off away from the park's entrance.

Beau and Marcel stepped under the weathered white arch with *Armstrong* spelled out in lights. They passed the old and gnarly live oak trees on the right, staying on the path past the center of Congo Square to the back part where cops usually didn't breach.

Lissette had limited her escape routes by showing up here, as most of the park was enclosed with black wrought-iron fencing. Maybe she hadn't thought she'd be seen or identified. As Beau spotted her, he could see why she might think that.

Her long hair had been chopped into a buzz cut, only about two inches long. While most women might not be able to pull off such a look, it made those striking and unforgettable eyes of hers stick out even more. She looked almost other-worldly.

Those eyes locked on him. Beau froze. Lissette froze.

Not Marcel. He moved with the speed of a jaguar until he was beside her. "Hello, Lissette. We've been looking for you."

"So I hear." She didn't run, but straightened and stared at Marcel.

Unfrozen by her turning away from him, Beau pulled out his handcuffs. "Lissette Bastien, you're under arrest for the abduction of Adelaide Fountaine."

Lissette smiled as Marcel rattled off the Miranda rights while Beau handcuffed her. "You think you have a chance with her? You're wrong. She'll be Dimitri's wife. I know this. The spirits have told me." She cackled as Beau walked her through the square.

"I suggest you utilize your right to be silent," Beau ground out.

She only laughed again. "Oh, she's got both you and Dimitri so wound, but I know things. The spirits have told me she will marry Dimitri. Why do you think I took the actions I did? Because she'll be Mrs. Pampalon."

Everything in Beau ached.

"Shut up, Lissette." Marcel jerked her out of the park and toward the back seat of their cruiser. "Nobody wants to hear your ramblings."

She glanced over her shoulder at Beau. "He does. He's in love with her, but she's just playing with him. Or maybe she does love you, but she'll choose Dimitri over you."

Marcel shoved her in the back seat, then slammed the door. "Don't you listen to her, man. Don't let her get inside your head. That's all she's trying to do."

"I know. I won't." But her words stung. Because they were mirrors of Beau's own concerns? The fear that kept him awake at night?

"Why don't you tell us what your big plan was? You had Willie abduct Adelaide, but then what? He wouldn't have killed her for you, you know." Marcel slipped behind the steering wheel and started the engine. "No, but the spirits had told me that all I had to do was get her someplace out of the way and leave her to starve to death. Kind of fitting that I had to fight for every meal I had, and she would be the one who ended up starving."

The voodoo stuff really had her mind messed up.

Beau buckled his seat belt as Lissette started in again. "Doesn't it bother you? That she'll break your heart just so she can get what she really wants? The hotel?"

He wanted to scream that Addy wasn't like that, but he wouldn't give even a little credence to Lissette's rantings.

Marcel, on the other hand, was a great instigator. "You know, Lissette, your spirits really should have tipped you off that you didn't need to do anything. Claude managed to mess things up all by himself."

Beau nodded and glanced into the back seat. "Yeah, if you'd done nothing, the forced-heirship laws would have given you at least a fourth of the Pampalon estate, including the hotel."

"But you just couldn't wait." Marcel turned the corner and let out a chuckle. "Your own greed caused you to get nothing. Zero. Nil. Nada." He glanced at Lissette in the rearview mirror. "Oh, you don't have anything to say now, huh?"

"Marcel Taton, may you—"

He slammed on the brakes, and her shoulder hit the back of the front seat. "Ouch. You jerk. That hurt."

"Gee, I'm sure sorry about that." Marcel eased back on the accelerator. "Maybe you should talk to some different spirits. I don't think the ones you've been talking to like you very much. They sure haven't seemed to help you out much lately."

Beau shook his head. "I can't believe Dimitri and Addy took up for you. They had your back, and you do this?"

Lissette let out a muffled scream.

Beau turned his back to her. "Whatever, Lissette. You're going to jail for what you did to Addy, and to Willie. You're just back to where you started—with no one on your side. Only this time? This time you did it all yourself." He turned back to the front of the car, ignoring the frustrated noises coming from her.

Marcel winked at him as he pulled into the precinct's parking lot.

Beau forced himself to smile back, but his heart wasn't in it. Sure, Lissette was bat-crap crazy, but there was no denying Addy and Dimitri had feelings for each other.

The question was how did her feelings toward Beau compare?

## ADDY

Why was she so nervous?

"You look beautiful without even trying, so stop fussing over your hair." Tracey laid across Addy's bed, watching her stress in the mirror.

"I'm just . . ." She shook her head and sat on the edge of the bed. "I don't know. Nervous. Excited. Crazy."

"Well, that last one I've known for years." Tracey laughed and sat upright. "I know. It's a date—a real date. Naturally you're nervous."

Addy stood back up and checked out her reflection for the umpteenth time. "Yeah. I want to just crawl in bed and bury myself under the covers."

"Girl, come on. Yeah, you're nervous, but this is Beau. *Beau*. You know, the guy you've known like forever. You share supper with him practically every Thursday night at your dad's. You think his cat, Columbo, is the coolest feline ever."

Addy smiled at her best friend in the mirror. "I do love that cat, and he is amazingly cool, even if he is fat."

"See. This is fine. Besides, he's probably as nervous as you are."

"Do you think?"

Tracey smiled. "I do."

A loud knock rapped on the door.

"He's here." Addy's eyes widened as her heart kicked up a gear. "I'll get it. You—" Tracey stood and pointed at her. "—don't throw up." She headed into the living room.

The door opened, and Addy heard Tracey talking, but she didn't hear Beau's voice. Had something come up? She left the bedroom to find Tracey shutting the door. She held a huge vase of flowers. Tulips.

"These are for you." Tracey set down the massive arrangement on the kitchen counter.

Addy grabbed the card and opened the envelope. Her heart fluttered as she read the message: *Be Responsible—D*

She couldn't stop herself from smiling.

"Are they from Beau?" Tracey studied her expression. "Um. No. They're from Dimitri." She handed her the card. "What does this mean?" Tracey asked.

*Bam! Bam! Bam!*

"He's here." Addy grabbed the flower arrangement and shoved it into Tracey's hands. "Take these into my room, please." She turned and waited until Tracey had disappeared before opening the door.

Beau stood there in a pair of worn jeans and a button-down shirt that either looked new or had

386

just come from the cleaners. His hair was still damp from the shower, and his cologne . . . Oh, mercy, but he smelled good.

"Hi."

Tracey was right—he was as nervous as she was. That knowledge let her breathe again. "Hi."

"Ready?"

She nodded as Tracey walked out of the bedroom. "Hey, Beau."

"Hi, Tracey."

"Where are y'all going tonight?"

Addy shot her best friend a look. "You don't have to answer that, Beau. It's none of her business. Lock up when you leave, Trace." They turned toward the door.

"I will," Tracey said. "And Addy . . ."

Addy looked back over her shoulder at her best friend. "What?"

"Be responsible."

# 34

BEAU

Addy had gotten more beautiful in the span of a few hours, if that was even possible.

Beau opened the passenger's door of the Charger for her. He didn't get to take his personal car out as much, but he loved the Dodge. Had spent many a weekend working to fix up the old muscle car.

"So where are we off to?"

Beau started the car and eased out of the hotel's lot. "I thought it was a nice evening for a picnic."

Her whole face lit up. "That sounds perfect."

They arrived at the Fly, and he grabbed the packed lunch and blanket from the trunk and gently led Addy to a spot under a tree looking out over the Mississippi River. The sun had just set over the river, and a few of the big boats, their lights making them seem more romantic than they really were, maneuvered through the currents.

"Oh, Beau, this is lovely." She settled on the blanket he'd spread out, smiling at him as if he was the only man on the planet. He lit the two fat candles in their mosaic holders, setting them in the middle of the blanket, and the space was lit enough for them to see, but still gave the ambience of intimacy. Just like he'd planned.

She made him feel like a million bucks—that hadn't changed—but his mind kept going back to what Lissette had said. Yes, he knew it was her playing mind games with him, but the sentiments still made him wonder. He shook off the doubts that threatened to overtake him. This was his and Addy's time, and no one would intrude. Beau refused to allow it.

"I'm actually really hungry." Addy grinned.

"Is that a hint? Well, your wish is my command." He opened the big basket he'd stuck the take-out in.

"Is that Broussard's? Oh, that's one of my favorite places." Addy's face looked like a kid's on birthday morning.

Beau chuckled. "Yes, I know." He handed her a container. "Your truffle chicken breast with wild mushrooms, artichokes, and herb-roasted potatoes."

"I'm in heaven." She grabbed the plastic fork and took a bite. "I think I could eat Broussard's every day and never get tired of it." She nodded at his container. "What are you having?"

"I'm having the chicken and andouille gumbo. Want a bite?" He held the bowl out so she could see.

"I do. It all smells so divine."

He dipped his spoon, filled it, then gently eased

it into her mouth. It dripped just a little as he pulled the plastic spoon from her lips. Without thinking, he wiped her bottom lip with his thumb. She swallowed, then he did. He couldn't take his eyes off her mouth. He felt flushed all over.

Beau set his bowl down, then eased the container from Addy's hands without breaking eye contact. He slipped his hands on either side of her face and dug his fingers into her hair.

She parted her lips just a breath of a space. He couldn't wait any longer.

Beau dipped his head and put his lips on hers. Slowly. Softly.

Addy leaned her head back and wrapped her hands around his neck. He deepened the kiss, gripping two handfuls of her hair. She tasted like salty sunshine and truffle oil.

Untold emotions flooded his senses as she kissed him back. He let go of her hair and wrapped his arms around her, drawing her closer to him. Close enough that he could feel her heart beating. Its erratic pounding matched his.

He gently ended the kiss and pulled back a fraction, resting his forehead against hers, staring into her eyes.

"You are quite the woman, Adelaide Fountaine." His words were a little breathy, but he really couldn't help that.

She smiled, tilting his world even more. "And you're quite the man, Beauregard Savoie."

He kissed the tip of her nose, then released her, putting a foot or so between them. "We'd better eat before it gets cold."

She nodded and picked up her fork, but he recognized the flush across her face. She'd been just as affected by that kiss as he had, and it had rocked him to his very core.

Somehow, knowing that he had as much of an effect on her as she did on him, well, it made him more confident and relaxed. He handed her a water bottle and set his on the blanket before handing her a biscuit.

Addy took another bite of her chicken and made little noises of appreciation as she chewed. "This is delicious."

"Well, save room for dessert."

"What do you have?"

He grinned. "Also from Broussard's, we have Creole Bread Pudding with Bananas Foster sauce and Chantilly cream."

"Oh, you are spoiling me." She stabbed a potato and popped it into her mouth.

"You deserve to be spoiled, Addy."

She laid her palm against the side of his face. "So do you, Beau. So do you."

He grabbed her hand and kissed the palm, then let it go with a chuckle. "I have another surprise for you."

"Aside from the bread pudding?" She opened her water bottle and took a drink.

He reached into the basket and pulled out the gift bag the lady at the store had done up for him.

"A present?" Her eyes lit up. "You know I love presents."

He chuckled. "I know."

Pushing aside the tissue paper, she pulled out the black traveler's notebook journal and pen set she found. She ran her hands over the smooth leather. "It's beautiful. I love it." She locked gazes with him. "Thank you, Beau."

"I thought maybe you could, I don't know, write some of your poems in there."

Her eyes shimmered with moisture as she pulled the journal to her chest, hugging it. "Thank you. It's perfect. You're perfect."

She leaned forward, pulling him in for a kiss.

If the good Lord was to call him home at that exact moment, Beau would have died the happiest man ever.

## ADDY

Oh, Beauregard Savoie was full of surprises tonight. A picnic at dark by the Mississippi with some of her favorite foods, including the dessert, and a journal for poetry. None of that was as much of a surprise as how amazing she felt being with Beau in a romantic way.

And the man could kiss like nobody's business! Mercy, but he could make her forget everything.

She finished off the bread pudding and let out a sigh. "That was wonderful. Thank you for a perfect supper." The night had been perfect.

"You are most welcome."

A breeze gusted off the river and she gave a little shiver.

"Come here." He pulled her against him, her back against his chest, and slung his jacket over her.

She tucked it over her shoulders and rested against him. She could feel his heart pounding in his chest. It soothed her with its steady thumping, and she laid her head back against him and closed her eyes. She couldn't remember the last time she'd felt this safe. This secure. This relaxed.

"Hey, I read something the other day I wanted to share with you. When I read it, I immediately thought of you." His chest vibrated as he spoke.

"Should I be concerned?"

He laughed, his breath almost caressing her ear. "You know better. Hang on, let me pull it up, and I'll read it to you." He reached around her to scroll through his cell phone. She didn't care—she was comfortable and didn't want to move. Maybe ever.

"Okay. Ready?"

"Go for it." She snuggled against him, curious what would make him think of her. She felt him inhale before he read.

Music travels in her veins the ability to
create vibrates her hands.
Her will is the only thing stronger than
Her spirit.
She sees life through a spectrum of colors
light and shadows.
Justice follows her.
She is fair honest compassionate.
But also determined.
She is bound in love fiercely loyal
Her heart branded For great things.
She lives her life proudly,
knowing tomorrow isn't promised.
She exudes the sweet aroma of Faith
of Hope
of Willingness.
Her smile brightens the world.
Her laugh rings out
like a beacon to those who are
sad downtrodden desperate.
Her spirit rises in her delivering
energy to fulfill the works of her hands
mind
and her Heart.
She is a force to behold.
She is beautiful and funny.
Sassy and sweet.
Open and introverted. She notices details
Forgets failures Celebrates victory.
She is the best advocate

one could ever hope to have.
She sings to her own songs Doesn't take
   herself too seriously And likes being
   alone.
She is fierce Faithful and Free.
She is herself and she is happy.


Tears threatened to choke her. She bit her bottom lip and sat up. He got her. Knew her. Understood her. And that he saw her like that . . .

"Hey, I didn't mean to upset you," he whispered in her ear.

"You didn't." She smiled. "That's beautiful."

"No, Addy, you're beautiful." He bent his head and covered her mouth with his.

# 35

## DIMITRI

Adelaide smiled as she held Dimitri's hand, lighting up an already sunshine-bright afternoon. "I love the zoo. This was a great idea."

He'd debated where to take her on their date, and while she enjoyed food and he enjoyed cooking for her, he already did that at the hotel as much as she would let him. He wanted their date to be something totally different. Something fun and carefree. A memory together they could look back on and cherish.

They certainly deserved some fun and carefree time after the week they'd had, and the Audubon Zoo seemed to fit that bill perfectly.

Situated in uptown New Orleans, the zoo offered an unusual mix of animals from around the world as well as beautiful, lush gardens. The Audubon boasted unique natural-habitat exhibits like Louisiana Swamp and Jaguar. While many people came specifically to see the highly endangered whooping cranes, Amur leopards, and orangutans, Dimitri had, since he was a child, always most loved the mysterious white alligators.

Standing before the white alligator display he was, as always, awed by their magnificence.

"So beautiful," Adelaide breathed beside him, as obviously amazed as he was. Just something else they had in common: an appreciation of beautiful, if wild, things. "I don't think I've ever seen him on any of my trips to the zoo before. Then again, it's been a long time. Is he albino?"

Dimitri shook his head. "He's got leucism, which is a rare condition that has translucent white skin and deep-blue eyes with a hint of pigmentation splashed here and there. Albinism results in pink eyes and no pigmentation at all. While there's only a few documented occurrences of leucistic alligators, they aren't a separate species, but they're considered extremely rare."

She nodded, staring at the large, beautiful reptile. "His condition is beautiful."

Dimitri rubbed the small of her back. "He is. Not nearly as beautiful as you are, though."

Her face flushed, and his gut tightened. He slowly turned to face her, lifting his hands to cup both sides of her face—her beautiful, perfect face. He leaned in, gently pressing his forehead against hers. Their breath mingled, and he swallowed against the strong urge to kiss her senseless.

Instead, he gently lowered his mouth to hers. Soft. Supple. Just a hint of the depth of his feelings for her.

He pulled back, catching his breath. Her chest rose and fell quickly, obviously just as affected by their connection as he was.

It took everything in him to release her and smile, when all he really wanted to do was get lost in her. "How about we grab lunch over at the Cypress Knee Café? We can either eat inside or on one of the picnic tables on the deck overlooking the swamp."

Adelaide nodded, her face still flushed. "It's so nice out today, let's eat outside. Pretty soon it'll be too hot."

Dimitri led the way through the Louisiana swamp exhibit to the little café. "What do you want?"

"Well, you're the chef. I trust you." She smiled at him, and all in the world went right for him.

"Okay, then crawfish pies it is. Why don't you grab us a picnic table, and I'll get the food?"

She nodded and headed out to the deck.

Dimitri watched her walk away, his heart suddenly demanding attention. The way she moved, the way she spoke—everything about her was perfect. This day together had cemented the way he felt about her. He needed her to know that. Needed her to feel how important she was to him.

He carried their crawfish pies and bottled waters to the table, said a quick grace, then smiled at her. He couldn't stop grinning. Dimitri knew he probably looked like an idiot, but he couldn't help it. Being around Adelaide just made him happy.

She took a sip of water and caught him staring at her. "What? Do I have something on my face?"

"Just natural beauty." Had he really just gone so cheesy and corny? She did that to him.

She blushed and looked down.

Her shyness made his stomach flip. He reached out and tucked the strand of hair that had fallen against her face when she lowered her head back behind her ear. She looked up, getting caught in his gaze.

The intensity in her face . . . the honesty in her eyes . . . the openness of her heart . . . Dimitri couldn't stand it. He leaned forward and again captured her mouth with his. Her lips were soft and supple against his. His arms wound themselves around her. Her hands were hot against his chest. He could kiss her forever, getting lost in Adelaide.

But he knew she needed to breathe, and he needed to control the pounding of his heart. He slowly withdrew, but kept her close. "Oh, Adelaide." He laid his head on top of hers, loving having her in his arms.

He could stay like this forever.

## ADDY

Oh, her heart.

This man . . . Dimitri . . . He made her feel like a cherished princess. She loved the way he

399

pampered her. But she also loved the way he kissed her breathless.

She held his hand as they strolled toward the jaguar exhibit. She adored the big cats. Always had.

In front of them, a young mother held tight to the hands of what appeared to be twin girls who were maybe five or six. Their incessant chatter amused Addy, along with the caliber of the questions they asked their mother. The mother's answers depicted an enormous amount of patience. Addy couldn't help but wonder what kind of mother she herself would be.

She supposed that should be a natural question to ask herself. After all, she hadn't had a good role model. Okay, truth be told, her mother had been no role model at all.

What if their family had a defective maternal trait?

"Have I told you lately how amazing you are?" Dimitri tugged her gently toward him, releasing her hand and putting his arm around her waist.

Addy chuckled. "Well, not in so many words, but I'm not complaining."

He leaned over and kissed her. It was a quick, gentle peck, but just that touch of his lips on hers made her legs feel liquidy.

"You are the most amazing woman I've ever known." His eyes were so intense that she felt like she could lose herself in them and not once regret missing anything else.

Just then, one of the little girls in front of them broke free of her mother's grip and took off running. For a little girl, she was fast. Really fast.

"Alexa, come back here. Right now." Her mother picked up the other little girl and started trying to run, but the child was clearly too heavy to be carried.

The little girl ran into the big cat exhibit and disappeared.

The mother ran as fast as her legs would take her. "Alexa!"

Dimitri released Addy and ran toward where the little girl had disappeared. Addy moved to the woman. "Can I help you?"

The woman gave her a stern look, shook her head, and kept running. Addy kept pace beside her.

"Alexa!" Tears came to the woman's eyes as the little girl she was holding started to slip from her grasp.

"Mommy, where's Alexa? I want Alexa." The child's cries felt deafening.

"We're going to get her, honey." The woman's voice was high pitched with fear.

And then Dimitri came out of the exhibit, Alexa's hand in his.

He smiled as he joined Addy and the woman.

"Mommy!" Alexa took her mother's hand again.

"Don't you ever run off like that again, Alexa. You know the rules." The woman let out a long breath. "Thank you."

"Of course. Not a problem." Dimitri smiled. He bent to the little girl. "Remember what I told you."

"Yes, sir." The little girl's head bobbed. "I hafta stay with my mommy so I don't scare her."

"Right." He straightened, patted the mother's shoulder, then put his arm around Addy's waist and gently led her away.

"You were wonderful," Addy whispered. The way he'd just acted totally on instinct. He was going to be a great father someday. Maybe even capable of overcompensating if his wife wasn't so maternal.

He stopped and turned Addy to him. "Adelaide, you are wonderful, and I'm blessed to have you in my life." He kissed her. Thoroughly. Completely.

The afternoon Louisiana sun beat down on them, but it was Dimitri that made Addy feel like she was melting.

# 36

## BEAU

The air outside the courthouse seemed even cooler, fitting for the day. Beau and Marcel had just endured what should have been a short hearing for Lissette Bastien to accept the plea agreement. Unfortunately, it'd been held in open court, so many of her voodoo friends had shown up in support. The ruckus had caused the proceedings to be halted for the bailiff to clear the courtroom.

Dimitri stood outside the entrance, turning to Beau and Marcel as they stepped outside. "So, did everything go as expected?"

Beau nodded.

"Once the crackpots were gone, yeah." Marcel shook his head. "My aunt was big into all that hocus-pocus stuff, and it drove a huge wedge between family members. I never understood why until now. They're crazy."

"It's what they believe." Beau shrugged. "Anyway, the judge accepted the plea."

"So, Lissette will be in jail for fifteen years, for sure? No early release or anything?"

"When it's a plea deal and both sides agree, they usually stick to it.

The judge accepted the plea and the recommendation, and her sentence is on the record for fifteen years."

Dimitri nodded but remained silent.

"I'm sorry," Beau offered.

"She conspired to kidnap Adelaide and planned to let her die."

Beau nodded. "But she's still your sister, and I know you cared for her."

"Thanks." Dimitri shoved his hands into his pockets and moved toward the road.

Beau fell into step beside him. "Have you seen your dad?"

Dimitri shook his head. "Not since his hearing. He's furious he was denied bond."

Marcel had also walked with them. "He has the means to flee. The judge made a good call to deny bond."

"Oh, I'm not arguing it. I'm just saying he was beyond angry."

"You know the DA offered him a plea deal, too, right?" Beau asked. "From what I understand, eight years."

Dimitri let out a half snort, half chuckle. "And anyone who knows Claude Pampalon knows he'll keep fighting until he wins."

"Illegal possession of stolen things, especially one valued at the level of that Van Gogh, won't just be pushed aside. Usual sentence would be about fifteen to twenty years. Eight was a gift," Marcel said.

Again Dimitri chuckled. "Not to my father. He'll never accept a deal unless it involves him receiving no time behind bars."

It was Beau's turn to laugh. "That won't happen. I can't imagine any jury finding him not guilty after seeing the video-surveillance evidence."

"And Jansen's testimony too." Marcel offered.

"You might be surprised." Dimitri stopped as they reached the parking lot. "Father seems to get away with the most awful things."

"This time, I think it's caught up to him." Marcel jangled the keys in his hand. "The deal Jansen got gave him five years."

"Another reason Father wouldn't take a deal. He holds Mr. Jansen more accountable than his own actions." Dimitri stared up at the rumbling thunderclouds overhead.

"What about the hotel?" Beau couldn't help but wonder if Addy's job was secure now that Claude had been denied bail. He didn't know what the legal ramifications were.

"We keep on keeping on. Father's lawyer sent me his power of attorney with all things involving the Darkwater Inn."

"So you get to make all the decisions?" Marcel asked.

"For now. The POA is specific in that as soon as Father is no longer in custody, my granted rights are terminated."

"But until such time?" Beau asked.

Dimitri smiled. "I get to run the Darkwater as I see fit. Well, Adelaide does. I'm perfectly content to stay in the kitchen and let her manage everything."

"She's good at that." Beau smiled, glad he and Dimitri both seemed to also be content at maintaining their uneasy truce.

"Have you heard anything about the princess?" Marcel asked.

Dimitri nodded. "Their laws are different in their country, but from what I understand, she's okay, even if she's having to face what she's done."

"And the crown? Is it official that it is indeed part of the Romanov crown jewels?" Beau shifted his weight from one foot to the other.

"Nope, and it's very unlikely that will ever happen. Despite many gemologists' agreement that it is, the Kremlin refuses to publicly accept that." Dimitri shrugged. "I guess that's better for the princess this way."

"What about her involvement in Luca murdering Jackson?" Marcel asked. "I didn't like that we couldn't charge her."

"We don't know. Every inquiry regarding that has been shut down, so I guess her country is handling it as they see fit."

Lightning flashed, filling the air with electricity.

"Guess we'd better get going to beat the storm."

Beau paused, then extended his hand to Dimitri.

Dimitri hesitated only a second before shaking Beau's hand.

Thunder boomed, and the skies opened up and spilled fat raindrops down in torrents.

## ADDY

Addy stood on her bedroom balcony, staring down at her city. One of the top ten most visited cities, New Orleans was in Addy's blood. All of the French Quarter, including Jackson Square—her love of the Crescent City was as deep as the Mississippi River flanking New Orleans itself.

The nightline lights of the people still enjoying carnival season below illuminated the sky. Beats from the zydeco music playing in the bars below drifted up to Addy's balcony. A lone saxophone played further in the distance.

Addy sat on the chair Dimitri had bought her. He'd had it made for her with a picture on the canvas material of their photo-booth snapshot taken at the zoo. She lifted the leather journal Beau had gotten her. Already she'd filled many pages with random thoughts, confusing emotions, and even a few lines of poems she was working on. Both men were amazing, and her heart was in constant flux over them both.

Addy hadn't had a chance for her heart to make any conclusions, but neither Beau nor Dimitri had complained. But she was in no hurry. She'd learned to appreciate life, every precious second. Choosing a partner to share her life could not—would not—be rushed.

Setting down her journal, she reached for the other book sitting on the table. She ran her hand over the worn leather cover.

Her old Bible. Once it had been her constant companion. And then she'd been so hurt and angry she couldn't bear to even look at it, much less open it. Now . . .

Well, now her life was different. She was in a better place. Maybe, Addy hoped, she had grown up a little. Matured a lot.

She opened the Bible, the thin pages flipping and making a soothing, welcoming sound. Her heart lurched.

Addy closed her eyes, and for the first time in a very long time, she opened her heart to the one above all others.

Her real true love.

# EPILOGUE

Her wings curl over her back not clipped
just not tested
Waiting for the perfect time to unfurl.
She takes a step
then two, full of confidence surety of self.
Steps she knows where the path leads.
   Success.
Her wings stay folded—feathers smooth
   and in place.
The seasons change
One segueing into the next the rites of
   passage of time of accomplishments
of victories
of disappointments.
Feathers a little ruffled
but still in place over her back.
Storms of life ravage years pass
She grows older learning
But still close to the nest Lest she fall.
The taste of the future sits on the tip of
   her tongue—sweet, yet tangy inviting,
   yet scary.
She takes a cautious step into unknown
   territory

409

a place where her certainty is unsure her
 confidence
not proven.
Her wings quiver as they slowly Unfurl.
Massive span as they spread.
She takes another step into the uncertain
 into the risk.
The strength of her wings lift her holding
 her securely
even as she looks back over her shoulder
to what is sure. What is safe.
But love looks back at her Smiling
 through tears
as pride lines the creases
of the weathered face of support.
And she knows.
She has been given
the support to forge her way Into the
 future.
She turns with a smile and strength in her
 wings.
She flies.

Dear Reader:

Thank you for returning to New Orleans with me and the crew of the Darkwater Inn. Louisiana is in my blood, and Cajun country has a large piece of my heart. If you get the opportunity to visit the area, I encourage you to do so. The laid-back, generous, and hospitable attitudes of most of the people who live in south Louisiana will steal part of your heart too.

I've loved sharing this second story of Adelaide, Beau, and Dimitri with you. Each of these characters surprised me with their growth and depth from the first book. They pushed me as an author to create their journeys filled with struggles and joys, just like we all face in life. I'm looking forward to the last book in the trilogy, to see how they all turn out . . . And yes, to see who Adelaide chooses romantically.

Family dynamics can be some of the most complicated relationships ever—I know this from experience. As this story came to life, I wanted to show how many instances can alter the course of people, even family who are loved. Thank you for letting me share these insights with you as the characters worked out their family issues.

The Romanov family history has always intrigued me. I took liberties in writing in the missing diadem. The photos in the album vs the

411

book are real, but the outcome of it being in the hands of any royal family is totally fiction.

Additionally, I took GREAT liberties in portraying characters from Liechtenstein. While it is factual that all in the royal family are princes and princesses, I twisted many more details to best fit my story.

I would love to hear from you. Please visit me on social media and on my website: www.robin caroll.com. I love talking books with readers.

Blessings,

# ACKNOWLEDGMENTS

Each book marks the accomplishment of an entire team who made it possible. I'm blessed to have worked with such an amazing group of talented people on this second book in the Darkwater Inn series. My editor, Leslie Peterson, whose talents helped make my book shine! I thank you so, so much for all your insight, suggestions, and accommodations.

Thanks to my agent, Steve Laube, who manages to keep me on track and sane in this ever-changing industry, and who respects my business decisions.

This book was brainstormed with some pretty amazing writers at a private retreat. My thanks for their input and excitement: Colleen Coble, Carrie Stuart Parks, and Lindsay Harrel. I had a great time hanging out with y'all and always look forward to being able to brainstorm with you. Thank you to Kara and Mark Davy, for letting me stay with you and play with Elijah. Thanks to Dave Coble, for carting us around and making sure we didn't get lost—because I have no sense of direction.

Huge thanks to fellow author Pam Hillman, who was the best sport on our research trip to New Orleans. She let me drag her through cemeteries, the French Quarter, and on tour buses. I'm so glad I didn't have to go alone!

Thank you to Tamara Büchel-Brunhart, Assistant to the Ambassador, Embassy of Liechtenstein, for information. The details I twisted were all mine to best suit the story, not a reflection on the information Tamara provided.

I'm forever grateful to my circle of "my people" who are amazing prayer partners, beta readers, and encouragers. Thank you so much, Pam Hillman, Heather Tipton, Tracey Justice, Cynthia Ruchti, and Cara Putman. You ladies don't let me get away with anything or take any shortcuts, and I appreciate each of you for that!

To my immediate family, who help me brainstorm, plot, and cause havoc in my poor characters' lives: Casey, Remy and Bella—*thank you* for taking the active part in my stories. I can't tell you how much it means to me for y'all to rock the fiction process with me.

Lots of love for my extended family's encouragement. I so appreciate your continuous support: Mom, my grandsons—Benton and Zayden, Bubba and Lisa, Brandon and Katie, Rachel and Thomas, and Wade (because you are more family than not).

To my true north, Casey...there is no one I'd rather walk through life and love with than you. Every day, you remind me of what is good and pure in this life, and how blessed I am. Thank

you for encouraging me to fly higher in cha
my dreams, every single day.

Finally, all glory to my Lord and Savior, Jes
Christ. I can do all things through Christ wh
strengthens me.

# ABOUT THE AUTHOR

-selling author of more than thirty novels, ROBIN CAROLL writes Southern stories of mystery and suspense, with a hint of romance to entertain readers. Her books have been recognized in several awards, including the Carol Award, HOLT Medallion, Daphne du Maurier, RT Reviewer's Choice Award, and more. Robin serves the writing community as Executive/Conference Director for ACFW.

*For More Information*
www.robincaroll.com

**Center Point Large Print**
600 Brooks Road / PO Box 1
Thorndike, ME 04986-0001 USA

(207) 568-3717

**US & Canada:**
**1 800 929-9108**
www.centerpointlargeprint.com